D0095428

THE
FAR SIDE
OF
VICTORY

THE
FAR SIDE
OF
VICTORY

Joanne Greenberg

HOLT, RINEHART and WINSTON   New York

Library of Congress Cataloging in Publication Data
Greenberg, Joanne.
The far side of victory.
I. Title.
PS3557.R3784F3 1983   813'.54   83-6196
ISBN: 0-03-063252-8

First Edition

Designer: A. Christopher Simon

Printed in the United States of America
10 9 8 7 6 5 4 3 2

ISBN 0-03-063252-8

*To the Ladies' Tuesday Ski Team
and Terrorist Society
in all their downhill glory,
and
to Pat Lewis, J.J., and Denny,
members in spirit*

THE
FAR SIDE
OF
VICTORY

I

What surprised him was how little actual pain there was. If he lay quietly in the bed, there was only a dull ache all over and a soft, floury pounding in his head like a horse's hooves in the dust of the road. They had given him something for the arm, which was broken, and the concussion. People came, looked at him, murmured, and went away. Sometimes he slept.

He didn't remember anything about the accident. He'd been skiing with Claire, who always had enough to pay everybody's way, and they were drinking cappuccino and brandy and roaring after each other down the back side of Pickaxe Hill. After they left the slopes there had been a party, booze and grass, another girl—it had gotten Claire angry, so he had left her at the party, but then there was nothing, nothing at all until now.

When a nurse came in, he asked her the day and the time. It was Monday, February 6. He supposed he should ask more questions, but decided against it. Arnie had learned long ago to go with the flow of things. Someone always let you know soon enough. The car. The job. He would get a nurse to call his supervisor later and say he was in the hospital. It would sound better than if he called himself. He slept again.

When he woke, the room seemed full, but there was only one man, a policeman, standing over his bed. The straps and buckles and belts and badges sighed as the man breathed in them. Now Arnie ached horribly. Everything had worn off; the raw light grated on his senses, pain pounded at his arm and in his head. He groaned. It hurt to breathe. The policeman stepped back. "They told me you were ready to talk about this . . ." he said, not unkindly.

Never! Arnie's mind cried. "No, that's okay," Arnie said. "I ache—it all hurts."

"Do you know—did they tell you?"

"Tell me what?"

"I thought they told you in the emergency room."

"I wasn't told anything."

The policeman looked surprised, annoyed at what Arnie didn't know. "Shit," he said.

"My car—"

"You are Eric Arnold Gordon, aren't you?"

"Yes."

"Never mind the car, just listen," the policeman said, "I've got to do this. Sunday morning, February fifth, at six-thirteen A.M., you were on Interstate Eighty-one eastbound out of Aureole. Three miles east of Aureole you crossed the double line and were going approximately eighty miles per hour eastbound in the westbound lane. A car carrying Charles Noel Gerson, thirty-six, of Omaha, Nebraska; his wife, Helen, thirty-one; their three children, Lois, twelve, Richard, nine, and Patricia, four; and another passenger since identified as Jackson Oliver Bressard, twenty-two, was traveling westbound. A witness said you must have seen him but steered left into the mountain, farther into his lane, and that because of your oversteer the car became airborne in the curve—your car connected with the oncoming car on your passenger's side . . ." The policeman paused, waiting. Arnie lay stunned and unbelieving in a white silence. "Do you understand?" the policeman said. Arnie nodded, sending a lightning tracer of pain through his head. The man went on. The words had a factual flatness, but he couldn't seem to make them mean anything. It must be a mistake. He was too ordinary a person to be part of such an accident. The words were meant for someone else. But as the policeman went on, Arnie became more and more frightened. Had part of his brain somehow become disconnected? A vital part of it wrenched loose, pulled away? "The driver, Charles Gerson, was killed instantly, as were the rear-seat passengers, Lois Gerson, who was on the left, and Patricia, thought to have been in the middle. The passenger Jackson Oliver Bressard was thrown over the vehicles and died behind the wreck. The other child, Richard, is in critical condition with head and neck injuries and trauma to the vital organs."

"Oh," Arnie said. He had become aware that the policeman was reading from his report. He, too, didn't want to know such things—his reading was the proof of that. No one wants to know a thing as bad as this. It made Arnie feel vindicated.

"The mother is in ICU with him," the policeman said, looking up from the paper. "She's been there all the time. She was struck by one of the kids flying around in the car and had her collarbone broken."

"So, uh, what's going to happen?"

"Well . . ." The officer seemed at a loss for a moment. "You've broken the law. When you leave here, you'll be taken before a judge and you'll be arraigned and bail will be set."

"You mean I could go to jail?"

"That's right. You'd better get yourself a lawyer."

"But Christ, I don't even remember any of it! I must have tried to steer away—you said I swerved to try to get out of the way—" His voice had risen, and at the sound of it his head was pounding so that he was blind with pain. He heard his voice, high and panicky.

"I'm not the judge," the policeman said primly. "It's up to him."

"I couldn't have done it—I didn't mean to do it—" Then he stopped. His vision cleared and something caught his eye.

Someone was standing in the doorway, blocked by the officer. He felt, without actually knowing who it was, who had come there.

The policeman caught his look and turned. Arnie had a quick flash of the woman, her arm bound. She was wearing a hospital gown under an open coat. "Ma'am"—the policeman turned toward her and blocked her from Arnie—"ma'am, you shouldn't be here."

She didn't speak. Arnie was afraid she would rush past the officer, curse him, scream at him. He was glad he had the policeman's shielding bulk between them, but still she didn't speak or cry. "Lady, I—" he cried into the policeman's back. "I didn't know—I didn't mean to—" But the policeman was already gently moving her out the doorway, taking her by the hand and uninjured shoulder, and murmuring to her. She was saying something to the policeman in a very low but urgent whisper. The policeman moved away with her, and as they left, Arnie could hear the sound of his placating words.

That evening he called his parents in Silver Spring. He had called before when he was in trouble and had heard once or twice the guarded note in their voices. Because of that, he had recently begun calling them in a more routine way, working at keeping in touch. He loved his parents, but had always felt that love should impose no responsibility; his parents always seemed to want more. His father was a lawyer for the government in the Department of Labor. He would know what was best to do.

His mother answered, surprised and pleased. "It's Dad's rehearsal night tonight—you've forgotten—but he should be home any minute."

"Oh, hell, I forgot."

"Every Tuesday . . ."

"Sure, I know." And he had the picture of his father lumbering up the front steps with the bulky cello. That picture was so clear, why could he get no picture of the accident that would rid him of this nightmare, excuse, exonerate?

4

". . . and he and Phil and Joe Dresser still stop off afterward," his mother was saying, "but he'll be here any minute."

"I need to talk to him, but—" Suddenly, he was overcome with affection for the voice that sounded so ordinary, so normal and usual that he didn't want it to stop. "Go on, Ma."

"How's Uncle Tony?" she asked. "Did you see the cute Christmas cards he sent this year?" Arnie was in Colorado because of his uncle, who was also a lawyer and was with the state attorney's office in Denver. Uncle Tony had gotten Arnie his job.

"He's fine. He and Aunt Florence are on vacation now out of town. No, I didn't see the card." He was fighting sickness, the nausea he thought he had vanquished this morning. His stomach heaved and slid away on the greasy wave of it. He tried breathing slowly and deeply to quell it. He began to sweat. He breathed deeply again. She did not seem to notice.

"I don't want to run up this phone bill," she said. "Suppose I call you back?"

"Well, Ma, I'm not at home . . ." He didn't want to go into it, to face it, to change the cheer in that voice, but in a sentence or two he knew he would have to. If not at home, where? He had one telling in him, one dry and ordered statement of the still completely unreal thing, and he knew he needed to save himself from a rising panic. His father would appreciate his being objective. Luckily, he heard the sounds of his father's arrival and his mother's voice away from the phone: "It's Eric. He wants to talk to you."

His father picked up the phone, warier than his mother had been. Sometimes he thought his father loved him less but understood him more. "Well, son, how are you?"

"Dad . . . ?" He began with what he remembered: Claire, skiing, the party, and then what he had been told. His father became very dry, all lawyer. He asked a few questions—at first they seemed irrelevant. Was his rent paid up? Did he have any outstanding debts? Was he involved in any lawsuits or other legal problems? Were there any other speeding or drunk violations against him?

"No."

"But you do drink quite a bit."

"Yes, I guess so."

"And marijuana?"

"Yes, with friends—"

"Have you been seen drunk by the neighbors?"

"I don't know—I don't think so."

"Have you ever been drunk or not yourself at work?"

"Sometimes. If we finish a job early we knock off for the day."

"I mean when you are working."

"No, not usually."

"Sometimes, then."

"Well, yes."

"You'll need a lawyer, a good one. Where's Tony?" Arnie told his father about his uncle's being on vacation. "Give me the number, someplace he can be reached. Where did they say they were going? Never mind, I'll get there as soon as I can and meanwhile I'll call his service—there's surely an emergency number. Make sure you stay in the hospital until I get there. That's in the town, isn't it?"

"Dad, could I go to jail?"

"Maybe that won't happen."

His mother got on again. She asked about his injuries. Did he have everything he needed? Would he need help when he got out of the hospital? With his clothes? Would he be able to work while his arm was in a cast? He hadn't thought that far ahead and he paused for a moment, imagining himself dressing in his small apartment, eating. Aguilar could pick him up and take him to work. As he started to frame an answer he heard a sound like steam escaping and then another sound and then his mother's terrible, rending sobs.

"And that poor woman!" she cried half into the phone. "That family! Forgive me, I can't help but think of it—that poor, poor woman!" And then the voice was cut off and his father had the phone again, his upset making him sound brusque.

6

"Time for that later. Plenty of time for that later." His father told him to rest. "I'll take care of things from here tonight, and be out tomorrow. We'll have to post bond."

"I have no money."

"I'll take care of that."

Arnie thanked his father. In the background he could still hear his mother weeping.

His father knew the moves. The law was like everything else in life—like skiing a new hill a little beyond your class. If you looked at the thing all at once, it was awful—terrifying—narrow and steep and full of moguls and gullies and falloffs in a flat light. But his father led him and they bent around the pitfalls, steered past the rocks, bending, tacking, traversing, slowing, finding the way through, the way around. After the hospital they saw the police and the judge, they spoke to bondsmen and called lawyers. Uncle Tony had given three names. One man was out of town. The accident had become these things, a series of interviews and papers to be filed, appearances in court—the moves. Without those moves, he would have been in jail. With them, he found himself out on bond, free, able to go back to his apartment, back to work. His car was wrecked, but he couldn't drive with one arm anyway. He called Aguilar, he called his supervisors. It was all in the moves.

There were times during the moves that his father looked at him in a puzzled way, and there were questions asked by the lawyer, questions about the party, for instance, that made his father start to say something and then stop. It seemed strange to his father that Arnie knew only Claire, and had only known her for a month or so, and that the others at the party had all been strangers to him. Arnie's friendships didn't last long. This didn't bother him because he liked the feeling of change and excitement. For a reason he couldn't figure out, his ease at getting by had always vaguely disturbed some people—his parents, for example.

He thought he had been agreeable to his parents. His father had wanted him to major in a technical field, so he had taken civil engineering, but he purposely attended a school with a weak engineering department and he avoided the hard work of the more difficult courses. He also did not invest himself deeply in campus causes or politics. He was pleasant and easy and was a popular student. He was careful to keep from being typed as one of any special group. Big business was vying for engineers, but few of the major firms came to his school, and he avoided those that did. His father, puzzled, waited for him to "find himself."

During a vacation one summer he went to Denver and saw there the kind of life he wanted. He renewed his acquaintance with his uncle, who had always liked him. After graduation he moved out to Denver, where his uncle got him a job surveying sites in the various mountain lands owned by the city and county.

He liked working outside, in different places, and the money was enough for him to live on. Now and then his uncle sent him a little extra work. The job was easy and there was no pressure from anyone. Even his legal troubles would not cause consternation to his fellow workers because they were work-release prisoners from the city jail.

Aguilar had done time for drunk and disorderly and had been hired by the city afterward to "coordinate" the teams under the surveyor. He was sympathetic to Arnie, listening as they walked the sites in the unseasonably mild weather.

"And I don't remember the accident."

"Even now?"

"No, I remember the day, skiing. I remember the party. I called the people I was with—we were drinking, smoking a little, nothing else, nothing much else. They said I wasn't that far gone. I started home about three in the morning, but the accident didn't happen until six. It's an hour from Pickaxe to Aureole. My lawyer says I need to account for the extra time."

Aguilar shook his head. "They ain't gonna get you—you

got pull, you get out of it okay. It's the people that don't have no pull got the problems."

The other men nodded. The work crew consisted of a rod man, a chain man, a "laborer" to pound the stake, and Aguilar, who had come up with them. They used a city car, not the blue-painted prison bus that unloaded the common workers from the jail who cut brush and picked up litter. Arnie's men changed as often as the men in the blue bus, but to be on Arnie's detail was the prize job in the jail, and he suspected that Aguilar took bribes for it.

Their surveying work could be done in an hour or two. If the weather was good, Aguilar and the men hunted rabbits that he sold in town. If they were near a place, they headed for the bar and played pool or went where there was a game. Arnie was good at cards. The money he made paid for some of his sports clothes. Sometimes they hit one of the meditative dark saloons in the tiny mountain towns they passed, guarding its single, all-day patron. As long as there was no trouble and none of them got drunk, no one complained. Once one of the men did go over the line, and the others, their jobs in jeopardy, beat him sober. Aguilar was more careful after that.

"I started to remember a little more, the part about leaving the party; then, there was a time, another time, when I was sitting in a snowbank, laughing. In the dark. I wasn't cold or anything, just laughing."

"You sure must have been drunk!" Aguilar said admiringly. "What did you drink up there?" Aguilar liked to hear about how the rich spent their time—the ski weekends, the women. Arnie had spun the stories into moonwinkle for him, but now he would have to get careful about everything; his lawyer, Rademaker, had told him that: no more drinking, no pool-hall afternoons. Play on city time was sure to get back to the judge. So he would have to make the crew stretch out their survey work as long as they could. There would be pop instead of beer.

"You got a good lawyer?"

"Rademaker. A very serious man," Arnie said.

"Don't let that bother you, man. I been around this business long enough to know the law does what it wants to do. If it wants you to go free, you will, and if it wants your ass in jail, that's what's gonna happen."

The others nodded. Arnie had heard this almost daily from the men at the jail. He didn't know whether he believed it or not. He never argued; they were serving the time, not he, and for the most part, even the serious criminals seemed agreeable enough to him. They all said they were innocent—and now he knew what they meant. They had not intended the evil they had done. They had not planned it, and if they had, they hadn't foreseen the reactions of the people involved or the consequences. Afterward, when the beaten wife lay bloody on the floor or the saloon was a shambles or the victim of the threats went beyond fear to an answering rage, they stood blinking and amazed at the outcome. He knew now. He had said to the lawyer what he had said to his father. "I never meant—I never wanted—if you knew me, you would know—" And they were the truest for him, the most deeply felt of all his words.

2

Rademaker, his lawyer, was the one his father had chosen. Arnie never would have made such a choice. It was hard to confide in so deliberate, humorless a man. They had had their first conference when Arnie "appeared" in Aureole for arraignment. Rademaker had heard the basic story then and had told Arnie what to expect. A week later Rademaker called him into the office in Denver.

"Who is Jackson Oliver Bressard? Why in the hell didn't you tell me about him?"

"I never heard of him."

"He was in your car when you had the accident. He was riding with *you*." Arnie had a sudden snap, a door opening on a scene he couldn't quite take in, and the door closing again. "Mr. Gordon, are you following me?"

"What?"

"The police first thought this Bressard was in the other car, but Mrs. Gerson says she and her husband and the three children were the only ones in that car. By the way, the other child . . . died." The lawyer riffled through some papers. "The—uh, Richard, aged nine."

"Oh," Arnie said. His mind pulled quickly away. Didn't they know he couldn't remember any children, any family, any other car?

"You don't know why this Bressard was with you, then?"

"No."

"Well, we're trying to find out. He *was* in your car—we know that. He was whipped through the front door on the driver's side, and he died in the explosion of a compressed-gas cylinder."

"What?"

Rademaker took out some pictures. Arnie nerved himself for the sight—tangled metal, shattered glass; they had done this to him before. This time there were only objects on a white background. "Do you know what this is?"

"It looks like some kind of pressure gauge—oxyacetylene maybe, for mining, or welding?"

"You didn't have it in the car, did you?"

"No. What is it?"

"It's the gauge from a tank of compressed gas."

"I don't understand."

"This Bressard was a dental student, and we suspect that he was carrying a cylinder probably containing nitrous oxide. When the car impacted, he was pulled out across your body, still holding the cylinder. As he left the car, the gauge hit something and broke off—the top of it broke off—this part, and was found in the car. He was thrown up over the cars, and when he fell, the cylinder exploded into his body."

They sat silently. Arnie was stunned. Bressard, Charles Gerson, Lois Gerson, aged twelve, dental equipment, gauges, nitrous oxide—what did any of it have to do with him? Yes, he had been a little drunk and there had been some grass and—something, someone else, but not this, none of this! It was a stream of facts he didn't remember and didn't wish to remember. Rademaker was waiting for some answers, but Arnie said nothing, and finally he looked at Rademaker and said, "I don't remember."

"Let me suggest some things to you. You were at the party at the ski lodge. You were pleasantly drunk, and the marijuana you had kept you and everyone else from realizing how drunk you were, so none of you felt any great anxiety when you started out for home. They say that was about three A.M. On the road, you picked up a young man, hitchhiking. Do you do that often?" Arnie nodded. "It was our Mr. Bressard. He told you he had something that made people feel wonderful. Perhaps you asked what it was, and the young man said that it would be better if the two of you stopped for an hour or so, and so you did. In the presence of pure oxygen, nitrous oxide wears off very quickly and leaves no residual effects in most people, but since you didn't have oxygen, you had to use the natural ventilation, which is only twenty percent oxygen. Perhaps you were not ready to drive again."

"There was snow—I remember sitting in a snowbank. I was laughing." This memory or feeling had come early to him. He didn't like remembering it, so he had put it away. Now Rademaker seemed to need it.

"And was someone with you?"

"I can't remember, but there was suddenly—the world got very big and the snow wasn't cold at all. I remember thinking we should have warm snow, that it would be good to have warm snow."

"And let me suggest that you got back in the car when neither of you was quite ready. You were, systemically speaking, depressed with alcohol and marijuana. Nitrous oxide is also a depressant. Recovery would have been still longer." Arnie was silent, passive. The lawyer sighed and went on. "Let me suggest that Bressard, beside you, said that the cylinder was empty. You'd had your party and it was time to go home. There was the cold, too, further depressing your brain function, rendering you still slower in clearing the effects of Bressard's tank. You started to drive. But the cylinder wasn't empty. Bressard had not closed the valve on it, or not all the way, and so you were there in the closed car with a dribble of the gas slowly accumulating, building up until you were unwittingly but almost completely drugged. Remember, it was only an hour or so since you had been drinking. An accident was almost inevitable."

13

"What will that mean for me?"

"The state is charging you with reckless homicide, which, if left as is, will mean a prison term and a heavy fine. But if we can find out more about Mr. Bressard and this gauge, I think we can plea-bargain and get a reduction to drunk driving—operating a motor vehicle while intoxicated. I think also that we can go for deferred sentencing."

"That means—"

"It means some kind of light probation and, probably, you'll lose your license for a while. The judge can't let you off with nothing. There were fatalities and you did contribute partially to your . . . condition."

"But not jail—I don't want to go to jail!"

"Well, your past record is clear."

"My Colorado record is clear."

"Good God!" the lawyer groaned, his routine manner whipped away in the wind of the surprise. "What was it—what was it?"

"I—when I started driving—some reckless-driving tickets and one failure to yield. I was sixteen. There were speeding tickets, too, but I left the state, so—"

"All right. All right." The lawyer sighed. "Maybe they won't look. If the judge asks you, tell him. Don't volunteer anything. There was nothing in Maryland like this, was there? Arrest, anything violent?"

"No."

"Maybe they won't go back for it. Plea-bargaining means pleading guilty to a lesser charge. You will be pleading guilty, so there won't be a trial. I'm going to try to postpone the hearing, preferably till the springtime. You make a good appearance. That never hurts." There was a slight, subtle tinge of envy in the tone.

Arnie knew about good looks. His were not the kind that would separate him from others; there was nothing theatrical or striking about him, but from the time he was fourteen girls had smiled at him appreciatively, sometimes longingly, and other boys went out of their way to include him in parties or on trips. He was tall and slim, his hair was dark and thick. It gave him a casual, relaxed look because he couldn't plaster it close to his head. His teeth were slightly irregular, but they were very white; his smile was good, his eyes were large. These features were a harmonious combination of the looks of two resolutely homely parents, who had given their worst features to his sister, Doris. Because of his good luck, his parents had idolized him a little. They wanted him free to enjoy what they had missed due to their plainness. His health was naturally good and made his looks even better, so that he had no need to be vain. That lack of need gave him the final gift, naturalness and grace; the whole was better than the sum of its parts. Some of his girl friends had told him this.

He talked to Claire that evening. First he had to apologize for the argument they had had, of which he remembered almost nothing. Claire had told him in the beginning that the relationship was for fun. Later—they always changed later— "You still don't remember? We had wallbangers, mostly. We had tequila in them. And salty dogs. I told that to your lawyer. You're going to get off, aren't you? I mean, you didn't *mean* to crash the car! I mean, you didn't even *know* those people!" Her excuses for him were the same ones he made to himself in his own mind. Why did they sound so weak and vapid coming from her?

His appearance in Aureole for the hearing had been set for the end of May. His parents had asked if they should come, but since it was only a hearing, Arnie told them not to. He didn't want the responsibility of them. He must, Rademaker told him, be careful and formal on his job for that time. It chilled his relationship with Aguilar and the prisoners, used to dreaming through saloon afternoons, playing pool, and drinking beer. They never considered his case like theirs. The rich get off, they said. Yes, the rich always get off. Rademaker had also told him that there would almost certainly be a civil suit beyond the criminal one, but he was insured and that would be fought out by the insurance companies. The wife would sue for the expectations she no longer had—the support of her husband. His family might sue, or hers. The law began to seem to him not like a whip in its punishment, the pain sharp and hot, but like a chronic illness, dull and long and blunt. Once he dreamt of being butted to death almost gently by a herd of woolly, soft-eyed sheep.

Much of the case had been carried on without him. As the months went by, March, April, Rademaker would call and tell him about this or that meeting with the D.A. "I'm going for driving while intoxicated, as we discussed. It looks as though they'll accept that because of the circumstances." In May he called about Bressard. "Apparently, this Bressard had nitrous-oxide parties all the time, and if they don't go for a guilty plea on the lesser charge, I'll have enough evidence in court to make a good case for your having been drugged without your knowledge or compliance, although I think the way we're going is the surer way."

A week later . . . "We've got it. They went for the drunk-driving plea. Now I'm going to ask for deferred sentencing. We'll have to hope the judge doesn't need to make some kind of example of you. We go up Friday—well, Thursday afternoon. The hearing will be on Friday and the judge will make his disposition after that. Now, I'll need to see you this week. I want to brief you for this hearing."

They had three meetings. Rademaker told Arnie how to dress, what to say—but even more important, what not to say. He was dry and businesslike; he didn't deal in feelings at all—the fear, the racing of Arnie's mind, and his attempts to keep it away from the fear were side effects barely acknowledged. At first, Arnie was relieved not to be asked to display his "finer feelings" to the judge, to weep, beg forgiveness, suffer aloud, but as the conferences went on he began to feel uncomfortable, as though something important were being overlooked. It was all routine, calculated—his clothes, his hair. "Oh, and no jewelry, tiepins, any of that. No rings—no, not even that college ring. I see the cast is off your arm—do you wear a sling? Better leave it off if you can— Now, when answering . . ."

It occurred to him that no one—except his mother, months ago—had expressed horror, had understood the meaning of what had happened, and she only for an instant before being silenced by the practical good sense of his father. "Oh, that poor, poor woman!" No one else had spoken of the pain to the woman, or castigated him for the ones who had died. He had not known what to expect, but he had certainly expected anger and recrimination. Wasn't anyone—lawyers, police, judges—horrified by what had happened? "Where will she be—the—uh—Mrs. Gerson?"

"Haven't you been listening to me? This is important. A judge will be studying you to see if he can judge the kind of man you are. If he decides you are a bad man, you will do time for it. If he decides you are a good man who's had some bad luck and are a man who can keep his nose clean for a year, he will free you. Is it fair? I don't know. It's probably as fair as any other method of judgment, but if you don't impress him, you'll be the one responsible. Mrs. Gerson is back in Omaha, for all I know. Please don't do anything as stupid as writing to her or attempting to communicate with her. I've told you that there will be civil suits arising out of this, and you will compromise yourself if you even breathe in her direction. Leave it alone. Now"—and he settled back, creaking the leather of his chair—"can we get back to the business at hand?"

They went up to Aureole early Thursday evening, Rademaker and his secretary and Arnie. After the months of waiting, it seemed a relief to be going somewhere, doing something. The mountains late in May promise spring, but it is only a promise. This evening the air was soft as a smile and only when the sun was gone did the cold come in to lie coiled in the canyons waiting for unwary campers from the flatlands. The great mountainholds lined the sky before them, sheer on either side as they drove. Arnie had always loved this trip, going skiing or camping. He remembered having marveled at it the first time—the great ramparts first seen from afar, then growing larger and larger against the sky. Those people from Omaha must have marveled, too, as they rode up this same canyon. Did they—oh, Jesus! He put it out of his mind.

They got to Aureole in good time and checked in at the hotel near the courthouse. It was one of the grand old Colorado Gothic places—high-ceilinged and comfortable, built in the exuberant days of the gold strikes for prospectors suddenly rich. Around them, vacationers going west or campers on their way to Pickaxe or Comb Mountain or Granite gave the place a holiday feeling. Rademaker briefed him again. "The hearing is tomorrow. They'll read the probation report and the judge will ask you questions. We'll be in a hearing room or in chambers, but it was a big accident—there may be some press there. Answer as I told you. I hear that on cases like these, Judge Hamblin likes to look at his man for a few days. He may question you tomorrow and then let things go and have us back on Monday to talk about deferred sentencing. If that's so, you'll have to stay here for the weekend and come back Monday. Meanwhile, rest up. We've already had the pleading, so the pressure is off. Just take it easy. I'll see you here for breakfast at seven-thirty."

Rademaker was so certain, so confident, that when he was with him, Arnie's fear dulled to what he had come to think of as his legal feeling, anguish blunted. Arnie had never been so frightened in his adult life. This fear evoked the terrors of childhood. He hated it—he thought he would do anything to escape it.

He went up to his room and took a long bath. There was no television but there was a radio, and he turned the dials

18

mindlessly, trying to become involved in something that would mute the fear. Claire, pot, easy job, parties, flowing, lessons of the ski slopes and the river, go with the power, don't fight what's bigger than you, blend. And now there was nothing with which to blend. He stared at the wall until his body rescued him with sleep.

It wasn't a courtroom. Rademaker had said it wouldn't be, and being smaller and less formal, it was less intimidating. But there were chairs around the wall and people were sitting there whom he did not know. Rademaker was sitting next to him and they waited for the judge.

"Who are those people?" They made Arnie more nervous.

Rademaker looked around at them fearlessly. "This is a public matter. They're the public. Relax. Some of them are clerks. That one there is a court reporter. Some must be press. Those two look like hobbyists. They're retired people; they come to trials and hearings as a, well, a pastime. My grandfather did that. The old fellow ended up knowing more law than Darrow. I got into the law because of him. That woman coming in there, the dark woman, is Mrs. Gerson, I think."

Arnie felt his ears suddenly begin to ring. His whole head rang with deafness. The room darkened a shade and he saw corpuscles flowing in the spaces. "Stop staring!" Rademaker hissed in his ear. Arnie closed his eyes and tried to make the fear flow away. When he opened them he saw she had selected a seat to the left of him and he was able, without actually seeing her, to get the sense of her in the peripheral vision of his left eye. Her movements as she settled herself were deliberate and purposeful. She put her purse down and took off her coat, arranging it neatly; then she picked up her purse and sat down and held her coat and purse in her lap. She didn't fuss or turn her head or look around the room.

He had had only that single half-glimpse of her in the hospital. This woman seemed entirely different. That Mrs. Gerson had been wild-haired and old, very old! His thoughts had turned her heavy, gross, and raging, a large woman, a looming fury. Could this be the same person? This woman was much younger, and she was delicate, compact, and was making ordered, deliberate movements that were pleasing to watch—like a dance.

"You're staring again!" Rademaker said in his ear. "Listen, you don't want to get on the wrong side of that lady. She may still sue your ass off!"

"Sorry . . ." And he looked away.

The judge came in. They all rose and sat again. The hearing began and its mundane quality quelled Arnie's fear, or, rather, gave it a place to settle. The judge excused himself and dealt with a sheaf of papers handed to him by the clerk. After several minutes the judge looked up. "This is the matter 6.262.4.65, the, ah, Eric Arnold Gordon, on February 5, 1967, to a charge of driving while intoxicated. The defendant has entered a guilty plea."

"Yes, Your Honor," Rademaker said, and he and the judge spoke. Rademaker explained the accident. The judge's expression showed nothing. Then Rademaker explained about Bressard and the nitrous oxide, and it almost seemed as though the judge was glad to hear about it, because he asked some questions. Perhaps the interest in it would turn him, charm him in some way . . .

"You say he had a cylinder of it with him?"

"Yes, Your Honor."

Arnie looked out of the corner of his eye at the woman. At least she would know he hadn't meant to do this, that his will had been stolen from him by a stranger.

"And the man was killed by the cylinder?"

"Yes, Your Honor, and the fall. Those cylinders can become like projectiles when the gauges have been broken off at the neck. Mr. Bressard was holding the thing when the wreck occurred and when they both went through the driver's door, the gauge was broken off. When Bressard landed, the cylinder exploded, uh, into the victim."

"My goodness!" the judge said.

Arnie sat, listening. He had in the last weeks begun to recover some memory of the accident, and the time before. He had not told Rademaker for fear of the lawyer's disapproval. He remembered that he and Bressard had stopped several times, once in a town, a small, sleeping town, at a shack where Bressard had a friend. Bressard had acted strange, speaking not in sentences but in phrases. He had said "the place, man," and Arnie didn't know if he had come from "the place" or wanted to go to "the place." He wasn't happy in dental school, he said. Later he said he wasn't happy anywhere. The police had shown Arnie a picture of Bressard's corpse for identification. Dead people don't look like the living ones they used to be, and there had been so little light . . .

"Do you often pick up hitchhikers when you are driving alone?"

"Yes, sir."

"Isn't that dangerous?"

"I've never had any trouble before, and at night they help you stay awake, talking, sir."

"I see," the judge said.

Arnie had another quick memory of that man, Bressard. He had worn a leather flight jacket with a sheepskin lining.

The judge asked some other questions. Rademaker had said he would try to introduce the deferred-sentence idea, but now he was doing something else, making a point Arnie could only guess at. A bailiff came in with some papers and the judge took time to sign them. Arnie sat silent, bloodless and cold. He had thought that his Uncle Tony would come. Uncle Tony liked him and his presence would have had an impressive effect in this courthouse, but Uncle Tony hadn't even called after that first session with Rademaker. Their monthly first-Sunday breakfasts had stopped. Arnie sighed and Rademaker at his side threw him a cold glance.

"Gentlemen," the judge said, "I've read the reports and I've heard you. There's a lot to consider and I don't want to deal with sentencing just yet. Let's meet on this matter again on Monday, at nine, right here. Clerk, make the note." They all rose and the judge left. Arnie opened his mouth to speak and Rademaker warned him, kicking his leg under the table. It was noon already, and warm, but Arnie felt icy air from somewhere, so cold he had to concentrate to keep from shivering. It was morning, but he felt as exhausted as if he had been doing some back-breaking work—cutting brush with the prisoners in the blue prison bus. "We'll go back to the hotel and talk," Rademaker said in an undertone. He began gathering his papers.

In the corner of his eye Arnie saw the woman get up, preparing to leave. When the doors closed behind her, air seemed to flow back into the room. "Did the judge know who she was?" Arnie asked.

"I don't know—probably," Rademaker said. He hadn't even looked up.

At lunch the lawyer was more relaxed. "I think we're doing well. I *thought* His Honor might want you to stay over here for the weekend. There's a conference I've got to attend in Grand Junction now. Get on the phone and call a friend to come up and stay with you. There should be someone—a good friend. Don't leave town. Don't drive, of course. Will you call someone?"

"Yes, I will," Arnie said, although he had no intention of calling anyone. It was only two and a half days, after all, and when Rademaker had said the word *friend*, Arnie knew he didn't have anyone. Claire would come, but he was afraid of encouraging her, of what her coming would mean. Aguilar would want to drink or gamble; the other casual ski friends or bar friends wouldn't want to make the effort. The family would come, but his father, he knew, would argue, and his mother would cry. "I'll call someone."

"Well, take it easy. Walk around town, go bowling, see a

movie, but stay out of saloons, and for God's sake, don't get into any trouble. Do you have enough money?"

Arnie nodded. His problem would not be money but time. The two days and three nights now opened before him like the waiting days of childhood—infinity. Rademaker left with his secretary. Arnie stared after them through the restaurant window until they disappeared up the street.

By that evening, he had explored all the downtown he wanted to see. He was bored. He had dinner and went to a movie—*Bonnie and Clyde*, with Faye Dunaway and Warren Beatty, and after the movie he walked back to the hotel through the now-dark streets. He had learned from his surveying work that few towns, even the smallest, were as dead as they seemed at night, eyes piously closed in sleep. Nightlife was there somewhere—you just had to know where to find it. There were whorehouses, late bars, strip joints, card joints, homosexual hangouts, anything Paris, London, or New York had, he guessed, but it was all hidden, private. He didn't know where it was, here, and if he tried to find it, there might be trouble. He felt shut out, alone. He walked back to the hotel, his steps ringing on the night pavement, a sadness coming up from the still-warm streets. Then, in spite of all he could do to prevent it, he thought about her, the widow. Would she go back to Omaha, to a house that echoed her steps, too big, too empty? Would she awaken at night because the house had hoarded the cries of her children during all their early illnesses to release them now very softly, one by one, into the total quiet? Last year at this time it was spring in Omaha, and that house was loud and busy with living people planning their summer vacation. The kids would have been taking swimming lessons, the husband cutting the grass in the front yard. They had flowers planted in back, and barbecues or picnics there on hot nights. And all of a sudden, there was nothing, and she was here, watching him. At least, he thought, at least she had heard that it wasn't his fault, that it was Bressard, really, who had done the wrong.

He didn't blame himself; he believed Rademaker. Bressard had made him drunker, without his knowledge or approval, or at least without his conscious choice. Bressard, who was really the cause, was dead. The policeman, his parents, people who knew him might have categorized him as someone who approved of anything that was easily done, so he had been drunk enough, tired enough, suggestible enough. He had let it all happen. But that is not sufficient, Rademaker had said, for conviction for a crime. Arnie knew this to be true. He wasn't guilty; he hadn't wanted any of it, but it was sad. It was really very sad.

And he didn't like sadness, so he put it aside and spent Saturday keeping free of it. He went over to the little city park and walked around and met two vacationing girls who were stopping over on their way to Denver and they played three games of tennis and got quickly, easily friendly. Then they went bowling and out for drinks and met a young couple, and they all went out for dinner and, afterward, to a club outside of town that had a good band, or an almost good band. It was fun to fit in so well that you could be in a new place for one day and find the means to end loneliness and keep your troubles separate from your life. He was sorry he hadn't done it sooner, that he had wasted Friday keeping to himself, as Rademaker had told him to do. They left the club at three and Arnie went with one of the girls to her motel room, and they made love once that morning in the dark and later again in the daylight, and then had a late breakfast. She and her friend had to leave, so Arnie went to the park again and found another girl. They played tennis, too, and he got quickly, easily friendly with her, although this time there was something nervous, calculated about it that she felt without being able to put into words. Still, he flattered her and jollied her along, so that she stayed with him for dinner, and the club, and an almost compulsive time in bed—urgency without hunger. It was 6:00 A.M. when he got back to his room. He took a long shower and had a big pot of coffee sent up. It wouldn't do to appear in court bleary and hung over.

24

But he did look tired, very worn and haggard. Rademaker looked at him and looked again, with the first sympathy he had seen from the lawyer. "Jesus, you were up here alone! I told you not to stay here alone! I thought—I'm sorry—really—there should have been someone with you." For a long minute Arnie stood stupidly, not understanding what the lawyer meant. It was only when they were standing for the judge's entrance that Arnie realized how Rademaker had misinterpreted his exhaustion.

The woman was there again, out of his line of sight, quiet and unreadable.

The judge went through some routine announcements and preliminaries. Then Rademaker spoke. The judge said, "I see you have applied for deferred sentencing."

"Mr. Gordon's record is good," Rademaker said. He showed that the accident had been beyond Arnie's power to foresee or stop because of a drug given him without his knowledge or approval. "I feel that the best interest of the law will be served . . ." he said, and on and on, and when he was finished the judge said, "Mr. Gordon, you have pleaded guilty to driving while intoxicated and the result has been the death of five persons. There were, however, the mitigating elements to which Mr. Rademaker, your attorney, has referred. I agree with Mr. Rademaker that deferred sentencing is appropriate in this case. You were, however, somewhat intoxicated when you left Pickaxe, and your actions, taken while rendered suggestible by alcohol, resulted in the death of a family. The court cannot in good conscience allow you to drive away, as it were, and therefore it revokes your driving privileges for fifteen months. You will also be required to report at stated intervals during that period to the office of probation and parole in this jurisdiction, or a jurisdiction so named." And they all rose and it was over.

He drove back to Denver with Rademaker and his secretary. To Arnie's complete surprise, Rademaker lightened up—joking and singing barroom ditties in a mellow baritone, funny old-time songs that Arnie had never heard. "Can you drop me at my place?" Arnie said.

"Yes, to be sure, but first we're going to see Uncle Tony."

"My uncle is pretty angry. I don't think he wants to see me. We haven't talked since the day after the accident."

"Your uncle is a careful man. It was not in your interest that he see you. What he did do, though, was to arrange for you to get Clement L. R. Hamblin as the judge in your case."

"Could he arrange that?"

"No, but he did. Clem Hamblin's only son, age twenty-three, died of leukemia some years ago. They also serve who only sit and grieve."

3

Arnie went back to his job. Aguilar picked him up every morning in his beat-up car. There were all kinds of ways of ducking the probation, Aguilar said; things would be the same as they had been. And it seemed to be true; the job was the same, the people the same, the weather nice, the mountains greening, but something had changed in Arnie. His old life did not content him any longer. At first he thought it was restlessness because he couldn't drive and because Claire had gotten tired of driving him places and had dropped him. It wasn't that; there were girls enough and cars enough. He had made himself stop thinking about the accident, but he couldn't stop thinking about the hearing, the weekend he had spent in that town, Aureole. He dreamt about the town and about Judge Hamblin, to whom he now felt, in a very odd way, related.

One weekend he took a bus up to Aureole and walked past the judge's house and went to the cemetery and found Martin Hamblin's grave, and had a strange feeling, being part of that old sorrow. He walked along the Ute as it flowed through the town, went to the offices of the two local papers and got copies, and went to the library and took a sunny seat at the tall windows and read about Aureole.

The town was bigger and more varied than he had thought. The gold boom had come and gone, silver after that, and in the fifties there had been quite a stir over uranium. That boom had gone the way of the others, but there were still active mines in the hills around town. To the south there were cattle ranches and the town was the gateway to the skiing and recreation areas west of it. Aureole was also the county seat of Hayes County, booming again because of its resort towns.

Objectively, he saw these things, but deeper in his mind were voices—Judge Hamblin's voice, police voices—and pictures of himself playing tennis with the girls, laughing and making love because he couldn't bear to be alone. It had seemed reasonable then, and fun. He had been proud of himself for escaping a bad weekend in a small Colorado "city," which back East would hardly qualify as a town, but . . . and he had a sudden stab of shame, seeing Rademaker's real concern at his haggard face when he had only been tired from making love too much and drinking too much. Maybe he had gotten off because he reminded Judge Hamblin of his son—a posture, a look—or because of helplessness, perhaps.

Suddenly, it all seemed to mean he belonged here. He had made a mark on no other place so much in his life, or been so affected by it. He had been in a hospital here, and a courtroom. He had gone through the cemetery and found a name important to him. He had been free here, but not forgiven, and the town was waiting for him.

Arnie looked at the job folders posted at the library from the state and county. He looked at the want ads in the papers. There were openings for surveyors and engineers. He looked through the local telephone book, getting a feeling for the town. He wasn't restless this time, needing girls or company, but he was suddenly aware that he was doing all this because of an impetus in himself, not because of someone else's wishes for him or because it was the easiest way. The feeling was a little frightening—no, exciting—like skiing in whiteout, where the way was felt but not seen, and meaning that he must feel more, concentrate more deeply, work harder. So he listened, felt, watched, and when the bus took him back on Sunday morning, he was tired and exhilarated and was carrying a list of the job openings in Hayes County and in Aureole.

Uncle Tony was incredulous. "You can't be serious! It's a *town*! There's no scope for anyone there. What would you do there?"

"It's bigger than it seems, and it's going to grow. There's something about the size I like—it's a place I can know."

"You'd be burying yourself. Listen. It's the accident, isn't it? People do things, crazy things after—well, when things happen to them. You can't let what happened change you."

Why not? No one wanted to speak of what had happened, not even the law. He stood before his uncle's strained patience and couldn't answer. He had no idea why he felt as he did, whether it was something in himself or the result of the accident. His own actions surprised him. He had never gone against the easy downhill flow of things, against the fall line. He had never taken unfamiliar territory as his own, especially the territory of his inner feelings. It was mysterious and exciting and sometimes he felt more alive than he ever had before.

From Aguilar: "*Aureole?* You crazy, man? In them small towns everybody gonna know your business. Drink a beer, you got ten cops on you—a piece of gum is missin' from the gum machine, they pick you up. An' borin'? What you gonna *do* nights?"

"I don't know," Arnie said dumbly, "but I asked my uncle if we could move the case back up there—I mean, if it was possible."

Aguilar hit himself on the forehead with impatience. "I always thought you was smart; you got *the* deal here, you don't do no work, you got money, girls, you family rich—up there, man, you got *nothin'*!"

"You're right," Arnie said, "I'm not the kind of person who takes chances, who does things the hard way."

"That's right, man, life is hard enough."

Arnie nodded in agreement and then said, "I can't apply

for any of those jobs from down here. I'll have to go there. I'll have to move there first."

"That's *crazy*," Aguilar said.

"It sure is," Arnie agreed. "So will you help me move?"

He had to ask his parents for more money. They had paid the lawyer's fee and the incidental expenses of the case and they had had to pay his hospital bill, because he had neglected to apply for the city and county insurance program and his accident had not been job-related. Now this, and it meant an explanation of something he couldn't explain even to himself, much less make clear to them. He tried to put it on a practical basis. His inability to drive would be less limiting in a town where distances were shorter. There was work in the town, which was growing, and a chance to be on his own. The reasons sounded as hollow to him as they did to them. Aguilar had been blunt and scornful; his parents were psychoanalytic: "The accident business is over. Don't let it ruin the rest of your life. Don't bury yourself in guilt." Arnie picked a reason out of the air: "It's a place to start, to get better experience at more varied work than I could do where I am. Later, I'll be able to come back into something better. I need the kind of work I can get here. It will look good on my résumé and since I can't drive, I thought I'd make use of the time to get this experience."

Not for the first time did the lie sound more convincing than the truth, but for the first time it saddened Arnie and made him feel lonelier than he had been before he had spoken to them. His excuses and justifications had always been those of convenience, easily given. This time he hadn't known what to say because he himself was unsure of his ground. His father sent him the money, which he added to the debt of almost $8,000. He went up to Aureole on the bus again. He applied for a job with the county and one with the office of the city engineer, and one he didn't really want with a private surveying firm. He got himself a dark, cramped room whose only virtue was that it was downtown and near his possible work.

The woman at the courthouse had suggested he go over and see the city engineer, a man named Cady.

The "office" was, surprisingly, in a private house, old and paint-faded, across the street from the county courthouse. A handmade sign was on the door. Arnie rang the bell and heard the jangle of it inside, and then thought that since it was an office he should walk in. He tried the door and opened it as he heard a cry of "Come in!" and a small, gray man appeared at the top of the stairs. "Hello, come on up."

As Arnie looked around he saw into what had once been a living room. It was full of filing cabinets and map racks and stacked against the wall were four or five army cots and a pile of blankets. There were also lanterns and three large dry-cell batteries. He went up the uncarpeted stairs. "Hello," the gray man said, and ushered him into what had been the master bedroom. There were two drafting tables there and more files, a bookcase, and stacks of papers on the floor. In one corner on a precarious table was a two-way radio. Arnie was about to say something when the phone rang. The gray man held up his finger and went to answer it. When he was finished with the call, he went to the radio. "Hey, Bischoff, Cady. 2162 Victory Pass Road. A whirlpool of water sinking into a hole in the street outside his house. Sounds like he found the shaft to Two Bore. See what that is, will you?" There were a crackle and a few expletives from the radio and Cady said, "Ten-four." Then he turned to Arnie. "Half that area is undermined with bootleg holes nobody knows about. What can I do for you?" He was smiling.

"I—uh—I was sent here."

"Oh?"

"I mean the woman at the courthouse—"

"Aha, you're the man who applied—well, yes, sit down—oh, there's no place, is there . . ." He was clearing a chair when another, younger man came in. "Roche," Cady said, "here's the fellow Joan called about." He turned to Arnie. "No need my being clever, we need a new man badly. The town council knows it, or they should. Sit down and tell us about yourself."

31

Arnie told them about school and his summer jobs, about Uncle Tony and the survey team. "What made you leave a job like that?" Cady asked.

Arnie took a breath and told them about the accident. "I won't be able to drive for fifteen months," he said. They were looking at him levelly, both of them. "The problem wasn't alcohol," he said. Not a lie, not really, not the truth, either. Well. "I want to do something . . . more. I want some real work." Right after he said that, he thought he should have said something practical—mentioned the debt. They probably saw him as a nitwit.

But their expressions did not change. To his surprise they didn't pursue the matter of the accident. Perhaps there was some fellow feeling in them that kept them from asking more. Everyone drives too fast sometimes, rolls past stop signs, barely misses another car. Everyone remembers . . .

"We do all the city's engineering," Cady said. "We send out pothole crews, do inspections and surveys, manage snow removal. Every now and then we'll get something bigger, designing, working with architects on city projects. We all do every part of the job—you get to know the city better that way. And there's the river to watch and the undermining of certain areas to stop. I've got a map—"

"Hey!" Roche said, and Cady laughed.

"Sorry. You haven't decided yet and there's the council to meet and talk to formally. Maybe you've applied to other places and maybe you thought this office was bigger than you see it is."

"In addition to which," Roche said, "we don't know your name."

Arnie got up and shook Cady's hand and then Roche's. "Eric Gordon," he said, and with that introduction, the days of his college nickname were over.

That afternoon he went walking along the river, first upstream and then down. Like all of Colorado's rivers it was a creature of flood and scarcity, of swelling surfeit and sudden lack. In the spring it turned eagerly in its bed, shifting for comfort, widening its banks, pulling its taut, roiling muscles up and over miles of the pillowing boulders its limbs had worn smooth. He saw it now as an engineer would have to see it, where they had diked it in one place, banked and shored it in another; no effort to control its uncontrollable power, but subtle arrangements like promises spoken in whispers to keep it from its excesses; the tact of modest men. He smiled.

It was a nice day. Eric walked out beyond the town limits, following the river. He did not go as far as the place where he had had his accident. Why, he wondered, had he not remembered how close the river had been? He had no memory of the water as he and Bressard rode beside it. They could have been anywhere. What a waste.

He used the time well, waiting for the day the town council was to meet. He went up the older streets studying the city's layout and problems. There was a large commercial street running parallel to the river and a smaller one crossing it where the largest bridge led from the highway. Sometimes he heard Uncle Tony's voice, or Aguilar's, telling him he was a fool for waiting, for wanting to "hide" where there could be no advancement, no career.

At the meeting, Cady and Roche introduced him. The council members asked questions—more than he had ever been asked for the jobs he had held before. The matter of the accident came up and he stated again the not-lie about its not being a problem of alcohol. They did not pursue it. They asked many personal questions, so many that there were moments when he was tempted to tell them off and leave, but the meeting ended and Cady came over and said quietly, "Welcome aboard. Forgive Brad Kimble and Hizzoner. They've been raising objections to things all their lives."

The next day Eric went to work for the city of Aureole. Cady took him through the cluttered house, explained the radio, showed him the maps and records, explained that they had eight men in the snow-and-repair crew but no secretary. Both Cady and Roche seemed to be serious, literal-minded men. They didn't laugh or joke. He had thought them humorless, but as the day went on, he saw that it was a different kind of humor than he was used to: quieter, more subtle, more dependent on shared experience, not a shimmer, a glow. Cady was showing him the key points of the city on a huge, detailed map he had to unroll.

"This is the sewage-treatment plant, the work of many minds. The river *here* has springs—see how close they put the elementary school. We're going to have to build a new one soon. Back in the forties I used to take young girl tourists out to that spot there to show them the airfield."

"Oh," Eric said, "was there an airfield there?"

"No," Cady answered, carefully, "no, there wasn't." It was said with such a quiet wistfulness, it made Eric smile.

They went out to lunch at a place across the square from the courthouse. On the way, Cady explained that the food was terrible, the service worse, but "city" and "county" and "business" met there and it was one of the ways things worked. "When we have something we want done or not done, it's there we talk it out. You'll see."

"About the food—" Eric said later.

"Serves a purpose, too," Cady said. "Keeps people from holding public office too long."

Eric learned the job slowly, following Cady and Roche day by day. Cady knew the streets and the history of the buildings and the land under them. In the areas that had been undermined, he knew which prospector had made which hole and by what method and who had staked the claim and where there had been night work, the furtive stealing of ore through a bootleg shaft. He passed off Eric's admiration. "I saw a lot of things as I came up in this town."

Roche was from Bluebank, a town up the river. He had grown up with its dying. "My folks knew I couldn't stay there, but they liked it and they couldn't afford to move." Eric had often passed Bluebank on his way to ski. He hadn't paid much attention to it. "But it's coming back," Roche said, "by a miracle. The work force that services the fancy resorts in Pickaxe and around it has to live somewhere. They're renting in Bluebank, building trailer parks and small houses. My folks have rented out their garage to a couple. All the old-timers I grew up with who were waiting for the next boom never dreamed it would be *people*."

Slowly, day by day, fighting his impatience and Cady's slowness, Eric began to learn the neighborhoods of the city. He began to do site inspections, riding a bicycle he had bought. People stared and it caused laughter for a week at the restaurant, but he needed better speed and range than he had walking, and Cady didn't seem to mind. Eric endured the laughter without seeming to feel it, and that helped. Once or twice when the weather was bad, one of the city's five policemen took him to an inspection. It pleased them that he wasn't cheating on his probation. Because the accident had happened three miles out of town, the state police and not the local police had dealt with it. His name evoked no pictures for them.

He wrote to his parents about Cady and Roche, the inspections he did, surveying the Ute's give and take. He didn't mention how dark and squalid his room was. He had gotten it quickly, in need, and because of the debt he was beginning to repay, he had very little money to spend. He didn't confide in Roche or Cady, because the reasons he couldn't spend money for a decent place all came back to the accident, as everything did. He still had pain in his arm when he overworked or the weather was bad, a dull, diffuse pounding up into the shoulder and down into the two middle fingers of his hand. He didn't tell them that, either, or that he had realized that taking girls out was almost impossible when there was no car, no money to spend, nowhere to take them. He had had dinner several times with Roche and his wife and kids, but he

hesitated to go too often because of his inability to recipro-
cate. Roche had to drive him home afterward, which also
embarrassed him.

So the accident had given him a punishment of social di-
minution, an outcome far too subtle for the law to have foreseen—not the whip or the wheel or the prison cell, but the
need, for some time, constantly to be dependent, and to
apologize.

One day Cady invited Eric to have dinner with him and
his wife. "We're not very social—Esther isn't well—but if you
can eat something simple and help clean up afterward, we'd
like to have you."

They lived in a big, old house two blocks from the courthouse square. There had been plenty of room even when the
kids had been there—two boys now oil geologists and a girl,
married and living in Portland. When Cady stood with his
wife for the introductions, he suddenly looked a decade older.
Esther Cady was tiny and white-haired and bent with arthritis. Her hands were clubbed with it and she moved slowly. In
spite of that, there was something appealing about her, a
simplicity that attracted Eric. She gestured painfully. "Such a
big house, and bigger now that the children are grown and
gone. Cady and I don't want to leave. Being old does that to
you—shrinks you that way."

"I notice you call him Cady, too."

"He won't hear the other name. Even in high school it
was Cady."

"Even in sixth grade," Cady said.

Esther laughed. "Cady's one of those people who have the
world convinced they're conformists, and waving that banner
he marches so prompt and straight and spirited in his own
direction that when he leaves the parade ground people think
it was part of the drill all along."

The dinner was simple. They ate in the kitchen, and to save
Esther movement, Cady did most of the serving.

"I get better than this, really," she said ruefully. "Sometimes I'm as good as I ever was. I wanted to wait before you came, until I was better, but it was so long this time, we thought—" And for a moment she looked sad and bewildered. "Anyway, here you are and it's nice to meet you, the new man from the city."

He liked them together. Their care for each other, their quietness together, their interest in each other, still, moved him. After dinner they all cleaned up and went into the sitting room. Esther explained that they now lived on the ground floor—the bedroom was the front room—because she couldn't take the stairs. "When I started to have 'winter weeks,' people came—my friends. It got harder, and slowly, they stopped. People called less and came over less. I'm a bit of a guilty secret," Esther said.

Cady laughed. "That sounds a little dramatic . . . skeleton in the closet."

"I wish I could hang my skeleton in the closet," Esther laughed back, "but people protect themselves. Take Cady, here. He wants to propose something and he's scared to do it."

"What's that?" Eric asked.

"He wants to ask you if you would like to live here—upstairs."

Eric was amazed. He had never discussed his living conditions at work—how could they know how bad and depressing his situation was? He had begun to look in the papers and had made a few disappointing calls. "Well," he said, "I . . . could I see it?"

Cady took him up. There were three rooms and a large front bedroom from which the furniture had been taken. It looked wonderful compared to what he had now. They went into the other rooms. "Any of this furniture that you want to use," Cady said, "but there are some conditions with the place."

"What are they?"

Cady looked away as he spoke. "I need someone here who will help us a little. I do the shopping and I take Esther places and I do some cleaning, but there are times when she may need help with the things she wants to do, and up here, no one has cleaned since she—well, since the winter before last. If you come, you'll need to help with things, carrying the laundry in when I'm not here—things like that."

"I'd like to give it a try," Eric said.

"Good." And Cady turned back to him. "What are you paying where you are now?" When Eric told him, Cady's eyes opened wide. "Good Lord, I wasn't planning to ask for that much. Pay me that and we'll have a maid."

"Mrs. Cady wouldn't like a maid."

"No," Cady said, "you're right. It would mean a kind of defeat for her—that I'd given up on her."

So Eric came back the next morning before work and looked again and reveled in the room's brightness and space. That afternoon he moved the furniture from what had been Cady's son's room, gave his notice at his old place, and began moving in his possessions. As he went through the rooms and down the stairs, he saw that the place did need care. The hall was musty and full of cobwebs. It was work he could do without too much trouble and he would be happy waking to the sound of summer birds in the shading elms and the play of light on the ceiling of his room. Soon the nights would be cool and the snow would begin to fall in the mountains. He could see the mountains from these windows, the year turning. He was filled with a new, odd kind of contentment, the sources of which he couldn't identify.

He chose Sundays to do the work of the house. He dusted the upstairs and wiped down the walls and waxed the banisters and dueled with the cobwebs and vacuumed the staircase. He saw how glad the Cadys were to have him there. At first he didn't know how to help Esther—he was shy and then flustered, did too much so that once they wrestled with the laundry, and several times she came upon him working away with a rag on a stick, dusting the hall ceiling, and they both acted as though they hadn't seen each other and later laughed over it. Then Cady tried to help them work out a plan. "Engineering," Esther said, and she and Eric joked about *that*, so it brought them together. He saw that her life was already too engineered. The illness was doing it, crushing the spontaneity out of her, closing away choice. He knew this as surely as he knew he had never before looked into another person's life, not his parents', not a girl friend's. It was as though he had accepted everything without ever asking the source of it. He saw that he had never hoped ahead of himself, and had closed the past behind him also, neither proud nor ashamed of the past he had made.

Lying in bed, thinking about Esther and the way her life closed in on her when she was ill, it came to Eric that this knowledge—secret knowledge, because no one had told him—this room that he liked, the people sleeping downstairs whom he liked, the job he liked in a town he liked and wanted to learn about, that all these things had come to him because of a family's death in an accident that had been the result of his passivity and selfishness. He felt, suddenly, an awful panic and terror. He tried in the midst of the terror to think why he should be feeling it, but no logic would yield an answer. He could only lie there and endure it like an illness until it slowly released him, little by little, to a clammy dread.

So this was what they had felt, his sister in high school, his roommate before exams. He had heard about the puckers, the sweats, the jitters, but he had never felt anything like this clutching, the beating of panic in him. Maybe he had never cared enough about anything to fear its loss. If this was so— how vulnerable he was now, how fragile everything was! He had been easy, easy and careless, skiing downhill in a life that had never before opened such sudden crevasses before him. Crime and *reward*? Death, a plea of guilty, and a room full of moonlight.

He remembered then, years ago, when he was nine and another boy had dared him to jump from the roof of his house across the walkway to the carport. The roof was sloping and so was the carport roof. The space between them was wide. He had shrugged and walked away and left the other boy screaming after him in the strange rage of children: "I dared you! I double-dared you!" Who was daring and double-daring him now in the serene ride of the moon, and daring him to do what, to leap to what far side? Was it to justify—explain, leap over the deaths of that family, in some way to transcend those deaths with his life? That other time there had been the dare and then the fear. Now he lay fearful before the dare.

He lay in bed all night, listening to the noises of the house, the sound of the trees against the window. This sound was different from the sounds trees made back East—he couldn't yet tell how—but the leaves of these trees, all planted by the settlers from back East, were smaller, scantier than those of the trees where he had been raised. The sound was . . . A little before dawn, the puzzle brought him to sleep.

But it was there the next day, sound in silence, smell in the air. I dare you. I double-dare you. And then the fear of it.

4

The autumns in Colorado are long and golden mellow. The snows come early and suddenly with snapping cold and black frosts, cold so sharp it tears at the lungs. But just as suddenly the cold is gone and the frost-nipped trees dry in their yellow dress; the days are warm again, not like spring, not like summer, not like any season the East has. Mellow days, cold nights, star-cold, cracking dry. No frost rises because no dew falls. The sun next day forgives everything.

On the high peaks the snows begin to move. Standing on any of the hills near town or looking out over the western ramparts of them, one can see the whiteness advancing downward, eastward, week by week, and the old-timers say they know by which hill is wearing new snow what week of the month it is. Another storm, locking the passes, marooning a thousand towns, and forgiveness again, a forgiveness of singular excitement and energy. The air turns winy as new apples, or smells like the sea; the mornings shine like pearls, the mountains echo, and light pours between them radiant from its slide down the powder snow of the mountains.

But the oscillation of noon warmth and midnight cold, a day of snow, a week of leaf-crack dryness, however invigorating it is for men, wreaks havoc on their possessions, and all the things they build and use. Sidewalks contract and heave, potholes yawn suddenly in the streets, asphalt cracks a dozen mocking smiles between the filling station and the corner. Wood dries to pollen-colored powder; plastic, eternal plastic, crazes, films over, turns brittle as autumn leaves, and shreds away. Building fronts weather to stone-dust, the fragile webbing of craze blooms over even granite and concrete, and once the breech is made, be it ever so delicate, the freeze-thaw finds it out. Fine fingers explore and open the hairline crack wider, and still wider, all through the equivocating long sleep of fall, and by the time winter comes . . .

So Cady and Eric and Roche oversaw the patching and the diking, the sealing, the filling, in a puny forestalling of the inevitable crack-dry, frost-heave, melt-freeze ruin of weathering all over town. They ran from place to place planning for repairs on the good days, snow removal on the bad.

He was learning the feel of the town and the river, its giving, its mercies, the wrongs of building and the revenge the mined earth takes. He knew which parts of town were windiest and which weathered in the sun, and he saw the plans of his predecessors and how they failed partly or failed fully or failed hardly at all. When they did not fail, they became invisible and were taken for granted. He had dived into the work, dived and drowned because it stilled the fear and because he had an idea that the work itself was part of the dare, the double-dare he had been given.

In November, between Halloween and Thanksgiving, Cady called Eric and Roche to the work table one afternoon and laid out a sheaf of proposal papers.

"What's this?"

"It's a new municipal building. It's going to move Hizzoner and the town council and the county people and you and me, Mary Ellen's health department, and everything except the court and the sheriff's office, out of the private houses and saloons and courthouse basement where they now reside, and into a new building. Boys, we are going to en-gin-eer a fa-cil-ity."

"We are?"

42

Cady turned to Eric. "Really, *you* are. I've talked this over with Roche, who says he'll do our part of the drawing, but he doesn't want to work the plan. What do you think?"

"I think I've never engineered a building before—I wouldn't know how—"

"I'll help you with that," Cady said, "and there are specs to help you, too. A building is the gathering and harmonizing of a bunch of details all put together, but they come one by one, really." He went over to the bookcase and got down a battered red volume. "This is a good place to start. Don't get scared, lots of the chapters don't apply."

That night they left with five of Cady's books and the two of them walked home together between the bars of warmer autumn light and the chill shadows. The first snow had fallen and dried away, and the second. The light was wan. "Back East," Eric said, "the leaves fall deep and people rake them into piles and when the kids have tumbled in them for a while, the leaves are burnt. Its a smell that—it used to make my mother cry."

"We can't burn these," Cady said. "If we burned the old needles or the cottonwood leaves, we'd set the town on fire."

"A building . . . has the architect made his plan yet?"

"The architect is L. C. Blaine—Elsie. You'll get to know him."

"What else has he done in town?"

"What else has he not done? Most of the schools, the bank on Main Street, half the churches. He's not a genius, but he's a solid man and he works well with people. As soon as he has a plan begun he'll be around."

"A building," Eric said.

Cady grinned. "Does that mean you'll stop waxing our banisters?"

"Could we go over there—I mean, to the site?"

"Sure. It's late, now, though. We'll go tomorrow on our way to work."

"I'm wondering . . ."

"What?"

"Why you gave this to me—you could be doing it yourself."

"I guess it's just something I've learned," Cady answered. "There's very little greatness in a small place like this—with the ratios it breaks down to one or two really gifted people, and there are relatively few chances for big things. The people who don't like that, the very ambitious or the very gifted, they leave. The rest of us who stay have to learn not to be selfish. We're not daring, because we have to live with all our mistakes, human and professional. I figured if I was going to keep staff, you and Roche, I'd have to be generous."

"Roche—"

"He'll get the next thing. He said it was okay."

"Did you ever dream of the big towns and the big jobs?"

The light was gone. The warmth fled from the streets like a thief. Eric in his light jacket hugged the books to his chest and shivered. They walked faster. "I was the only college man in my family," Cady said. "My dad had dreams for me—bigger things. I guess you'd say I was a war casualty."

"You were wounded?"

"I suffered a severe puncture of the ambition. I did a great deal of work during the war. Few engineers get to do as much as I did."

"How come?"

"I was a Seabee."

"CB?"

"Navy engineer. We laid out and built airstrips and troop encampments, launching areas, depots all over the Pacific. Sometimes we got there while the marines were still taking the damn places, and twice, before they got there. Much of the ugly ruin you see from the Philippines to Okinawa has my name on it and I make no apology for any of it. Three airstrips, three repl-depls, eight field hospitals, six hazardous-material dumps, ten supply landing areas, and six battalion HQs."

"Good God!"

"It cured me of the build 'em and leave 'em idea. I came back here and did the municipal water system that we still use and I put in all the retaining walls, shoring the south bank of the river. It was a good job. When engineering is good, people work better, but they don't know why. Good engineering means that the air *doesn't* stink and traffic *doesn't* jam up and the front of the bank *isn't* a skating rink in winter. Invisible, inaudible, unsmellable."

"Too bad," Eric said, and he and Cady looked at each other and laughed.

The fear came and went, slowly diminishing. It had leapt up in him when Cady gave him the proposal and it was waiting for him in the cold upstairs room where he went to read after dinner. But as he read, it gradually slid away and a shy, newborn excitement took its place. It could be done. Step by step, measuring, weighing, testing, figuring, it could be done. And he could do it. And he would do it. Suddenly he was aware how cold the room was. The summer's coolness and serenity had become a winter chill, stiffening his fingers and aching up the bones of his legs. He went to bed and worked there, reading until he fell asleep.

They went to the site the next day. Eric's neck was stiff; he had felt his back crack at the shoulders as he leaned over to wash in the morning. He worked it gingerly as they walked.

"What's the matter?" Cady asked.

"The bedroom's drafty as a forest."

"The warmth from the furnace never did get up there. I guess I forgot how bad it was. I weatherstripped it last year and the room's got storm windows, but what it needs is heat of its own. You know, there's a fireplace in there. It was bricked in years before my folks bought the house. Let's find it and uncover it."

"You mean that?"

"I do. We'll have to go to the county offices to get a permit, though."

"Thank God!" Eric said.

The site for Eric's building was a block east of the courthouse square. Eric tried to unsee the houses on it, three of them clustered at one corner. It was impossible to see the land bare, waiting for its building. Cady was enthusiastic. "Building is lovely, but I'm doing the demolition. Look at it! Wonderful problems, wonderful!" He walked around the empty houses, planning his moves, his face and gestures animated, anticipating this before that, measuring with his eye. Trucks would stay here and large equipment move through there. "That equipment's by the hour, you know; make a mistake in positioning, get a crane before it's ready, and it can cost you five hundred dollars an hour—"

"—and the scorn of the corps."

"—and the scorn of the corps. This one's going to be smooth as a dance, move by move."

"And no one to know how smooth."

"Only the fortunate few."

They walked on to work, to the common repairs and the calls, but Cady's enthusiasm had put a glow on the morning, and Eric found himself thinking of how kites are pulled and pulled and suddenly begin to lift in a breeze invisible to the astonished person pulling and then, suddenly, are airborne. Cady would be daydreaming about tearing down three houses and carting the rubble away, and Eric smiled again into the phone as the voice on the other end complained about the fence that had gone down at the city dump.

At lunchtime Eric went to the courthouse and down to the basement where the filings and permits were issued. Now he was glad that Cady had made him go out of his way to meet all the city people and the county people. He said hello to Alice Ivers, the county clerk. "Permit to uncover a fireplace—that would be remodeling. Makes no sense at all," she said cheerily, "to have this stuff on permit. Just a sec—I'll get the paper you need."

Another woman came in with papers then, a small, quick woman, with dark hair piled up in a sort of Greek style. She wore a rosy lipstick and had large eyes. There was something about her, a gesture, that made him remember—what? He thought he must have seen her before at some county meeting or other. As she saw him looking at her, she inclined her head to him the slightest bit in acknowledgment but without smiling, and put the papers on the desk. Alice came back and said "Oh, yes, thanks" to the woman, and the woman left.

"Who was that?" Eric asked.

"Oh, she's new. She works for the county commissioners. Helen."

"She doesn't talk much."

"No. She's taking Peggy Slater's place. Peggy left to have a baby."

The woman's image stuck in his mind. He went back and asked Roche, "Do you know the new secretary at the commissioners' office—a small, dark woman?"

"No, but come to think of it there is someone new, isn't there?"

"Peggy left to have a baby," Eric said and sighed.

Cady had planned to spend the weekend working out his demolition. Walking with Eric past the block again on the way home, Cady had looked and looked again, measuring with his eye, walls, ways in and out. As they stopped for a moment, Cady turned to Eric and said, "Oh, I've called Fred and Elbert up to help unplug that fireplace tomorrow. It'll make a mess, but I think we'll like the result."

They worked all weekend and by Monday there was only the chimney cleanup to do and a trial burning. Eric went back to the county office to arrange for the inspection.

"Good God!" Alice cried, signing the paper. "You and Cady! Look up the thing and see if you can make out the evening star when the draft's open. Tell Esther hello. Tell Cady the town's so full of goddamn engineers no one makes sense anymore!"

On his way out, Eric looked into the commissioners' office. There she was at the filing cabinet, her back to him. He wanted to get her attention but for some reason he didn't dare. She had been on his mind now—the feeling he knew her, a desire to—and he had never been shy or slow before. Why didn't he go in and start a conversation? Why was this different from his usual, easy, pleasant way with women? The fear that had been sleeping in him began to slip coils, slowly, not yet fully awakened, its sensing, forked tongue tasting the currents of the air—he ducked out quickly. She had not seen him.

The fireplace made all the difference in Eric's room. He kept his wood in the old bin under the back eaves. He carried wood up and ashes out and because of the mess it made, he found he had to vacuum the upstairs hall and the stairs and that inevitably led to his vacuuming all the rooms, taking the work from a grateful Cady. Esther was doing less, now that the winter was upon them. He had never been necessary to anyone, truly needed. It made him grateful in a way he had never been before.

It occurred to him again that he had his accident to thank for the way he now lived. Had he been able to drive, he would have chosen a place where there were young people, a gleaming, efficient bachelor apartment. No one would have needed him there—he would have been part of nothing. He had, in steps he didn't know he was taking at the time, begun to change himself. Somehow, in some way, he had begun to discriminate between what was ordinary and what was something more, to reach toward—what?—a self he might be but wasn't yet. The house was part of it, Esther and Cady were part of it. Serving his trivial punishment was part of it, even the fear. Yes, the fear, too, was part of it.

The budgeting for the demolition had hit a snag. The commissioners had meeting after meeting over it. Cady waited, patient in a way that Eric looked on with wonder. "Get the virtue, boy, or working with government will kill you," Cady said through gritted teeth. The routine work kept them busy enough, but just out of sight was a building that would be built on land that wasn't yet cleared. Nothing existed but in Elsie's mind and Eric's, building without shape, a gathering of challenges, and like a meeting of wraiths, more powerfully conjured at midnight. Eric dreamed. He had learned engineering principles in school easily, automatically; the numbers didn't speak of real bridges, buildings in which real people lived. Now . . . One weekend he took the bus to Denver and spent all day in the library.

The evening gave him a chance to see Uncle Tony and his family. They seemed surprised at him in some way. He wanted to assure Tony, as he had his father, that whatever money had been put out for him would be repaid. He had begun to send his father a monthly sum, but he had no idea what Tony had spent and he wanted an accounting. "It will take time, but I'm making a steady income and spending almost nothing."

His uncle seemed embarrassed. "Aren't you bored up there?" his aunt asked.

The question amazed him. He hadn't had a serious date in months, he hadn't been skiing or out to a club or bowling. He lived in a big house with two old people and worked with one of them all day. "I should be, I suppose . . . I'm not. I wonder why I'm not." They felt sorry for him and took him out to dinner.

"I've brought you a present," he said to Cady when he got back. "A little spray of figures I happened on at the library.

It's about how much money we can save by getting started on the new building *now*. Think of the rent saved on the hollow trees we all live in."

Cady laughed. "They won't be hurried, but you can try. The commissioners are meeting again tomorrow. Go up there and get 'em. You can also tell 'em, subtly of course, that they'd better get on with it because I've got wind of two new developments wanting to come in. Forty houses on Divide Road and a shopping center by the new high school."

The commissioners met in the courthouse. There were so many people included that the meeting went slowly and was cumbersome. Sitting there in the drone, Eric began to doodle in his notebook. He had watched the movement of people downtown in Denver when he was there, and he had begun to formulate an idea that— There she was again, the secretary. She had come in with a sheaf of papers for one of the commissioners, walking quickly, unobtrusively up the side aisle to hand them to him. Her hair was down this time, pulled back in a kind of bun. She turned and faces merged—Oh, God, God, it was Mrs. Gerson—it was the woman, the mother, the widow! He stared at her. She saw him staring and gave the shadow of a nod of recognition. He looked away quickly. He felt awful, pale, gone green; his heart was pounding, his stomach contracted. Around him, he knew, words were being spoken, but he had ceased to hear them. He knew that he must soon get up and give his presentation; Cady had alerted the two friendly members and Tyrrel would call on him. He knew his figures weren't earth-shaking and would be used only to validate what the council already wanted to do, but this appearance was his first official one before the group and he had wanted it to go well. Now all he could think of was that woman. His hands were freezing, his heart still pounding in his throat. He wanted to shout at her, "Why did you change your hair? Why did you use makeup, rest, walk quickly? To trap me? You got me into the open, without defenses, and—"

And what? He tried to control himself by thinking slowly, rationally. What was he afraid she would do to him? The case was over, the decisions had all been made. The insurance companies had met and agreed; there was nothing more. His lawyer had told him so; Uncle Tony had told him so. What could she do, turn and point at him and cry out an accusation? Follow him in the street, crying aloud for what he had done, what she had lost? Nonsense. He tried to slow his breathing. She was working for the commissioners and he was working for the city engineer. She had changed her hairstyle and her eyes were no longer ringed with grief. She had known him at once; now he knew her. He breathed deeply and looked around. No one seemed to have noticed, no one was staring at him. The meeting was droning on. It quieted him. He was embarrassed, uncomfortable, even a little frightened, but there was no real danger. He looked again. She had been passed several papers and was gathering them. Now she was leaving. He breathed easier.

He heard his name. Tyrrel had been speaking and suddenly here it was. "Mr. Gordon, from the city engineer's office, has something to add, I believe." And Eric got up. He was off balance and suddenly unready, but he did his best, trying to slow his heartbeat by keeping his words deliberate and even. The presentation was short and soon it was over. He sat down and Tyrrel thanked him.

He saw her three days later in the commissioners' office, where he was delivering a water study. He had nerved himself for seeing her, expecting she would be there, but she wasn't, and he was almost giddy with relief. In the middle of a few words with Mr. Hume, she came in and he began to stumble over what he was saying and had to recover himself quickly. Two days later he saw her on a line at his bank and he slipped away before she saw him, as though he had forgotten something.

The commissioners began to include her at their table at

the restaurant now and then. Eric got in the habit of watching for her. Her presence chilled him. He couldn't laugh when she was there, or joke with Cady and Roche. His eyes went to her; he couldn't help it. He felt her presence at his back or to the side, and the talk died in him. When he had to acknowledge her, he did so, clumsily. They never spoke.

Cady's demolition had been approved, but before he could begin it, three huge snowstorms broke over the city. Two days before New Year's a sinkhole opened on Divide Avenue and the holidays were a blur of work. Cady, Roche, and Eric moved into the office, grabbing naps on the cots in the chilly downstairs room, staying up so they could coordinate the road crews and help the linemen, who worked around the clock. When it was over and Roche had a four-day beard, Cady shook Eric's hand and said, "Well, if you still want this job, she's yours."

"I'm too tired to make big decisions like that. Let's go home and sleep."

"Esther's sister comes to stay when the weather's bad. I wanted to take all of us out for a meal. What meal is this?"

"Lunch, I think."

"I'm too beat."

The town looked different to Eric as he and Cady walked out in it. Hunched over the radio, he had had a picture of anarchy, or catastrophe, as the calls had come pouring in, frozen lines, flooded areas, impassable streets, backed-up sewage lines. Now, with the Christmas decorations gone, Aureole looked ordered, calm, stripped to essentials, as he had been. He felt proud in his exhaustion, like a veteran of a secret war. He fell half asleep as he walked beside Cady. He didn't remember getting home.

They slept, woke, ate, and slept again.

January was cold and dry, but at the end of the month three huge snowstorms kept the office open day and night. He and Cady and Roche all but moved down there, grabbing sleep when they could on cots set up in the back storage room. The days after were sunny and bright. Then a soft, deep snow fell.

"You know, it's perfect weather for the slopes," Cady said. "Look out the window. I saw the skis you have stored in the basement. They looked pretty well used. Why don't you go skiing?"

"No way to get there."

"I'll take you. We can be there by ten and I'll pick you up at four."

"But the office—"

"Not today. It's Lincoln's Birthday."

The day was perfect, blue and blue-white, the snow six inches of new powder on packed powder, so that his skis had almost no sound except the lightest susurrance, like long fingers stroking velvet. The lifts weren't crowded and he wasn't in a hurry. Alone, he had no one to impress, no other skiers to challenge, no need to do anything but what he enjoyed doing, loving the moment-to-moment play of perfect control against speed and excitement, the moves that were natural, a flying dance with the contours of his hill. He had always taken the expert slopes right away when others were with him, needing to prove something, to be quicker and more daring. This time he let himself sail easily downward, finding a serene pleasure in his speed and the incomparable snow. Even here, he saw he was changing, making himself or allowing himself to change— to be—what? Not a chicken, he cried, and went up again and took the hill of hills: the hardest, full of sudden-decision chutes and headlong gulleys and places where he went tree-bashing in the joy-peril of uncut trails down and down, to joining trails where he soared and sailed at ease, finding the places, as the birds do, where the upward turns have loft enough to give another and still longer sweep down the generous arm of the hill.

He stayed on the higher hills all morning and didn't come down until one. He was hungry and took off his skis quickly to go to the snack bar. The food lines weren't long by then. He bought two sandwiches, cake, and two coffees and took the tray to a quiet table near the wall. He was unloading it when he stopped to wonder at what he had done this time.

Always before he had come with a group—the bigger the better, all young, all attractive. They always took a big table at the very center of the room, and there they would be laughing, preening, girl watching, very much on display. Look where he had gone now, by himself. The difference interested him. It was an engineering problem, actually, a problem of people in their spaces. He would soon be designing the spaces where people met or through which they passed. This ski area, this eating place, was a problem—it used its spaces for many purposes. Were there human laws that applied here—laws of grouping and flow, access, special problems, different needs for different size groups? How do people naturally group and separate in the spaces made to contain them? Were there studies of the social spaces of a—

"May I speak to you?" It was she. Oh, God, it was she, Mrs. Gerson. The grace of the morning fled.

"Uh—oh—uh—sure." And while he was trying to move over on the bench, his jacket, which was beside him, was swept to the floor, and while he was trying to pick it up, his sleeve upset his coffee onto the sandwiches. "Oh—" And a man passing with a tray walked on the jacket.

"I didn't mean to startle you," she said. She didn't smile or laugh as people do when they want to ease a bad situation by making light of it. "I wanted to tell you something." She didn't say any more until he was finished cleaning up the mess. One of the sandwiches was still wrapped in paper and was salvageable. The other had been ruined, and there was coffee all over the table.

"Will you—uh—save my place?"

Still without smiling, "Yes, surely."

He waited in the food line again, wishing he hadn't come in at all, wishing something would happen that would interrupt them, would stop her, would take her away. He reminded himself grimly that there was nothing now that could happen to her to take her away from where she was and what she wanted to do. He sighed. Maybe she would think better of all this and be gone when he came back, but there she was, and he went back with the fresh coffee and sandwich. She was eating, slowly, her movements small and orderly. He sat down again, careful this time of his jacket, his gloves, his goggles, his tray.

"I wanted to tell you," she said quietly, without preamble, "that there is no need for you to stutter and turn pale when I come into a room or to duck away when you see me coming. The insurance company has made the settlement, I asked my lawyer what more there was to do, and he said, 'Nothing.' "

"Oh, God, what happened was—"

She went on. "He told me that I should begin a new life— start over. I came here because I liked Aureole. I didn't expect you to be here."

"I didn't recognize you—I'd only seen you out of the corner of my eye—your hair—you'd changed it—you didn't look the same."

"No. After you did recognize me, I saw you going through various—embarrassments. People noticed. They have begun to talk about it, so I had to say something. I have a job here. So do you. I like my job. I don't want to start over someplace else, so I won't move and you won't move. If that's so, you're going to have to see me without cringing."

He thought he flinched. She seemed not to notice.

"Does anybody you work with know—"

"No," she said, "only that I'm a widow."

"No one knows about me, either, only that I can't drive— that I'm serving a probation and can't drive."

"Then that's how it is," she said, "that we are people who know each other because of our jobs." She got up and picked up her hat and gloves. He noted that they were new. "Goodbye," she said, and moved away. He opened his mouth to call her back and then realized he had no reason. There was nothing he could say or do, yet he wanted once more to state his case, that he hadn't really been guilty, that he was changing, trying to change, that . . . He realized that her beauty had also touched him, and her grace. There was a dignity about the way she moved. He had been busy and happy without a woman for some time, whether because of guilt or expiation he did not know, but now he was aware of a longing he hadn't felt half an hour ago.

He was glad there were still a couple of hours left to ski. A few good, hard runs would clear his head and make him too tired to think about the widow or sudden longings. He went out into the bright, cold day and up on the lift, to Tumbleweed and Sidewinder and Juggernaut, the toughest runs on the hill. Coming down fast and hard from his second run, he gritted his teeth at having to slow down on the lower slopes where the novice skiers were. One of them was standing in the middle of a trail with crossed skis. "On your left!" he cried, and the skier sprawled, as though expecting to be struck. "I'm sorry—" He turned and stopped perfectly. It was Helen. "Oh." He moved back up to her. "You were right in the middle of the trail—"

"I know. I couldn't get my skis straight."

He helped her up. "How often have you been skiing?"

"This is my first time. There was the holiday. Everyone at the office skis; I thought I should try. It is necessary to try new things."

"You haven't had a lesson?"

"I didn't think for a sport—"

"How did you get up on the lift?"

"They stopped it for me, getting on and off. I don't think I can get down."

"Let me help you to get down. I'll teach you the simple things. How to turn and how to get up when you fall, so you can make it to the bottom. You'll get hurt otherwise. Please."

She looked at him without smiling. "I'm beyond my depth."

"Come on. Bend your knees . . . look downhill and then you turn . . . this way . . . weight your downhill ski . . ."

She was diligent and serious. She came toward him tight

with panic, her brows creased, her jaw set, her body tense. When she was within five feet of him she fell again. He didn't help her up, but fell beside her and showed her how to get up. She did, and fell again and a third time. They went slowly. "Go with the hill, bend. Now, unweight . . . turn . . . bend, see? Yes, but sooner . . ."

"I put my edges the way you said—"

"Yes, but you were frozen in the position you started into and the hill changed and the old position didn't fit anymore. Please, please have fun with the hill, feel it under your skis, relax. It's what this is for."

Slowly, slowly they came down. Her seriousness moved him. Her gritted teeth moved him. He admired her will. On the sixth fall she said, "You're patient. You haven't laughed."

She had none of his insouciance, his luck, his ease, but she had in abundance something toward which he wanted to move—simplicity and directness. He wanted to tell her he admired that, but he didn't dare. "You—you're frightened and so you freeze up, but I've seen you move and you move well. When the fear is gone, you'll have that grace to soar on these hills."

She was falling a little less often when they reached the bottom. She made a move to take the skis off. "Wait a minute. If you quit now, you'll never get back on these things. Couldn't you just let me teach you how to get on the lift and off and to go down the practice hill? You haven't given this a fair chance." She stood still. He couldn't tell what she was thinking from her expression, but as she stood there he had the knowledge, like a scent on the breeze, of her unutterable loneliness. She had that formal manner that was surely seen as cold, and she seldom spoke—he'd heard that from the secretaries at the courthouse.

"I don't think we should," she said.

"You mean because of who we are?" She didn't answer. He went on. "Who we *were* is not who we are. The light's still good, the snow is perfect, and you wanted to learn to ski.

You've rented these for half the day and there's still all this time—"

"When I came over to you it was because I wanted you to know that people are watching you—watching us—only that."

"Shouldn't we learn, then, to see each other without so much pain?"

"Yours isn't pain, it's embarrassment."

"How can you know that?"

"Then you've changed."

"No, not yet, but I'm changing. I've never had to talk this way to anyone whose—I don't know how to act about this. What you said about us both living here is true. In our jobs we'll be seeing each other, but I don't want it to be as the people we were—" He felt the fear again, flicking its tail. "Now, I just want to show you how to get up these hills and down again without falling so much." She turned toward him and fell again on the flat surface near the lift. Some teenagers skiing past guffawed. Eric had been such a boy and had laughed that way. "Come on." He smiled down at her.

She looked up at him and he couldn't tell whether it was resignation or whether she had seen the merits of what he had said, or that all her falls had made her too tired to argue. Falling flat on skis is harder to get up from than falling on a hill. He helped her and they made their way slowly to the lift. She must suddenly have realized as they were scooped up by the moving chairs that the ride up meant ten minutes or so with nothing to do but sit beside him, surrounded by breath-taking beauty and silence. She gave a little start but they were already riding up, and there was nothing to do but be where she was.

Knowing about the lift ride, he had foreseen her discomfort. He talked about skiing, using the time they rode to teach, being friendly but objective, an instructor, no more.

When they reached the top of the lift, a light snow had begun to fall. The sun had gone into the sudden snowcloud, and in the late flat light it was impossible to distinguish level from slope. She turned from him, and before she could move she fell over in the snow.

"How can people ski in this light," she said, "when they can't *see* anything?"

"They have to feel what's right, and they have to depend on that, to ride the hill on what they feel."

5

Cady was overseeing the demolition of his three buildings and the job kept him out of the office most of the day. Eric began to pore over the requirements of the new building. He walked the site, trying to unsee what was there, to imagine the noise and trucks and wreckage gone, the ground bare the site cleared, the size and presence of a new building with its parking areas around it. Months without a car had sensitized him to distances. He read books on construction and studied traffic patterns. At work he found he had to apologize to Roche. "I've been leaving all the routine stuff to you—"

Roche shrugged. "I don't mind. I like maintenance—working with the crews. Besides, Cady's a good teacher. I'm learning a lot. I want to sit in with you, too, when you talk to Elsie. He's bringing his drawings over on Friday. We'll all take a look."

Cady mentioned it on their way home. "Elsie's not a genius," he said, "you may be disappointed."

"You've told me about the geniuses going to Denver."

"He's a competent architect, though, and he's not threatened by engineers the way some architects are."

"Do you really think I'm ready to be responsible for something like this?"

"In a huge office like ours, with hundreds in staff, there might be someone who could give you a little help if you should need it," Cady said.

Friday came and with it Elsie and the plans, and Eric, forewarned, fought a terrible feeling of anticlimax. The building was ordinary-looking, a standard public structure, "modern," which meant that it could as easily have been a bank, church, welfare office, or school. Brick and glass. He had wanted, Elsie said, something more open, more gracious, but with the budget he had been given, there was room only for an open area by the steps and, inside, a small area at the entrance. They asked questions, murmuring quietly, visualizing the spaces being used. Every so often Cady looked over at Eric, who had taken it all in silence. Elsie left a set of plans with them, joking with Cady and Roche as he left, but he looked at Eric a little quizzically. Eric sighed. Cady must have told Elsie how sharp his new man was and here the new man stood, blank and silent.

"I'm sorry," he said, as they walked home. "I was disappointed and it showed. It wasn't the building, it was something else—something I don't even know how to describe."

"Well, the thing is no Taj Mahal, but details will ease some of the stiffness in it. It's not too bad, really; it's a simple building. Did you notice the various sizes of offices and the groupings? Very well done, I thought."

Eric walked along, a sorrow increasing in him. Here was Cady, trying to apologize in his own way that Eric's big chance was really routine, "his" building ordinary, and Elsie nothing like a genius. Eric wanted to tell Cady that it wasn't that at all. Something was stopping him from acknowledging even the ordinary usefulness of the building. "I need to know more, lots more," he said. "I didn't mean to be rude. How is the demolition coming?"

"Like a ballet, like the circus, like the Rose Bowl parade, exquisite choreography, a thousand delights!" Cady said.

"Speaking of a thousand delights, I won't be around to help with the laundry tomorrow. I want to go skiing."

"That girl from the commissioners' office—Helen?"

"I'm teaching her how to ski."

"Aha!"

"No, no aha."

"Oh," Cady said.

She picked him up in her car. There was a hard moment when she leaned over and opened the door because she didn't smile in greeting the way women do, and he was aware that the two of them were in a car together for the first time. He wondered if she had any fears about driving now, but she didn't seem to and he was unable to ask. Instead he proposed a plan: that he pay for the gas and that he teach her in the morning and they go to lunch, which they each pay for, and that after lunch she practice alone while he went to the expert hills. That way he thought it would seem less like a date, more like a lesson from an acquaintance. She agreed, nodding, and he sensed her relief. He sensed, too, that she liked formal, clearly defined relationships.

But something in her charmed him, a shyness, a sense of mystery. And there was her loneliness, too, for which he felt responsible. He had been so well liked, so successful, that he had never needed to be gallant. In some small way he could make amends by being a gallant friend to her. She didn't smile easily or laugh, and as the day went on, he saw that those responses would be all the more prized for coming slowly.

They spent the morning together on the novice hills. He watched her and the other neophyte skiers move along with an inimitable combination of terror and determination showing on their faces. "Don't look so desperate!" he said to her, smiling. "Please. This is supposed to be fun."

She made her traverse and fell again. "I never—I don't have the habit of doing things simply for fun."

"Didn't you ever play at anything when you were a kid? Didn't you go skating or sledding or swimming?"

"We were ranchers," she said simply. "We were poor."

They skipped the next week and he felt the lack, missing the day with her. They skied the week after and riding up on the lift for each run he tried to find out about her. It had become a challenge to him because she was not talkative, unlike all the other women he had ever known. She had grown up on a hardscrabble, hard-luck ranch in Nebraska. There were four older children and nothing extra in possessions or affection. The father had been a rodeo rider who had wanted to breed and sell fine stock, but his luck was bad and he was never able to get the animals whose foals would bring good prices. He got what money he made by going to shows and buying for other people. Helen's mother had been a beauty queen and Miss State Fair in 1924. By the time Helen was born, Charmaine Wingate's trophies in the attic were tarnished and flaking and she had been defeated by Plains loneliness and Plains poverty.

These facts he got from Helen slowly, by patient questioning. She seemed happier listening to him and he told her about Cady and their work, about the new building and his restlessness with it and how exciting it was. His talking to her seemed to crystallize the problems, define them for him. The questions she asked were apt and probing and made him see things he had not seen before.

In the afternoon he let her practice alone at her own pace while he went to the expert hills, carving the moguls in tight, swift strokes, leaping sudden rocks, his two tracks often the first in the perfection of new snow. In those high places he let his old nature reassert itself for a while, careless, lifting joy. The unconcern that had been his life's ground had been passive, a sin of omission. Now he made something positive of it, a flinging outward, a dare to gravity, and he soared, swooped, wheeled, bent, landing on gliding wings that seemed barely to kiss the snow. He read the mounds and ridges beneath their winter shawls, all the bones and hollows of the earth, leaping or gliding as they came, in a rhythm, right, left, a dance which at that intensity is so much ego it seems to be none at all. Then, when the light drew off the back slopes, down and down until three o'clock, when the light went flat and a chill came up from the snow and iced the low places. Then it was time for the last descent into the world of responsibilities and ties, loyalties and judgments, slowly, a little sadly down, down to the lower places where the neophytes were, so that he had to go carefully, slowly past them, and still farther down to the new, careful life.

In the evenings he had begun to leave Cady and Esther after he had helped with the dishes and go up to his room to study Elsie's plans and the plans he had to make himself. Would the ground beneath the building bear its weight without sinking or moving? Where were the water and power and phone lines? Would they need to blast or shore? The contractor would orchestrate the movements of the builders but he had to know the specifications of each component of the building. Sometimes Cady grinned; he saw Cady grinning, even from the back, but neither of them mentioned the work.

Elsie met with them again and this time he was impressed with Eric's knowledge of the plan and his preparation. Still there was something missing. Eric hesitated several times, as though he were about to say something. Elsie waited, Cady said, "Go on," and Eric had to demur and say, "It's nothing— I'm sorry."

"Tell them," Roche said, after Elsie had left. "You don't have to be so polite."

"It's nothing I *know*," Eric said miserably. "Something wants to be said, but I don't know what it is."

Days went by, weeks. He dreamt about the building, but the dreaming did not give him the answer to his restlessness about it. By the time Elsie was ready, he would be ready with all his standards and studies, frustrated as ever. So be it. He tried to put the project out of his mind.

They had another snow and Chinook winds after, so everything melted and there was flooding, and the school gym was under a foot of water. Cady and Eric stayed overnight in the office coordinating cleanup crews. They had sent Roche home because his wife, Phyllis, was expecting again, and they had set up the army cots in the downstairs front room. They got to sleep around three and slept until eight. Eric woke stiff in every joint, with a pounding headache. The room, usually ice-cold, was sweltering because Cady had turned the heat up before they went to bed and the thermostat had gotten stuck somehow.

"I feel awful . . ."

"A shave and a shower will fix you up." Cady kept shaving supplies in the filthy bathroom. Eric took a shower and then gave in and went around to Stark's drugstore to get some shaving things of his own. Then he sat moodily at the upstairs office window waiting for Cady to finish. It was a bleak day, cold and windy. Now and then the old panes rattled. Cady was singing in the bathroom. He sang Stephen Foster songs in a light tenor voice. The coffeepot was down to oily dregs. Eric's eyes hurt with tiredness.

Outside on the sidewalk two girls on their way to school had stopped to talk. They carried their books against their chests in a way Eric remembered from his own high-school days. The girl in the red coat was bending her knees up one after the other, to warm her legs briefly under the coat. The girls were in the middle of the sidewalk. Passers-by had to go around them. They were talking animatedly, spiritedly. He could see their heads moving to nod or shake. Why had they stopped just there? Look at that—without their being conscious of it, probably, they were circling slightly, in a thirty-degree arc, back and forth, keeping a certain set distance between them, a yard maybe, but always face to face. The house, he thought; they are in the lee of the house to be out of the wind, but the circling, that—the circling . . . "Cady—"

"I'm *com-ming*."

"Cady—"

"Though my head is bending *looow*."

"Cady, where are the plans, Elsie's plans?"

Cady came out of the bathroom. "There's a set somewhere. You have a set at home."

"Where is the set here? I need them now."

"Look in the file under *B*, 'Bigger than a breadbox.' What's this all about?" Eric was going through the file. "Give me a clue," Cady said.

"Breadbox," Eric growled.

"Give me another clue."

"Here they are. Put on your shirt, Cady, I want you to look at this with your shirt on." Eric was at once fully awake. He felt the same high, clear feeling he had when he had air under his skis and all the mountain down. "Cady, the breadbox, the beautiful-ugly breadbox, is facing the wrong way!"

"*What?*"

"Look—" Eric pulled Cady to the window. "The girls, look at the girls." They were gone. The street was bare.

He got Cady back to the plans. "Look at this. Straight facing on its lot. Good old Elsie; and the wind cuts across it the same way it does to all the houses on that street. You ought to know with that icebox we live in facing the same way, nothing personal. While with a twenty-degree, no, make it twenty-five, angling, see what we have—more sun, fall and winter, less wind, more room for meetings, talking outside—benches *here*, trees, maybe, for an added windbreak and no glare. You won't have to cover the idiot windows and flood the place in fluorescent light and—what do you think?"

"Take a breath, you're turning blue," Cady said. He took the plan. "Get me the scissors," he said.

They cut the building out and began to set it angled on the site. "It looks better. Somehow it looks less boxy, too."

"I'll be damned," Cady said, "if it doesn't make the space part of the building."

"Before we decide if the main entrance is here or on the other side, I'd like to do a traffic study. Do you think the commissioners would pay for one?"

"Don't need to. I'll call Pete Yerby at the high school. If we go up there and explain the problem to his math class, they'll take it on as a school project. Write up exactly what you want to find out. They'll love it."

"And Elsie, what about Elsie?"

"Actually, we're not changing his building at all. This is partly an engineering decision and all we have to do is tactfully show him why."

"There's going to be less ice build-up on this—"

The phone rang. "There's our public," Cady said. "Why don't you go shave."

When Roche came in they tried the idea on him. Looking at the plan, he saw it and cried out, "Why didn't we think of this before?" And they all laughed. Through the morning of taking calls and radioing the crews, they thought of reasons and refinements, questions, details. Before noon Eric called the commissioners' office to talk to Helen. "Can I see you? I need to see you. Can you have lunch with me?"

"I don't know where we could go to be private—where there wouldn't be talk—"

"After work, then."

"I've got to take the car in to the shop."

"I want—I have something to tell you."

"All right, at one I'll meet you in the archives room. It's here in the courthouse on the third floor."

"Thanks."

He got away at lunch and went quickly to the courthouse, up to the seldom-used third floor. He had called her in the second wash of his enthusiasm and joy, because right after Cady and Roche he had wanted to share the news with her, to see her face as he relived the sudden opening of his inspiration, the tiredness, the gray day, the cold, the girls, the wordless connection of picture to idea and then words to go with it, and, for her alone, what it meant for him. But when he faced her he didn't know how to begin.

"I, uh, I feel silly, keeping you from your lunch."

"What's happened?" she asked. "Only half your face is shaved and you look—"

"How do I look?"

"Tired, tired and shining."

"I feel just like that, tired and shining and half-shaved. I was sitting by the window this morning, because we stayed at the office all night . . ."

He told her all of it. She stood quietly, saying nothing but listening very intently, her eyes never leaving his face. When he finished with the events of the morning, he went on and said the thing he hadn't told Roche or Cady. "I was never very serious about work. I went into engineering because my dad thought it was a good idea. I never felt any call to be an engineer. In school I could see some of the guys who were excited, really excited by their futures, and I envied them in a dim way for it. But this—this thing that's happened is like a message, what I saw and know because of that girl turning to try to get out of the cold was a message to me that I belong here in Aureole, belong to the work I do—that these things are part of me and that I'm part of them."

She was smiling. It was a shy smile, a smile of quietly controlled delight. It made him shy again. "And you're giving up your lunch to hear all this. I wanted to tell you because you know the problem—the problem I was having with the building. I'd already talked so much about it and I thought—"

The room was defeating him, high-windowed and dusty, rows of bound county records, smelling of mushrooms and disuse. The two of them stood there as though having a tryst in a mausoleum.

"I'm glad for what happened," she said, "and that you told me. Later I would like to see the plan, the way the building will be. Remember, I'm going to be working in it."

"And Saturday we're skiing, aren't we?"

"Yes," she said, and smiled, and turned and left.

He stayed afterward. He had wanted to touch her. His hand had come up tentatively and he had felt the wish to reach out to her arm or her shoulder. When she had said the words about working in the building he had had a quick picture of her moving into that protected, windless, sun-warmed space, her coming in every day, his gift to her. He knew then why he had called her and asked her to hear him. He had thought it was only the excitement and her having known about the problem his hesitancy made with Cady and Elsie. "Oh, God!" he groaned into the dusty room. He had told her because he had wanted her respect and approval. Because . . .

His triumph had worn away in tiredness. He rubbed his face. She had been right—he was only half-shaved. Then he remembered her smile, the quiet, intent way she had listened. Sighing, he went down the stairs and left the building and went back across the street to work.

It was Cady who "engineered" the way they would introduce the change to Elsie. They traced and retraced power lines and sewage lines, the parking areas and the traffic patterns on the two major streets, all the technical problems of the building's presence on city property that were their responsibility. Every time there was an advantage in the new way, they listed it. "Hurry up," Cady said to them, "Elsie has to hear about this *first*, before it leaks out. If it comes from anyone else, he'll think we've bushwhacked him."

Eric gulped. He had told Helen. Why shouldn't she mention it casually to the commissioners? At noon he called her. She didn't sound annoyed, but he felt clumsy, swearing her to secrecy. First the archives room and now this.

The building focused what he had noticed before, harnessed the questions to a purpose. "Watch people," he told her as they put their skis on. "See where they gather. Watch them in the lunchroom, how they move the chairs and tables. See where they sit, who in the corners and who in the middle. We build shopping centers and schools and hospitals and ski slopes and public buildings and we never think we're part of a neighborhood."

"Has anyone written about this?"

"I'm trying to find that out now."

"I could help you do that," she said.

Now it was his turn to be shy. "I . . . I'd like that."

Later they skied the west side of the mountain. From its height they could look over the intervening hills and into the canyon where Aureole lay along its river. "What a beautiful town it is," he said quietly. He was conscious that he was speaking of something few others saw. Around the town lay hill after hill, scoured and defaced by mounds of yellow tailings, tumbling breakers, collapsing mine shafts. There were hills where even after a hundred years only a handful of scrub weeds found enough soil to grow in. "I love this place."

"People love the places where they're happy," Helen said.

"Yes, but there's something else about Aureole. It allows itself to be known. It's not self-conscious. For all the talk of Cady's about its founders being exploiters out for gold, for all its history of boom and bust, it's not small-spirited."

Helen said, "Well, it isn't Cory, Nebraska, I'll give it that."

"You really hated Cory, didn't you?"

"I wonder if I would have liked it if I had had friends there like you or like Ernestine, my friend in the office. Maybe they were there and I just didn't know how to find them."

"You're happy here, aren't you?" he said.

She skied away a little down the hill. "I'm not sure what the word means," she said, and tried to turn and cut her uphill edge.

He saw her going wrong and put his hand up, too late. She went sprawling. "Be happy," he murmured and went to help her, "please be happy."

They met with Elsie. Cady was masterful. He presented the changes as engineering problems. Roche explained savings in water and sewer lines; Eric, the obvious savings during construction; Cady, the ease of maintenance, even greater if they extended a windbreak of shrubbery on the northwest and angle-parked the cars in the lot. No one mentioned a word about the building's increased beauty or interest or of making something of a meeting area in the space they'd gained. It was a trap and Elsie fell into it as easily as if forty-five minutes earlier he hadn't called the ideas trivial. "These steps look silly with the building turned. You'd need a longer, wider entrance"—and Elsie began to draw, sketching quickly, seeing more as he went—"much better balance, a focus here that leads the eye up and in . . ."

Cady grinned at Eric over Elsie's head as he drew. "I never thought about the aesthetic qualities," Eric said. Cady's heel came down hard on Eric's little toe. Eric bore his pain in absolute silence.

"You nearly lost it all!" Cady cried at him later. "Elsie's not dumb. If he hadn't been so deep into it, he would have heard you."

"I'm sorry." Eric laughed. "Old ways die hard. You give great noogies, though; I nearly fainted with pain."

"You deserved it," Cady said primly, and the three of them laughed aloud. "He went for it all, the wide courtyard, the shrubbery. I could see him opening his mouth to say 'wasted space' the first minute he came in here. Next week we *all* go to the commissioners about *Elsie's* building. Got it?"

"Yes, sir."

On the way home Cady said, "I know the idea was yours. Roche knows it, too. The county men won't know, but they'll suspect it isn't Elsie's or mine. In twenty years we haven't come up with anything like it, but we can't say it's your idea—it's got to come this way. I hope that's enough for you." Eric probed into his mind as deeply as he could. He read no hunger there, no anger, and no sorrow. Surprised, he nodded his head. Cady put a hand on his shoulder. "Gets your name on the plaque, though, right where folks come in, right under the commissioners and Hizzoner and devil knows who else and Elsie and me and baby makes three."

"Sounds good." Eric laughed.

"Brass," Cady said. "Engraved right in. One thing more, something serious. You've been taking that Helen skiing Saturdays—"

"Yes."

"Esther's got the wind up. She feels we've fallen down somehow on the hospitality."

"Oh, no, it's not—there's nothing—"

"You're not listening. Nobody's interested in your murmurings. This is a woman thing. Cake and tea. Their sound has gone out, as the Bible says, and it is your job to lie still beneath that sound and endure." He grinned at Eric. "Sweet Jesus, I feel good!"

Eric put it to Helen, carefully, when they left the next Saturday. "Would you mind—Mrs. Cady wants us to stop by with them after our skiing . . ." He saw her pause, weigh. She didn't answer for a long time. He knew she had been raised on hard equations—and that their being together was one of them. A spontaneous yes or no would have been as foreign to her as that weighing and measuring was for him.

At last she said, "It would be bad manners to refuse, wouldn't it?"

"I think so."

"In that case, it's important that we go."

She skied well that day, and by cautious, subtle questioning over the weeks he was learning more about her family. The father had died; Curtis, the oldest brother, was on the ranch with his wife and mother; Buck had gone away somewhere after a fight with Curtis. Frances and Mary Anne had married local men; Mary Anne lived in Cut Bank and was the only one with whom she had contact. For the first time, Eric raised the subject of her days in Omaha, her meeting with Charles. She said only that she had gone to Omaha to work after high school. She had worked in the insurance office for almost six months before Charles asked her out. They married six months later and began their family almost immediately. Lois, Richard, then Patricia.

That part was too painful for him to pursue. What he had learned had been given, a sentence or two at a time, almost as though she were ashamed—the explanation of a preference or a dislike revealed, quickly, shyly. He admired her courage and tenacity and told her so, and thought to himself, No wonder it's so hard for her to relax and be easy when somewhere likes and dislikes are being weighed and criticized by some invisible judge, and only facts are to be trusted.

"That's what skiing's for," he told her, "to glide past things, to turn and bend and sail and fly free and play with mountains and look down the edges of the world, playing."

"I'm not used to playing," she said.

He dreaded the afternoon with Cady and Esther. They didn't know who Helen was. What if they offered something besides tea and cake? He had never taken a drink in front of her. Perhaps in some part of her she connected his ideas about "fun" with the boy he had been, the careless, stupid . . . Maybe Esther would ask her how she had come to be in Aureole, and the whole, awful story would come out. Accident. They knew there had been an "accident," but how different that was from seeing the widow and knowing she now stood absolutely alone, and that it was he, Eric, who had caused . . . His afternoon skiing was badly off form. He had several serious falls and spent the last hour on the easier slopes with Helen. Nothing for it but to go and live with what would happen.

"Perhaps I should go home and change—" she said when they started back.

"No, this is very informal. They know we've been skiing."

"Mr. Cady seems like a nice man."

"I think you'll like his wife, Esther, too. They've been very good to me."

"People are nice to you," she said, and looked at him levelly. "People like you." It was said with no rising or lowering of the voice, without anger, rancor, or envy that he could hear—only as a fact.

For an instant he began to demur. With anyone else he

would have; her honesty and what he owed her forbade it. "I know," he said.

She came into the house shyly, but her shyness had none of the coy quality Eric had seen with shy women. She followed Cady's small gallantries gravely and was happy to go with Esther and help get the snacks. Cady made her a gin and orange juice, which she had never had before. Eric had a drink then; it followed naturally; she seemed not to notice. Cady told about the fireplace upstairs and Eric said, "Getting the permit was how I really met you, Helen," and she smiled one of her rare smiles. Roche came by. Phyllis was home with a sick child and he could only stay for a while. They talked about skiing, and Eric praised Helen's progress and described the faces of the skiers on the learner's hill. Then Esther told about a new health store, the first one in Aureole. "They saw my arthritis and caution was thrown to the winds; out came all the remedies, the roots, the bracelets—all of it."

To Eric's surprise, Helen said, "I used to shop in a store like that. Once, when I got to the counter the man said, 'How come you never come with the other Adventists?' I told him I was not an Adventist. He said, 'You don't have to hide it—only Adventists buy those crackers.' " She hadn't embellished the story but she seemed pleased when people laughed. Roche asked her if that was in Denver. "No, Omaha."

"Oh, did you grow up there?"

"No, I came from a small town called Cory. I went to Omaha to get work after high school."

"It must have been hard, starting out like that," Esther said.

"Yes, it was."

Cady smiled at Helen. "Do you feel like a heroine?"

"I don't believe in heroism," she said. "What I had to do, I did; there was no other way."

Eric felt another question coming from Esther, something kind, but something that would open the road to that buried husband, those disappeared children. With her frankness,

Helen wouldn't dissemble and the friendly, casual group would darken with the oncoming night into the agony she had suffered at the hands of a drunk, drugged, consenting . . .

Because he *had* consented to it all. Not two hours ago, beetling down the narrow chute of the Juggernaut, the hardest run in the area, off his form with that other anxiety, he had remembered Bressard. Suddenly, a full picture had come, complete, unbidden—the wild, stripped-gear fun of driving into the dawn, laughing, singing, beyond control. He had taken Bressard someplace in that extra hour or two—they had gone into a sleeping town, and there was a shack of some kind, and a friend of Bressard's, and they had had some kind of pill or other; a man and woman were there and they refilled that tank of laughing gas and "Arnie" had consented to it all because it was there, because it was easy, though he knew in some part of him . . . And in the middle of the chute on Juggernaut his rhythm had broken, his concentration had shredded away upslope, and he had fallen end over end and lay for several minutes in the snow until another skier came by and asked him if he was all right. He had gotten up and put the knowledge of that night away again, out of his mind as he had always done with unpleasant things. There was nothing to be done about any of it now, and he had laughed uneasily with Helen at the bottom of the hill—"See, even expert skiers fall"—showing her the telltale snow on his pants and back. But right now he wanted only to stop Esther from summoning the ghosts of that night, so he told them an experience he had had in Boulder when a peace marcher had begun to harangue him in a health store. It wasn't a great story, but it moved the conversation away from Helen's life and she shot him a quick, grateful look as Cady began to talk about the war, which puzzled them, President Johnson, and the protesters.

The talk turned to John Kennedy and where each of them was when they heard the news of his being shot. Eric had been in class and two kids from the dorm had rushed in. No one had known then how bad it was, but no one's attention was on hydraulics, and the professor let them go. Cady was out on a prospecting project for a friend, up in the hills near Cold Spring. He found out the next day, when he came upon a town numb with mourning and felt he had been away for years instead of days. Esther had heard the news on TV and had sat mesmerized all afternoon as report after report had come in. Helen said she heard it from a neighbor.

The talk went on, quiet and friendly, until the light went and it was time to go home. Eric saw Helen out to the car. "You covered up," he said. "Your Kennedy story was half a story."

"I did hear from a neighbor," she said, "technically."

"Tell me."

"Why should it matter?"

"Because we're friends—we're getting to be friends in spite of ourselves, and it's the right time and because it's Saturday evening just before supper, which is my favorite time."

"It's cold."

"We'll sit in the car for a minute, while you tell me."

They sat in the dark. "I was taking my neighbor to school. We were going to pick up our children early." Her voice was level. "Richard was in kindergarten, then. Some of the teachers were gathered in the halls—they had heard, and there was an awful feeling in the air, a shock-feeling. The older children were upset. The kindergarten teacher was weeping at her desk. I thought the children should know why, even though they were so little. I told them that the President had been shot. They were very quiet, but three of them raised their hands to ask a question."

"What was it?"

"They all had the same worry."

"What was it?"

"They said, 'Who will take care of his children?' Only that."

"Helen—"

"Yes?"

"A careless stranger destroyed that life—someone who didn't know you, who didn't know your family or what he was doing, someone who's not the man I am now. Can you—could you ever forgive me?"

She looked at him levelly. "I had to, at first, in order to stay alive, but now I want to. You are different, I think, from the boy who did those things. I saw you in the hearing room. I saw you again in the commissioners' office. Something had changed in you. Both of us are trying to make a new life here. I can't live here and keep on hating you. Yes, I can forgive you. I think I already have."

He knew she had only one other friend—only Ernestine among the secretaries. He still heard Helen described as "snooty," "odd," "standoffish." None of her strengths made her easy to be with. He knew she must be lonely and vulnerable in a way he could only guess at. That loneliness, he thought, the simple need for someone else who cared and was interested in what she did, was dictating her forgiveness. Let it be, then. Had he been given the choice, he would have made her popular and easily befriended, and made the world such that her virtues could be easily seen. Whatever the reasons for her forgiveness, let them be. He was more and more attracted to her, more and more hoping for her approval, more and more in need of sharing his thoughts with her.

Again he wanted to touch her, as he had done so many times when she had gotten up from a fall and needed steadying, except that now he was the one who was off balance and she was the one who stood secure.

6

The ground was cleared and the digging was started on the new site. Cady laughed at Eric. "Did they come up with ten new tests since I left school? You've done tests on that ground and structure I've never heard of."

"You'd want to know how the river—"

"The river's a mile away—"

"Nine-sixteenths of a mile," Eric said. He knew that Cady's joking was pride in his meticulousness. Linder, the contractor, was a tough, weathered block of a man with what he declared was "blood pressure." Eric lived in fear of Linder's finding out that this was his first building. He read the specs a dozen times, checking them against the materials brought to the site. When he sent back three-quarter-inch rod that should have been seven-eighths, and five-inch pipe that should have been six, Linder raged. Eric yearned to give in. Maybe Linder was right, that the specs were artificial and not cost-effective, but in the end he couldn't take the chance. He stuck by the specs and earned Linder's rage and respect.

He had never worked where there was a natural tension between the workers because of the differences in their jobs. His work in college had been under a boss; he slid by with minimum stress, doing just what the job required and no more. His time with Aguilar—he saw it clearly now—had been a sinecure, a boy's job, requiring little besides his presence and the minimum exercise of his trade. Here he found himself having to argue form against practicality with Elsie and specifications of weight and density, wind resistance and heat loss with Linder, who needed to come in under budget. The water commissioner and utilities men were both on the take—Cady had told him that. "Not for this building, they're not!" Eric cried, and Cady smiled and said, "They can't do it without you." So Eric went early and late to the project to make sure of what had been done and he stopped by at odd times on his way to other things.

Footings were dug, foundations poured. The change in the building's orientation began to show its virtues. Trucks were able to go front and back without blocking the street. The work went faster. Linder was grudgingly impressed. Sometimes he would look at Elsie quizzically—the very conventional building sat at so rakish an angle. Elsie neither confirmed nor denied that the changes were his; neither did Eric.

And Saturdays he skied with Helen. As he watched her body and face and hands, knowing when she was tired and would fall, watching the moves being made—too soon or too late, moment by moment—he began to learn to read her gestures and her face. Helen seldom spoke. She didn't like talking about her emotions and there was pain for both of them in her memories, even though he urged her to tell him about her years with Charles and the children. She never did, but her voice said more than her words and he began to learn what pleased her and what bored her and what angered her by the slope of her shoulders, the gestures of her hands, the expressions that went quickly across her face. Her family had been a cold one, an angry one; she had learned to keep her face carefully blank, her body still. But the feelings were all there for someone who wanted to see them, in the careful voice, the resonances, in the face held still, the changes—pleasure, tiredness, annoyance, delight. The more he learned, the more he wanted to learn.

If she was mostly silent with him, he had never confided so much to another human being. For all the girls he had had, all the trips up ski lifts and to and from the rivers or the slopes, or dancing or making love, he realized he had given very little of himself.

He told her about the building, about Elsie and Linder and their natural divergences, about what he was seeing in the way people grouped and moved. He asked her about the offices in which she had worked—about the physical conditions that made the work easier or harder. He was formulating a theory about neighborhoods and he told her about that. She listened and he saw the ripples of interest and sometimes humor move on her face—there and gone, but there.

He saw also, over her head, that the sun was warming the snow. It would soon be spring. Their skiing was now his excuse to see and be with her. What would happen when their reason for being together was gone?

"When spring comes, real spring, let's go rafting," he said. She looked at him quizzically. "It's all around us," he said, "some of the best water in the state."

"Why?"

"Well, because it's fun." She didn't reply. He felt the need to tell her. "I like being with you. We can't ski in June. There is no snow. How am I going to see you, then?" She didn't answer but looked down at her mittened hands.

He wanted to plead. He wanted to say "I've just learned to read you from the back, your shoulders and neck—when you're tired and when you're frightened. I'm beginning to understand, to understand and love. How can I waste that knowledge now?" Damn all seasonal things! They could have drifted on together becoming more and more natural and easy with each other until the natural ease made itself apparent to her, too. "Well," he said at last, "there's still time."

The next week Cady said, "Elsie's building is causing lots of interest. Commissioners have been getting calls. A couple of people thought someone was drunk the day the footings were poured. Tyrrel's been feeling a little left out of it all and he wants us to have lunch with him to talk about it."

"Elsie—"

"He'll be there, too. Bring some extra money, will you, he'll bring O'Brien or Forbes with him. I'll pay for his lunch. You can pay for the other one." To Eric's look, Cady laughed and said, "Son, when a commissioner 'has you to lunch,' *you* pay. No commissioner ever pays for anything during the daylight hours and only half the things at night."

Tyrrel was a big man who had, years ago, worked for Cady on a road crew. He had been very popular in high school. Eric knew this from the way he used his body. O'Brien was nondescript. They made pleasant talk for the beginning of the meal. Eric was beginning to wonder if it all wasn't a waste of time when Tyrrel said, "Y'know, a place like this—everybody comes here, though God knows it isn't for the food. It's convenient to the courthouse and there's that window so people can see who is in and who isn't. Kind of casually. I guess people need places for casual meetings." Across the table from Eric, Cady bit his lip. Elsie's mouth dropped open. Eric, too, was surprised. Had Tyrrel been reading their thoughts, or had he seen the plans and figured all the open space in front?

They talked about the features of the building, careful to indicate Elsie and say, "We thought . . ." and "Elsie's plan calls for . . ."

"I guess things like, well, planning, is something officials should start looking at," Tyrrel said. Eric nodded.

"Elsie says—" Cady began. Elsie stood up and excused himself to get back to his office. When he left, Cady continued. "Elsie says—"

"Oh, come on"—and Tyrrel laughed—"Elsie's been doing buildings for years and he never mentioned any of this stuff before."

"We all live and learn," Cady said. The men finished their meal and got up. They thanked Eric and Cady and stopped at at least five other tables on their way out. Cady fingered the bill, grinning. "See?" he said.

Eric was amazed. "Where did he read—did he study the plan and see what we were getting at?"

"Tyrrel's not a student, never was. My guess is that he talked to someone, picked a brain."

"Elsie's?"

"No, not Elsie's. Helen's. I think it was Helen."

"How did you make it happen?" he cried to her. "The man was listening, and later he said that business about public spaces—I nearly fell off my chair."

"I didn't do very much." She looked down. "You'd told me enough about the differences in the building—your general ideas—"

"I could kiss you!" he said, and all of a sudden, it seemed possible to do so, like a friend, he said to himself, like a dear and cherished friend, and he kissed her enthusiastically once and then again. "What are we going to do—what are we going to do when the snow is gone?" He was holding her shoulders, smiling down at her, but the question was moving closer, touching at the edges of their clothes like the warming winds of spring, a consciousness that there were a few moments longer in the warmth of the day. The skiing would soon be over—the excuse of his teaching her would soon be gone. She didn't answer him and the moment passed.

It was time to let his parents know that he was planning to stay and make a life in Aureole. He had written and called with general news, on anniversaries, Christmas. Their enthusiasm for his new happiness, his energy and seriousness, was cautious; they were still hoping that with his fifteen months over, as they would be this coming fall, he would move back again; back East to settle down near them. He had told them about Cady, the building, he had mentioned Helen ("my skiing student"). "I want you to come out," he begged. "Come

in June to see my friends, Cady, the building, the town . . ."
They said they would come, and with his new way of hearing
he heard their unhappiness.

"Cady, how can I get them to see what I have here?"

"I don't know. They only know you're not going to be close
to them. Our kids moved away. For a year or two Esther and
I pretended we were glad—just think, we said, it's an excuse to
go to Portland, to Iran, to Mexico, to see and be part of all
the things they're doing—but none of the big ideas about
traveling came true. Your folks didn't expect you'd stay,
probably."

"Did you?"

"The truth?"

"Yes."

"I didn't think you were the type to like it here."

"Why not?"

"I thought you were what my dad used to call a summer
soldier. You were pleasant and easy with people; I didn't
mind giving you all the pothole calls because you were so
good at it, but . . ."

"Go on."

"Oh, I don't want to say all this—characterizing people
flattens them out somehow . . ."

"I asked you; go on."

"I had the feeling you didn't care much about anything,
that you weren't, uh, serious. Then I began to see I was
wrong. You worked hard, then you moved in here and you
were so good to Esther. I saw, too, how much you cared about
Elsie's plans, about the building, about doing it right. I knew
then that I'd misjudged you."

"No, you hadn't. I *was*—what was it—a summer soldier.
Then, well, then there was the accident. It changed things."

"I never asked you—it must have been serious, your not
being able to drive for so long . . ."

"Yes. Some, uh, there were people killed. The time's about
half over and so much has changed."

"That's a terrible thing to have happen. Was that where you hurt your arm?"

"Yes—how did you know? I was out of the cast long before I started work here."

"When you're tired, very tired, I've noticed you favor your left arm, that it must be hurting."

"It does—I guess I do favor it—I didn't know it was that obvious."

"I'm the husband of an arthritic wife, don't forget, and at sixty-two I have my little twinges. I thought the injury must have been recent. My dad used to say, 'It's when you're old that the body remembers its insults.' You're not old."

That Cady should have seen him so close, seen through the flesh to where the bone was knitting itself, alarmed Eric as much as it moved him. He had spent all his life hiding from other people's expectations of him, hiding his selfishness in an easygoing cheer. Could his weaknesses still be so readable to others? "I'll have to write to my parents again," he murmured, "to tell them that the building is going on." Then he smiled at Cady. "I use the pain to tell the difference between right and left."

"When the pain goes," Cady said, "I'll tell Esther to sew a little bow on your shirt cuffs, because that and up and down are the four things an engineer really needs to know."

His letters to his parents were trying too hard to convince them and sounded either manic or stiff. His mother wrote back, parrying. "Don't make a final decision until you are sure." Eric wanted to let them know that he was sure, and was looking forward to the years of his new life, the repayment of his debt to them, a relationship with Helen, being a part of the town—gifts of the accident, good out of evil. They were terrible letters:

I am very happy living here; I like my work. There is a ~~girl~~ . . . woman . . . ~~whom I~~ . . . with whom I am friends.

84

The letter gave none of the flavor, the sense of discovery, the hope and anguish he had been through, the fear that still struck him from time to time, and the dawning knowledge that the relief of that fear lay in his active dedication to changing himself. He wanted to be like Cady, who loved and cared for Esther and was happy in his assistants' challenges; he wanted to be like Esther, who bore her pain quietly and tried hard to do things in the house; to be like Helen, who was quiet and never shallow. None of the letters spoke of those things.

They called on his birthday. His mother sounded equivocal over the phone, his father less enthusiastic than he thought he would be. "You got them to change the direction of the building?"

"Well, just a twenty-degree change in orientation. I found we could get more space, a protected space for people to meet outside in good weather, and great savings on heating and cooling because of the change. I guess it's not a beautiful building, but to me, it seems well designed . . ." He felt the work of it, trying to convey the excitement he felt.

"But why *there*?" his mother cried. "Why can't you come back here?"

"Because it's happened here; I don't think I can re-create the conditions of it anywhere else. Please come out during the summer. It's a nice town, bigger than you think."

He had a sudden, joyful picture of their coming. Maybe they would feel a heart-rise driving up Gold Flume Canyon to that revelation of the Front Range, or the horizon-to-horizon openness down from Victory Pass. Maybe they would see what he saw, would feel the grandeur of it all, the sky, spread out to the bending of the world. "Please come out soon . . ."

They said they would come. He said he would meet them in Denver and they would drive up together, up and over Victory Pass. As he spoke he thought that perhaps the pioneers named that pass for all the boys who grew up on the journey west and went down the other side of those mountains changed. He took a deep breath and said, "There's a woman, too—someone I've met—her name is Helen."

When he hung up, he realized that this was the first time he had "introduced" a woman to his parents, named a name. He had never mentioned Claire or any of the others by name; he had said, "I'm going out with a girl." Years of "girls" gave him no guide to his behavior now. He felt shy with his parents, tongue-tied. He knew they would be horrified if they found out who she was—had been. The easiest way would be not to let them know. At least not yet, until they got to know her well.

But the conversation with his parents changed something in his relationship with Helen. He knew he was falling in love with her; his words had made him sure. It was everything he had heard about and never believed—the anguish and joy, the fear and need. He began to "see her" in earnest, asking her out for dinner after they skied, for lunch when he could. At these "dates" he was courting so self-consciously she was forced to mention it.

"Flowers again; I don't need flowers."

"Take them to work with you and put them in the office. Let's go dancing. They're having a dance at the Elks on Thursday . . ."

"The whole office is gaining weight with all the candy you bring over there. Myra, the statistician, is all broken out." He laughed, and then so did she.

Her laughter was self-conscious but he loved eliciting it. She was naturally reticent, preferring to listen to him rather than talk about herself, but he read her enjoyment in the way she turned toward him, her comfort with him in the narrowing physical space between them, the positions she chose, sitting down beside him, her small unspoken choices. These things seemed louder to him than the words she never said.

She didn't like excess, confrontations, dramatic scenes. In the movies and plays they went to, grand emotional bravura left her incredulous or bored. She liked comedies, musicals, although she admitted they were unrealistic. "People don't fall in love that way, but I like to see the dancing." She liked ice shows and horse shows; they went to everything that came to Aureole and they sometimes drove all the way to Pickaxe to catch something. He liked the special quality of what they did; the special behavior of "seeing someone" was new to him. They went on a hayride. They went to Pickaxe to go up in an airplane.

And he found out that she kept a journal in which she listed all the things they had done. "I never knew anyone who kept a journal," he said. He asked her if she used it to confide in—to list her triumphs, cry aloud, to rage or admit to fear, all the things he had always assumed women did so easily.

"I use it to forget," she said.

"What?"

"I keep the books so I don't need to keep the events. When it's written down, it's gone."

"But you can go back over—"

"I never go back over. I was eight when I started it—I felt then that I was writing down the days. I thought that gave me a kind of power, a way of keeping a thing the size of its words."

"Does it still?"

"No, I learned that it gave no power, but there's a kind of clarity and then there's forgetting."

"What is it, one of those five-year diaries?"

"No," she said, "a habit like that is a collection of little habits. I started with a line composition book and twelve books later I'm still doing it that way."

"When you were eight?"

"Yes," she said, "it was 1944."

He was startled a little. He had forgotten that she was fully eight years older than he; that she remembered at least part of a war he had only heard about, that she knew about that "good war" in a way that he did not. "Did you write about the war?" he asked. "The Second World War?"

"The war in Cory," she answered.

He was grinning. "Tell me about the war in Cory."

"Many people in Cory got rich from the war because prices were kept up and everyone sold his cattle and grain to the government. My father got very little good out of it, so he turned against it. My brother Buck was exempted from fighting, but Curtis went to get away from home. My father never forgave him."

Her words shocked him. "But I thought everyone was patriotic then, sharing, the spirit of that war was so good—"

"Not everyone," she said quietly.

The building had been excavated and footings poured with concrete that smelled sharp and filled Eric with a feeling of exhilaration. He found he loved the elemental smells of building: the blueprint paper, earth, cement, iron and wood, welding smells and the smells of the earth-movers. He inspected, suggested, sometimes argued. The sealed-window argument took weeks; Linder called him a hippie and fresh-air fiend, and Eric got Elsie to design something that would slant the windows so the rooms would need less air-conditioning in the summer. Cady laughed but Eric saw his approval even when he didn't agree with the fight. It made him care even more that things be right.

Electricians came and studied and made patterns of the building's nerves, rough carpenters framed its bones on scaffoldings of stel and concrete, plumbing and heating men planned for the secreting of its ducts and chambers within the walls the carpenters and plasterers would make. Linder orchestrated it all like a dance, and when the parts didn't come together in the right combination of laborers' time and money, he would beat his head with his hand. Eric laughed because he had heard the nickname "Flathead" used about Linder.

Now there were changes day by day and Eric went to the building on his way to other jobs: a row of houses leaking raw sewage into a ditch along Grant Street, water problems, culvert calls. Evenings he read specs, fire codes, safety codes, health department regulations, all of which contradicted one another in details great and small. Sometimes the Cadys heard him pacing, and when Esther mentioned it, he bought a rug for his room. But the house was old and the floor squeaked anyway. A week of bad weather stopped the work and put Eric back on snow detail. The pipes froze at the courthouse, the streets buckled at Divide Avenue, there was poor drainage at the hospital, and there were always the water problems.

The snow that Eric and Helen skiied took on its April texture—gummy or grainy. Bare patches appeared, and sprigs of dried weeds. The season was ending. Soon only the diehards would be skiing; in two or three weeks the area would close. Their being together would lose the comfortable excuse that he was teaching her to ski. He wanted to move forward, but would she? He wanted to make love to her, to hold her, caress her—but he dared not say the words to begin to ask her. Never before had it been important, a thing he could be refused and not recover from the next day with another girl. He cursed himself, afraid to ask more of her, afraid to play any of the games with which he had charmed his women before. It began to trouble him. The strain made him curse himself all the more.

Colorado's springtime is equivocal. Budding lilac branches break with sudden snow; spring beauties bloom in the lace of ice; torrents of water from melting snows unlock their hundred gulleys and break down the doors of silted creeks, pouring in flood down and away, and two days later choke black in a freeze. The wind beats like winter and ravages the leaves of trees not made for mountain country. Flowers the flatlanders planted in last autumn's homesickness heave in the freeze and die even before the bone-dry summer has its time with them. The towns along the Ute blew green and froze, greened and froze again. A four-foot snow fell on the third of

May and a secretary at the typing pool burst into tears as Eric arrived with a sheaf of reports; she was grieving for the roses she had planted at the balmy end of April. "When will it be over! The damn, damn, damn . . ." Tears flowing down her face, her fists clenched. He stood staring helplessly and then moved toward her and held her as she sobbed out her frustration against his chest.

An hour later Roche heard about the incident from the secretaries and kidded him. Cady heard about it from Tyrrel before lunch, Helen from the secretaries, and Esther from God knows where. In his own frustration he called Helen from a pay phone the next day and shouted at her, "Why wasn't it *you*, crying in the office? Why can't I comfort *you*!"

"Cory's winters went on forever," she said carefully, her voice controlled above the office sounds behind her, "and I learned not to cry years ago. Perhaps we could meet after work without the tears."

"Please have dinner with me."

"All right."

He knew she was speaking quietly, flatly, so as not to attract the attention of anyone in the office. He couldn't see her face, but he thought he heard something in an undertone— but he wasn't sure.

Helen wanted to go to a place that wasn't as nice as he would have liked. She always insisted on paying her own way and she said that because of the skiing she never had any money. They stood bundled up against the weather, arguing about it, and he saw the winter strain on her face as well.

"I won't be going home tonight," he said. "I'll be staying at the office to dispatch the snow crew, grabbing some sleep on the cots we have."

"When do you have to get back?"

"Eleven or so . . ."

She looked at him levelly, without coyness. "I have a quiet room. You can be with me until then."

He stopped. It was a moment sinking in, and then he took

her in his arms and kissed her, smelling the smell of snow in her hair, feeling her nose icy cold. "I love you," he said. They didn't eat supper that evening at all.

Her room was small but private—they went to it by a set of stairs outside the house. It was very neat and very spare, severe almost, and as he looked around he saw nothing of the past, no picture, no widow's relic, no mommy-gift—clumsy ashtray or construction-paper Christmas card—propped against the mirror. He wanted to ask, Had she cleaned them away yesterday, this morning, knowing? Had she gone through the room taking down those pictures? Surely there had been a picture, the family standing in front of their door, while a neighbor snapped the shot—

There was nothing of them here. On her single bed was a plain white cover. The room had a stillness about it. It quieted him. She took off her coat and turned on a small electric heater and went to a corner where there was a hot-plate and put up some water for tea. Then she turned and she smiled at him and came back toward him, but she didn't speak at all as she moved closer and then away from him, taking his coat and hanging it up, adjusting the heater, closing the drapes. When she moved toward him again, he stopped her and took her in his arms and they held each other for a long time before they kissed. "I want to do this right," he said, "it's so important."

He saw that she was weeping. The tears were soundless but they were falling quickly down her face. He had never been with a sober woman in tears. He had no idea why she was crying or whether it was for or against him, but when he clung to her to comfort her, she let him hold her and then take her to the bed, and there she undressed, still weeping, and when she was partly undressed she turned out the light. He had wanted to see her and let her see him, but with the weeping . . . He sensed that she would not or could not tell him why she wept.

She lay facing him. He took her in his arms, caressing her.

91

She trembled. He felt her readiness. He had been continent for so long, he came almost at once, a deep, complete spending. She shuddered under him and he whispered, "I'm so sorry—it's—uh—I've been a long time without anyone. Would you like me to—to help you?"

"No," she said, "it's all right. I can love, but I don't have orgasms."

"Never?"

"No."

"But surely all the years—"

"It isn't necessary for a woman," she said.

"Is there a reason—something medical—something I could do?"

She was smiling then, he heard it in her voice. "I don't think so. I like being with you, I like—"

He touched her hair. She had taken it down in the dark and when he caressed her, he had moved his hands over it, marveling at its sensuousness. "I want you to have all the pleasure I do—"

"You have all of me that there is to have, all I can give."

"I didn't mean—I only meant you—"

"Never mind," she whispered. "Sleep for a while."

As he drifted off, he relived the softness of her hair, her hands—he thought she must have taken off her wedding ring.

At four in the morning he was up monitoring, listening to the drawn, disembodied voices of the road crews, thinking of warm Helen's cool hair, about the quiet room, her turning off the light. He would have to teach her a little wantonness, a pleasure in her own hair, a delight in letting him see her. Maybe then . . . and he saw that his wish for her orgasm was as much selfishness as love. He wanted her to have pleasure but he also wanted her bonding, her fidelity, and he thought he could assure it by knowing she responded to him fully. When he was in school they used to talk about it late at night in the dorm bull sessions: Could you trust a woman who didn't like it with you? Wouldn't she keep looking? "It's only our first time," he had said to her, "next time we'll be together longer; we'll have lots of time to learn each other." She hadn't seemed disappointed. Her voice had been warm in the darkness.

"There's no pain, no numbness. I like having you. The orgasm—it's not essential to a woman."

But she hadn't lied, he thought. How many women lie because it makes their lovers feel good, or their husbands shut up? How many of his girl friends had cried out with passions they didn't feel? Helen felt loving, eager for him, and she had not lied. What more did there need to be? Is orgasm love?

Because in the blue gloom of the predawn, where he sat in the dark listening to the radio, tired, bored, dry-mouthed and jittery with too much coffee, he knew he was more deeply in love than he had ever been or ever thought he could be. His quest for himself had led him to a woman older, quieter, more serious than he had known before. And suddenly in the dimness he laughed. Older. He was older, too, and, he hoped, quieter, deeper, more serious. Not an affair, a love; not a halfway thing, a full gift—all of it, whether she felt the same or not—nothing less, nothing held back. For a moment he felt fear in the chilly room. Not the fear he had felt before—this fear was twined in the love it came with, smaller, cleaner, sharper, gone in a moment, overtaken.

7

Learning her: learning to read her moods in the air around her, sound of her footsteps, echo of her voice. She loved stillness, order, form, formality. She mistrusted spontaneous acts and surprises. He thought that even before the destruction of her family she must have been hurt or denied many times; so many that she no longer trusted the world to reveal a pleasant truth to her. She slept with her arms over her face, on guard. She didn't like gambling of any kind, lotteries, "winning." She had a strong urge toward justice, the cause and effect that sudden winning or luck seemed to upset. She shopped with a tenacity that awed him and came from the battle victorious and exhausted. She was fearful of jokes and said she never understood them. When he had first told her a joke, she had looked frightened. He "taught" her a dozen good jokes and found her using them not as currency but as secrets between the two of them, as a form of language. She had said, "People used to tell jokes about us, about the people on our side of town. I would take off my coat or open my lunch box and everyone would laugh. I never knew why." Thereafter he kept his jokes gentle. She was indifferent to holidays and told him that the Wingates had never celebrated birthdays or Christmas. Charles's family? "They always had big parties. They had big parties for everything. I never liked big parties and I don't think Charles really liked them either, but he felt we should go." She liked movies and stories in which virtue was rewarded, evil punished. She loved to watch any kind of dancing, she liked parades, baton twirling, gymnastics, ice skating, fireworks. Sometimes he would see her later, furtively practicing a move from a dance she had seen. He loved to watch her move. He remembered that first impression of her in the hearing room, the neatness of her movements. He took her dancing. She was hesitant and stiff until he said, "No one's watching us; they're all here to dance themselves." She began to follow step for step, turn for turn. "My God," he cried, "you're a natural!"

So they went dancing, square dancing at the Grange hall and on Saturday nights at the hotel. When one of the high-school teachers started a group that did the old-time ballroom steps, they joined it and found they were good together—neither as creative and venturesome as he would have liked nor as formal as she would have liked, but they made a good team. They moved together so well that soon people were watching them when they danced and they began to make small variations all their own, comments on the steps, private jokes in motion.

But if he expected that dancing would open Helen to orgasm, he was mistaken. She was physically modest to the point of prudishness; it was only after long pleading that she allowed him to watch her undress. What could her years with Charles have been like? he wondered. Did they undress in separate rooms, creeping to one another in the dark, furtive as moles? He judged Charles's ghost harshly, but Helen herself seemed to prefer undressing alone or in the dark. If he asked she would please him dutifully, and the next time go back to the way that was obviously natural to her.

She didn't like contact sports. When Cady and Eric settled down to watch a fight on TV, Helen shrugged and went into the kitchen and worked with Esther. She had learned how much Esther needed help and she began to come over on Saturdays to iron or clean. It was a generous act, but somehow it made Esther uncomfortable. Eric only felt this and didn't know why. Helen was, by her own admission, a terrible cook, and didn't try to take over that job in the kitchen. To all outward appearances the women got along well.

The better he knew her, the more deeply he admired her tenacity, her courage, integrity, and patience, and he saw that what she lacked he could teach her: a sense of fun, of ease and spontaneity, a way of being that wasn't always careful and on guard. If he taught her these things, might she not help him toward becoming the self he wanted to become—someone stiller, deeper, more patient?

And there was the building. Eric's delight grew daily. The money saved by giving access on both sides allowed for changes in the quality of the materials they were using. The building was framed already; it had its shape and in the third week in May it got its eyes. The glaziers came, and when they were done the shape was alive. "It's a real place now—empty, sleeping, but real," he said to Cady. "I can begin to imagine people moving in it, I can imagine *us* in it—cabinets, typewriters . . ."

"Won't you miss the old place just a little?" Cady asked.

"Of course I will, overheated half the year, and giving chilblains the other half, drafts so strong you could fly a kite in them—yes, I will miss it, but God, Elsie's damn breadbox is beautiful!" And they laughed.

Early in June, Roche invited the Cadys and Eric and Helen to visit his parents in Bluebank. They followed the river through valleys and mountains. The terrible floods of spring that had crumbled foundations in town and flooded basements as far as Divide Road only greened the mountains here and quickened the water. "Three weeks like pictures of Switzerland," Roche said, "and the rest of the summer like pictures of Spain. Did you know"—Roche turned to Eric—"that the camel and the llama were both tried in Colorado, down south?"

"No, what happened?"

"I don't know, but they didn't take."

"They had better luck with plants," Cady said, "the improvers. They brought the tamarisk. It was so successful that it took over all the lower parts of the rivers and forced out all the native growth, willow and yampa, that had been here before."

"Then the Ute looks different from the way it did when the Indians were here?"

"Down from the mountains, yes. The Indians hunted here in summer but they had no permanent camps. Too short a season. Even for them this area was boom and bust and they were tourists, too, never staying."

"When did settlements begin here?" Helen asked.

"When gold was discovered. Before then people moved through on their way to California. They moved through for fifteen years without settling. Then gold. Boom and bust. Then silver and boom and bust again, and in the fifties uranium and another boom and another bust and now tourists and vacation land, but the mentality is the same."

"Developers dress better," Roche said, "but they have prospectors' eyes."

Phyllis Roche looked at Helen. "I'm from Dakota," she said. "They weren't like the people who came here. I don't think your Nebraskans had prospectors' eyes, either."

Eric knew he would have to learn not to be anxious every time the subject of Helen's background came up. They had all been moving along in an easy and friendly way together, Esther in her first big outing of the season, sitting up front with Cady, who was delighted for it; Roche expansive as he drove; Helen, Eric, and Phyllis in the back, kids on their laps enjoying the day. There had been an awful moment when Phyllis Roche had thrust the middle girl, Marie, at Helen, saying, "You wouldn't mind taking her on your lap, would you?" And Helen had taken the child with practiced ease, replying, "No, of course not." He had ached for Helen, looking at her and away quickly, and then he had had a sudden stab of fear that the others had seen how easy she was, how natural, with a child in her lap, a child who had curled into her arms in complete trust. Now and then he had glanced over at her, but her expression was gently remote and unreadable. There was talk, casual conversation all around. No one else seemed to notice anything. Suddenly it was there again, a question that could, in the natural, easy flow of such things, open his horror and her grief. Helen was answering quietly, as she always did, after a pause, measuring the words. "Most of the people in Cory had stock and they farmed feed grains, but now I understand my brother has become a prospector."

"In *Nebraska?*"

"He has three oil derricks on his place—the ones that look like big, pecking birds." Something in her tone made them all laugh and the tension fell away from him and he noticed again that the valley was green.

Roche's parents' house stood right in the middle of town, a small old house in a row of small old houses, gentled by trees, but all very much alike and too close together for the usual Colorado street. Eric was surprised—it was almost like a suburb back East, and all the more incongruous because around them mountains and the long river valley opened huge wide arms.

"Didn't you know? This was once a company town," Roche said. They went between the houses to the tiny, almost prissy, backyard where the Roches were serving a picnic lunch. "Look down the row—fence, yard, fence, yard, like any high-density suburb."

"Company town?"

"Sure, mining. Of course, these houses didn't belong to the miners. They were two streets down, shacks that fell in years ago. You'd call this row middle management, I guess, clerks and personnel men, the town telegrapher and the schoolteachers and the company doctor. People like that. Lots of gold mountains or coal mountains had towns like this. Blue-bank just stayed on a little longer. Look up on that hill—see the piles of tailings? Get rich quick and get out quick—big hopes, then cut your losses and get away when the bottom falls out. The houses here are close together because anything that wasn't built on was staked out to be mined—gold first, just like the towns we were talking about, then silver, coal, uranium, now—"

"Now, skiers."

"The cribs are still here, discreetly, three hundred yards outside of town."

"Cribs?"

"Where the prostitutes stayed, one-room places just big enough to hold a bed and a washstand. The johns are out back. Hippies live there now."

"With no water?"

"They get along. They patch up the places and make do. That street was still operating during the fifties when the uranium boom was on."

"As what?"

"Cribs."

Before Eric thought about what he was saying, he asked, "Do you go down a little draw—down behind a larger building? And then the road turns and they're all in one straight line?"

"Aha!" Roche cried. "So you've been down there, have you . . ." He was free to say this; Phyllis Roche and Helen and the kids were setting out the picnic things on the sunny side of the garden. Esther and Cady were talking to Roche's parents.

"I, uh, I got lost here one night on my way back from Pickaxe, skiing. I turned off the road and went down . . ."

This was the place—it must have been. He had been with Bressard in that predawn visit to an unknown blind and shut-tered town, to a shack where he sat on a wooden floor while Bressard dealt with the shadow couple, a man and young woman, talking about drugs. He remembered the grit on the floor—there was a mattress there and a kerosene lamp, but its glass was so dirty that it hardly gave off enough light to see. He had paid something and Bressard had paid, too, and there had been tanks they filled outside somewhere, or in an outbuilding, and a joke about the man being a welder. Where had the drugs gone that Bressard had taken with them? Lost, blown up with Bressard, or lost somewhere in the wreck, overlooked by people not trained to look for them? He must have seemed pensive, because Roche laughed.

"God, that ugly line of cribs haunts my youth. We were told to stay away from there so often it became the most important place in town, after home and school. When we were teenagers we went there all the time. Of course, that was in the late forties, when very little else was happening. The whores were gone, almost all of them. Things didn't pick up until the boom of the fifties, and by that time I was in college. Are you curious about the place? We can take a walk on over there."

"Oh, no, the people who got me back on the road wouldn't remember me."

"Probably, and the place itself will be gone soon. It's too valuable to leave to squatters. Developers have bought most of the land around here—there's a system called condominium, I'm not sure what it is—they're talking about shopping malls and a whole instant city."

"Big doings." In some part of him, Eric was relieved. The sin would be paved over, built up, covered, buried under the progress that Roche wanted. But he was still curious about the cribs. "Is this the only town on the river that had those cribs—I mean, there are towns up the line between here and Pickaxe—did they all have—were they all the same?"

"Actually, this is the only one," Roche said. "Granite was, believe it or not, a nineteenth-century religious settlement. Callan was a mining town, but it was made up of prospectors, shirt-tail individualists with pocket-sized claims. There was a furious rivalry, even after the busts, after the company pulled up and left. We looked down at Callanites as the descendants of wandering trash. They looked down at us as the descendants of company slaves. In the fifties, of course, all that changed."

"How could the towns have been so starved, so narrow?"

"I don't know. All I know is that it seemed natural then to love us and hate them, to know everyone you saw and have that number shrink instead of grow, as you grew."

"Did you ever *feel* poor?" he asked Roche, thinking of Helen.

"Not here, not in town with my own, but when we went to high school, yes. Cady'll tell you everyone was pretty much equal in school, but that isn't so. Cady didn't see the social differences because he was on the top side of them and being the kind of person he is, they meant less to him. They were there all the same. It was why Phyllis left her town and, I guess, why Helen left hers."

Eric nodded, and said no more. He looked over at Helen, sitting with Esther and Phyllis, the senior Mrs. Roche, and the children. She was beautiful as she sat there, quiet, attentive, listening, but she was the smallest bit distant physically. She was part of the circle of women and children but almost out of it, turned toward the center but like a planet responding to a gravitational pull no other part of that system felt, and so being pulled the smallest degree away from the others.

They themselves seemed not to feel it; they laughed and chatted, including her in their comments, and she showed interest in what they were saying. He knew people in the office still thought her cold and standoffish. It was that physical thing, he thought, that slight unwillingness to commit her presence fully, a caution of body by which she stood, unconsciously, a little apart.

And it was her unwillingness to commit herself in talk. Even as he saw these things objectively, he saw deeper to her honesty and love of beauty, the part of her quietness that was serene and contemplative, her gentleness. As he looked over at her, watching, Esther, who was facing him across the small yard, caught the look and looked back at the other women, and Phyllis turned then. Helen, who practically had her back to him, had to turn the whole way around to see what the others were looking at and he was caught, so he grinned and shrugged and they all laughed. Later Esther came over, getting the men to the table, and smiled and took his hand. "Your love-eye is showing," she said, and he answered, "Well, I guess it is."

The next weekend he took Helen rafting for the wonder of the sun broken into shimmering fragments on the water, the flexing-releasing sinews of the river under their boat. Because the boat man knew him, he let the two of them go out with the smallest raft. Helen said it was playing at nature, and Eric knew it, since there was no need for their travel and they would have to be picked up at the day's end and brought back upstream. He showed her how to avoid sleepers, the almost submerged rocks, and how to paddle and how to ride white water. She learned well and did well, but he saw that she was frightened and puzzled at the sport and he smiled to himself, thinking he understood. That family of hers in Cory had fought nature and lost; perhaps pitting oneself against a river held little charm for her. But their children wouldn't read heartbreak in every change of wind, or despair when the rain fell too hard or didn't fall at all.

"Maybe we can find a backwater somewhere and swim."

"I never learned."

"My God, no wonder you're scared. I thought everyone could swim."

"You thought wrong," she said, "but I have this life jacket and if I don't let go of this oar I can't drown, can I?"

"Paddle, not oar. Let's get married," he said. "I want to teach our kids the backstroke."

"Be serious," she said. He looked into his mind and saw that he was.

The last week in June his parents came out. He and Helen had designed their visit as one might design a park: a series of views and vistas, details and overviews, things to do. They were shown the river, following it through town. He knew his father would be interested in the relationship of its engineering to the town's legal problems, and he got Cady to talk to him about some of the cases of years past. His mother liked scenery, so they planned a raft trip out on one of the quiet stretches and Helen said she would pack a picnic lunch. By then, she would have seen them at a play and with the group the Cadys would have on Thursday evening. He arranged for them to stay at the same hotel Rademaker had used last year. These plans were made to show them his new self—serious and stable, part of the town, belonging to a life he had chosen. He wanted, gently, to let them know that he planned to stay. He wanted, gently, to introduce Helen, to let them learn her silences, to ready them for what he hoped would happen. He was falling more deeply in love with her every day. He was in awe of his good fortune and there were times when what he felt was nothing less than rapture.

The weather was perfect. They went on the raft trip on Saturday, starting at Bluebank and ending just north of town. Helen had made a lunch, which they ate near Callan, beaching the raft on a sandy spit and walking up to a cattle meadow ringed with snowcapped mountains.

As they sat at the picnic, Helen that slight bit apart, Edith Gordon began, no doubt as a way of making conversation, to ask Helen questions. Had she grown up here? No, Nebraska. What had brought her to Aureole? Helen answered that she had seen it once, and later thought she would like to live here. Eric's heart went out to her. In vain he tried breaking in, but his mother—innocently or not—drilled on. Had Helen seen the town just once and then moved, just like that? In a sense, yes, Helen answered, she had been married and then widowed, a move seemed sensible. Remembering Aureole, that it was a growing place with jobs available, she had thought to settle here. A widow? Edith Gordon had the bit in her teeth. Eric's sorrow turned to dread. Helen might dissemble, but he didn't want her to lie. He didn't know if she would. The question was hunting her toward the edge. He felt helpless as his mother, rapt as a stalking cat, moved down terrain she didn't know was full of crevasses. To his immense relief, his father came to the rescue. Looking up into the mountains he announced, "It's interesting geology you have around here."

"Yes, people come from everywhere to study these mountains."

"Izzatso?"

"Oh, yes, as a matter of fact . . ."

Later, he said quietly to Eric, "Try to forgive Edie. She gets started and can't stop. I looked at your lady and she looked back at me like the defendant in a custody case."

"I'm grateful," Eric said.

"Don't mention it." And his father grinned at him. Eric was glad when the day was over.

The next morning he met them alone for breakfast at the hotel. It was Sunday, church-bell Sunday, and the hotel was full of summer tourists and people going into the mountains. His mother studied him across the table. "You've changed," she said.

He laughed. "I hope so. I thought you would be delighted."

"I am—we are, it's only that—well, that it's *here*, that you're making *this* your home, and—"

"—and Helen."

"Well . . ."

His mother began to choose her words. She chose so carefully that Eric saw into her anxiety and dislike as he never would have had she erupted in a blast of disapproval. "I think she's been part of this maturing in you—her quietness must be part of that, and I see her as a very *capable* woman—"

"Don't be so careful, Mother, please."

"She's so much older," his mother said sadly, "and a widow—a middle-aged widow, and you're still so young—"

"I'm twenty-four. It's true that Helen is older, but not that much older, not middle-aged yet, and I love her and want to marry her."

His mother sighed deeply. "Has she accepted you—are there plans?"

It was said so sadly, so resignedly, that Eric had to fight down an urge to temporize. "She's a widow. I want to give her time. She wants time. I know she's quiet, reserved, but if you only knew her—"

"I imagined you with a sweet young girl, that's all. I suppose in my mind I didn't picture *your* wife as much as *my* daughter-in-law." She wanted to say more. He could read the feeling, measure it. She had a picture of two young people, the young family, a daughter-in-law who was pretty, charming, coy, playful, appealing in an open-eyed way. Helen was older than he, quiet, direct, serious to the point of gravity, and, unknown to his parents, had once been the mother of three. And there was the secret part—how he had met her— which he never wanted them to know. He and Helen hadn't talked seriously about marriage—yet. He didn't know what she thought about it, or about having children, or what she saw as her future. Did she want marriage? Did he want children? He only knew that he wanted her.

His parents left the next day. The visit, for all his work and Helen's, had not been a comfortable one. Everyone had been polite, appreciative, artificial, and unhappy. The trip on the river, the visits to the site of the new building, the drives in the country, only showed the Gordons how truly happy and involved Eric was in the life of the town. The dinner the Cadys gave confused and depressed his parents. Eric remembered then how different the humor and how strange the conversations had first seemed to him; how much less important politics and social trends were here and how much more important local and regional concerns were. The pace of conversation was slower, more meditative, the laughter less at wit and more at humor. No one was brilliant. "If you're brilliant, you go to Denver," Cady had said. It wasn't true, but his parents thought it was. He was relieved when they left.

"I suppose we tried to do too much," Helen said. "They needed to adjust to the truth that you aren't coming back. That would have been enough for one trip. Then, later, me."

"You're not unhappy about their . . . discomfort?"

"I expected it. It's only natural."

"I suppose so. Only . . . when are you going to take me to meet *your* family?"

"I don't know that I ever want to do that."

"Why not?"

"They aren't like yours."

"I hope not!" He had been half joking. Her response was quiet, matter-of-fact, her tone almost without inflection.

"When Charles and I married, I wrote to them. They didn't answer. Only my sister Mary Anne wrote back. When each of the children was born I wrote. Only Mary Anne answered. Then, when Charles and the children—when there was the accident, I wrote and told them. My brother wrote back then, to tell me I had no claim on them or the farm. Mary Anne's husband wrote that I was not welcome to 'live off' them, but that I should take up teaching or useful work."

"Dear God!"

"They live in Cut Bank, Mary Anne and her husband. If we ever go through there for any reason, we could let them know . . ."

His heart ached for her. There was nothing of the pitiful about her, nothing waiflike or whining, but who could live a life like that and not have been desperately lonely in ways he could not even imagine? If she seemed too careful, too involved in cause and effect, if she lacked spontaneity, it was surely the legacy of her early life, and could be changed with time and love. She needed the part of him that was still a little careless, open, a man who made friendly, habitable spaces.

It would take time. His parents had raised their carefully tactful eyebrows only the slightest bit when Helen had unwrapped the lunch she had made for their picnic: for each, one small can of punch, one dry cheese sandwich, one gingersnap, one apple; lunch—nothing more. All that he could give he would give her and perhaps the giving, the generosity, would open her sexually, too, and she would blossom as she had never been allowed to do. Now he pitied Charles Gerson, who perhaps had not tried hard enough.

8

A week after his parents left he proposed again. They were in bed in his room this time. They had fallen asleep in front of the fire, wakened later, and had gone to his narrow bed and made love. She was warm and responsive beneath him, ready, he thought, but though there was her shudder he didn't know if she had come or not. He wanted to talk about their love-making. Perhaps there was something she wanted. But whenever he tried opening the subject, she would demur. It occurred to him that if her reticence was one of the things he loved about her, he couldn't expect her to confide readily on a subject about which even voluble people were silent. He felt that she was happy with him, although she never initiated their lovemaking. It was part of her reserve not to. Before dawn he had wakened and seen her standing over him look-ing down, and then, very gently, she had touched his cheek and very, very gently leaned over and kissed him, just the lightest brush of her lips against his cheek. He thought she had not known he was awake. Then she slipped away sound-lessly, leaving him tear-blinded with love.

It was Sunday. He called her. "I don't want just to be in love. Let's get married."

"Don't joke about that."

"Say yes."

"Aren't your parents right, that I'm too old?"

"Maybe you don't love me enough."

"That's not the point."

"It is the point, the whole point."

"You said you'd wait."

"I mean to wait until my probation time is up—that will be in September, but I want you to say we'll get married then." There was a long pause at the other end, then, "We'll talk about getting married then."

He felt brilliant, as though he had figured cleverly and won a prize with the right answer. "There'll be time to find out about what we want—a house, kids. You'll see, it will be good—it will be wonderful, you'll see!"

"It makes you happy, then—"

"It makes me very happy."

Elsie said the city and county building would be finished just two weeks past its date. Eric was impatient, Cady jubilant. "It's a miracle!" he cried. "A big building like this, a dozen small changes at the last minute—I've never seen a building finished so near the completion date, certainly not a government building. You should be doing nip-ups."

"How long has this been going on, this sloppiness?"

Cady laughed. "Four, maybe five thousand years. There was a two-hundred-fifty-year extension on the pyramids, fifty years on the Taj Mahal."

"I'm still mired down in details; the doors were all hung wrong, opening in. Linder missed it."

"Don't lie, you're having a wonderful time with all of it."

"I've been trying to keep it from showing."

"Why is that?"

"Looks bad—yippee, a building!"

"Dignified satisfaction is what's called for, but there is going to be a *do*—two of them. When the engineer makes his grand final inspection, he and the contractor and the architect usually send out for the works after it's over, and they're joined by whoever's still there or wanders in. Then there's the formal thing, at the dedication. Town dignitaries, suits, ties, wives, speeches."

"Oh, God."

"Him, too."

So that night Eric worked late and went over to the new building after everyone had quit for the day. With the trucks gone it looked even stranger standing, as Elsie had described it, catercorner on its site, but he liked the look of it, even without its softening landscaping and the windbreak shrubs he had planned. He walked around it, noticing the modifications that Elsie and Linder and he had worked out. Cady was right; the best parts were secret and would never be noticed—ventilation in the building, shading overhangs, but a feeling of light, secret details, the secrets visible but unnoticed.

He went around to the door, opened it with his key, and went in. Painters would come in soon, the men with the floor tile and the carpets, decorators and furniture people, and the building would become theirs. He had this hour or so to look at it when it was still his, or somewhat his. He knew how it rested, how its weight was distributed, which members bore it, how much and how strong, how flexible, how open, how contained, all the secrets . . .

He went from room to room, even into the ventilating attic space and the basement crawl-spaces where the heating equipment was. He thought he would come back later this evening or tomorrow and bring Helen, showing her the secrets, maybe allowing himself to show off a little: "This was my idea. I thought of that . . ."

There was a sound—he heard laughter down a hall and behind a door. He went toward the sound cautiously, moving as noiselessly as he could. Some of the workers drinking? Elsie or Linder working late? The sliding door was half open. He came around the ell that gave this inner office some privacy and looked in. They had brought sleeping bags, Linder and the woman. In the heat of the late afternoon they didn't need covers. They were hard at it, Linder's bare buttocks almost

110

glowing in the afternoon light. Eric ducked back and moved away quietly to the front and out the door, which he locked, turning the key with a proprietary snap. Linder, too, wanted to demonstrate his ownership, a *droit du seigneur*, a claim to what he had created. Eric felt in his pocket and came up with a roll of mints. He opened the roll carefully, spilling the mints into his pocket from the aluminum foil, which he flattened and cleaned with his shirt. Then he carefully made the prints of the five fingers of his right hand. Rolling the foil carefully into a tiny tube, he wedged it into a crack beside the door jamb.

When Helen appeared with Eric at the building's formal party, "the town" took notice. He hoped she would see that the difference in their ages didn't cause any raised eyebrows. She had used it as a reason why they shouldn't marry. He had been clever and turned it to his benefit. "You don't look thirty-two; only your clothes do. You're attractive; you could be stunning. You wear gray all the time, dark blue, dark green. I'd like to see you in something *vivid*; I don't know what they call those colors . . ." He was gratified when she got something brighter to wear, a dress she said was powder blue. He imagined her in something brighter yet and went nervously into Howard's and earnestly confided in a saleslady there and came out with five scarves in five bright colors. She was wearing the pink one, hot pink she called it, and it made her look beautiful. Even she had seemed surprised. "See"—he grinned—"what a couple we make now?"

Afterward, when she drove him home, he asked her about a family. "Will you want to start over—I mean, children?"

"I thought—I assumed we would."

He wanted to say more, to ask about more, but all he could say was, "I'm in debt—you know that. A big debt. I've been paying it off bit by bit, but it will take a couple of years and then—"

"It's all right." He felt her moving in the dark beside him. "We can do what we need to do."

She began to speak slowly. She told him she had received a

settlement from Charles's insurance. She had been living so humbly, so modestly, in so pinched a way that he had totally forgotten how wealthy she must have been all along. The image of that picnic cheese sandwich, ungraced by even a shred of lettuce, flashed through his mind as he heard her speaking, and stayed there like an afterimage.

"I'm not going to use a cent of that, not for us. I can't. You can understand that, surely. For the kids, maybe, their college, if we have kids, but not for me. None of it for me." There was anger in his voice that he hadn't meant to direct at her; it sounded like anger but it was nothing less than superstitious panic—Charles's money, smoking and stinking in his hand like the silver coins of Judas, leaving burned circles on his open palm. Throughout his tirade she didn't move in the dark; she gave no sign. It was their first disagreement and it was being resolved in a way that Eric would come to see was typical; Helen surrendered immediately, a capitulation so absolute that he wondered how real it could be. The wish stated, if simply countered, ceased to exist, blown out like a match leaving not even its smoke in the air. It surprised him. It warned him. Who had taught her such abnegation and by what savage means had she learned it? It would make him careful, very careful how he argued. Because she gave in immediately, without another word, it was only after he left her that he realized her capitulation meant that they would be living on their salaries, and because of his debt to his family there would be no house for years, no extras, trips, luxuries, that his superstition, masquerading as integrity, was costing Helen as much—more—than it cost him. She had made no argument, offered no reasons, asked for no compromise. It was, after all, her money—hers, not his, to use or to save as she wished. He had won and felt only guilt and frustration in the winning.

She did the same when they decided where they would live. He had asked her what she wanted. A small house, she had said, but he only mentioned his debt and Esther's need and she blew out the wish and left him in the dark. "Of course we'll live with the Cadys, then."

"Please," he cried, "don't leave me here all alone."

She took up the problem dryly. He was, as he had said, still in debt and would be for several years. Financially, it would be in their interest to stay. They could walk to work, then save money by helping the Cadys. There was room upstairs for her, cooking could be arranged.

That was all he was able to get from her. When she was impatient or irritated, she had a way of flattening the ends of her sentences, so that they went leaden, into silence. Her approval had an aftertone; it reverberated slightly for a barely measurable time. Her disapproval revealed nothing but itself. Her logic was impeccable. He did not see that wish again.

In August everyone moved into the new building. They packed their boxes of records, threw away fifteen boxes of outdated or duplicate pieces of paper, and began to shift everything into the carpeted offices, the new filing cabinets in the new file rooms.

Eric's first act in the new building, he thought, should be important, symbolic. He waited until Cady and Roche were back at the old place and called Rademaker in Denver. It was a moment, he thought, before the lawyer remembered him. "The time is coming close—my fifteen months will be up pretty soon. I wondered what you wanted me to do . . ."

"I'll come up there. I have to get in touch with the judge and see when we can meet. It shouldn't take long. There've been no problems, have there?"

"No," Eric said, "no problems."

That evening he went home and began to frame a letter. It was a letter to Judge Hamblin and to Rademaker. In a sense it was to Helen and to Judge Hamblin's dead son and to Charles and Helen's children. He wrote about coming to Aureole, about taking a job that demanded seriousness of him, about his care in not driving, about his citizenship in town and his marriage plans. He couldn't tell them who Helen was, and for a while he struggled with the decision to leave her out, fearful that they might question him about her. In the end, he had to tell that he had found a "fine woman and made plans to marry." It was too much a part of his redemption to leave unsaid. He saw the letter was too long—eight pages. He spent the next days refining it, trying to make it shorter without losing any of the essential facts or the heart of what he was saying. Helen's journals were day by day. If she had chosen to read them, she would see a reality emerging. In his statement he had to compress his reality into the smallest space possible. He came out with five pages, which he typed in good form, carefully, in the office after hours. When he saw Rademaker three weeks later, he handed him the papers with a pride he couldn't help but feel.

They had met in the old courthouse in a conference room half an hour before the judge was due. Rademaker took the papers, riffled through them and shrugged. "I won't need any of this—none of this matters—I mean none of it is relevant. This is a matter of form, of law. All you need to do is appear." And he flicked the pages back to Eric across the table. Fifteen minutes later Judge Hamblin appeared, looked at Eric, nodded to Rademaker, signed some papers, and left. As the law had paved over Eric's act of horror, it paved over his act of redemption. He was wordless. For a moment he found the face of Aguilar grinning cynically at him from the corner of his mind: "The law does what it wants to do. If it wants you to go free, you will." He hadn't known until now what lay in Aguilar's smile. He felt it now. It was despair.

So it was over, officially, that year and some, on which all his years would turn.

Cady wanted to give him a party, to invite Helen and some friends, to celebrate. Eric couldn't tell him how bad it would be—Helen at such an evening, any such an evening in this town, whose roads still bore, however faintly, the marks of his

114

impact, the cries of . . . He stopped Cady. "Please, no. It was an awful accident; I don't want to remember it, but Helen and I will want to set our date soon. Maybe we can have a little party for that." His statement won Cady's nod and silence, a sign of his growing respect, and the fear, like a small, scratching animal, ran across the corridors, so that Eric's breath was harder for a moment.

But Tuesday evening, the day after his sentence was up, he proposed to Helen again. "You look tired," she said. He *was* tired. The hearing had exhausted him in a way he couldn't explain. Rademaker had stayed over for lunch and had heard from his Uncle Tony that there was "a girl," and Eric had walked along the sheer edges of seven lies to keep the lawyer from knowing who the woman was. Even description was difficult: small, dark, graceful. Would Rademaker see in his mind to the side of the hearing room where Mrs. Gerson sat in that quiet self-possession—small, dark, graceful? He told the lawyer about the city and county building and the growth of Aureole, and afterward he lay awake most of the night with the fear-ferret running and scratching in the passages of his body.

"I want you to put this in your journal: 'Today Eric asked me again to marry him and we set a date.' "

"All right," she said. As he embraced her, he felt for the fear and it was gone.

He called his parents and Uncle Tony. Helen wrote to her sister, the Cadys gave a party, but to Eric it had a quiet feeling, his and Helen's engagement, an almost autumnal sweetness; Helen's widowhood precluded a big wedding, which he didn't really want, yet . . . He reminded himself that a big wedding would mean big questions: Helen's family, Helen's past. The county secretaries gave her a shower. Her friend Ernestine took them out to dinner.

They got their license at the new city-county building, where they both now worked. They were married by Judge Gambier and spent a weekend in Denver as a honeymoon.

His parents wanted to cancel the rest of his debt—he had paid more than half of it and with a wife to support and a family to begin . . . "No," he said over the phone, "Helen agrees that we should start clean. She'll go on working and for now we're staying with the Cadys. Be glad for us, please." They sounded so far away and helpless over the phone, wishing for his happiness and Helen's.

After the honeymoon, she moved in with him—it was easy; she had almost nothing. She made few changes in the rooms at first, but because she was neat, orderly, and precise, the rooms took on that quality. Things began to find places and a clean-surfaced harmony began to make itself felt.

Things weren't easy for the Cadys. Helen's reserve seemed to worry Esther, then annoy her. Helen took over the washing and ironing; she did it promptly and well and there was never any argument about it, but now and then Eric caught a look, a glimmer between Esther and Cady or a sudden silence from Esther when Helen was around that made him think that Esther was uncomfortable with Helen there. They were often at supper together, although he had made a space for Helen to cook upstairs with a toaster oven, an electric skillet, and a crockpot. "As soon as the debt is paid," he told her, "as soon as we can—"

"I know," she said, and nothing more.

The day of the first snow Helen told Eric that she was pregnant. It was late September, a bright blue-gold day that held them in a town-wide ring of light. All around them snow was falling, the passes showed weirdly in a strange purple glow reflected from low clouds. The city seemed cherished in the palm of an angelic hand, centered in light. Helen was wretchedly sick in the morning. "Flu?" he asked.

"I don't think so. We're going to have a baby."

Just like that. The earth heaved under his feet. "So soon?" It was all he could say.

"I thought, being as regular as I am, I thought there were safe days—"

"But you used—I know you can't take the pills, but you used—"

"Yes," she said. "What do you want me to do?"

He knew it was a test. "Be glad, I guess," he blurted and then he found himself dizzy and out of focus. "They give you nine months to get used to it, I guess."

"Not quite. I think the baby will be born in the spring, in May." Outside, the light went as suddenly as it did at sundown. Snow began to fall. Later, when he counted, he realized that she must have become pregnant before they were married.

Whatever misgivings he had, whatever fears there were, were set aside in communal joy. He supposed this was the reason for such enthusiasm, the shouting and back-slapping. When Cady heard about it he cried out to Esther and they came up for a toast, and Esther reminisced about their own children, now married and two of them parents themselves. The next day Cady told Roche, whose wife, Phyllis, was also expecting, and Roche told the road crews when they came in, and out came all their pictures and the stories: "My wife sent me a letter!" "My wife waits until my folks come up and she pours out the beers, one extra, see, and she says, 'To the five of us.' "

Their stories mirrored the same surprise he had felt. Some were angry, some proud, but all acknowledged the power of their women. Men may cheat, but they are found out, crudely, because they can't fake the passions they don't feel. "No lift-off," one man said, laughing but rueful. But no one truly knows what his woman feels. Listening, he thought, Helen didn't feign that—Helen had not lied. "We've got five kids," one man said, "and some of 'em might even be mine!" And the men laughed and waved him away. Eric laughed, too, but knew the man was telling a truth he recognized, that as loud as they might shout, as firmly as their steps might ring in their houses, it was women's voices that uttered the most important words of men's lives.

9

The baby was a son. They named him Mark. Eric lived through the birth in an unbelieving daze. After the excitement of the delivery came the baby's actual presence, a presence so total and pervasive that it seemed to consume everything else. Helen was exhausted and milky, Mark crying all the time; Eric escaped into work with a guilty relief. Donnigan, on the road crew, saw his red eyes. "I remember those days!" He laughed. "The fuss, the noise, baby this and baby that. Breastpumps and Kotex. I wondered what I ever saw in *her*, and why the hell she gave me *it*."

"Isn't there supposed to be more? Aren't I supposed to feel—something else?"

"I didn't—not in the beginning. I know what they tell you, but I didn't."

"Does it ever get any better?" Eric had been frightened by his lack of love for his son, that it might be some part of his old self beyond his power to change. He had tried to force the feeling and had had moments of terror because it would not come.

"Sure," Donnigan said, "the kids save themselves. They get faces, eyes, smile—they get their own faces, see, and one day they smile, maybe, or they grab your finger—"

"And you wanna be hooked," Sperber said. "You been hoping it would happen, so when it does, you try real hard, and later, why, later the kid grows a little and then *it* can love, and then it *does* love, and then, well, by that time—"

"I always loved my kids, but I was jealous," the new man said over lunch. "I loved the kid, but I couldn't get no relief, you know, six weeks they can't help you, and my wife, she didn't want to do nothin' special, you understand."

"My wife did."

"My wife wouldn't."

It gave him the courage to endure.

Gifts came from his sister and his parents and the aunts and uncles and cousins. The Cadys gave them a night out every week together while Cady and Esther watched the baby. But if they went to a movie, Helen would fall asleep, so they went dancing.

Because they were good at it, no dance hall was crowded for them; people gave them room. He had not thought to be singled out with her, to have the special pride of a man who is married to a beautiful woman. Helen was older, so he had not thought of her as being beautiful in the same way a younger woman would have been. Now he saw admiring glances from other men, young and old, and it made him feel proud, protective, a little nervous—the way a man feels who owns a rare but uninsured masterpiece.

Days, weeks, a month, two. He hadn't wanted a child so soon. He fought his fear with work until the saving thing happened, as the men had said it would, one Sunday morning when Helen was at church. She liked that morning out and arranged it so that Mark usually slept through. Ernestine came by and picked her up and they both walked to church, Ernestine's loud laugh echoing out the door. Eric had gotten into the habit of sleeping late on Sunday, then getting up and going downstairs for coffee. As he went this time, he heard Mark in the next room. The baby wasn't crying, but talking to itself, making soft, gurgling sounds. Eric thought suddenly that there might be some danger—the gurgling might lead to choking, and what if the baby choked to death while he was alone with it? He went in.

The room was on the dark side of the house, so Helen left a light on in there all day. Eric saw the baby's feet sticking up—it was playing with its toes. It—Eric tried to make himself remember to think of "it" as a he, as Mark; he moved close. The baby seemed suddenly better formed, suddenly more like a tiny person than a squalling bundle. As Eric moved, the tiny human saw him, turned his head and looked up at him, and then, remarkably, began to wave both legs and arms as though in recognition. Eric stood over the crib, reached in, and touched. The baby—Mark—began to make still louder noises of what seemed like pleasure. His fists came up, trying to find, then finding, gripping Eric's finger. Eric put his other hand into the crib and reached under the little shirt to stroke the little chest and stomach. The flesh was smooth and warm. He felt the heart, quick as rain, and a feeling of wonder, wonder and gratitude, flooded over him. The awe that had eluded him so far washed over him and brought him to the verge of tears. Mention of the little fingers, the tiny eyelashes, the perfect articulation of the tiny bones—none of it had spoken of the aliveness—breath, heart, all counting the rhythm of life. As he stood, his eyes blurred, the baby's face suddenly contracted into a horrible grimace, a look like an old man in agony crossed its features as Eric watched helplessly, and then the face as suddenly relaxed. Eric laughed. The baby smiled and for the first time, ineptly, Eric changed his son's diaper.

Then the time, which had measured itself out endlessly as he waited to become comfortable as a father, began to flow with increasing speed. Every day there was something new, every month a change. Mark laughed, Mark walked, then talked, then played games. Eric's life got fuller at work and at home. By the time Mark was two, their debt was paid and they took out a loan on a house Helen found. There was a second baby that Helen, terrifyingly sick, miscarried, and in the sad need of her loss, another, Karen, born, Eric felt, too soon. Then, Anne. His life opened outward.

What surprised him most about his growing children was their difference from one another. He had never imagined when he had said "children" to himself that he would come to know three separate individuals with personalities that differed so completely that he was unable to find the causes of their difference in their birth or nurture. They were, from the beginning, themselves. As he grew and developed, Mark was bright, daring to the point of recklessness, energetic, a little bossy, and fascinated with the way things moved and worked. He charmed Cady, who took him places and got him toys. Sometimes Eric saw in him a combination of Helen's perseverance and his soaring.

"Doesn't he seem—isn't he exceptional in some way?" he had asked Helen when Mark was five. She had answered defensively.

"Every child has some peculiarities, some differences. They can't all be the same—"

"I meant, are children his age that bright? Doesn't he seem brighter than the average?"

"There's nothing wrong with him," she countered. "If he seems ahead of himself it's because you and Cady explain things, take him to jobs, show him . . ."

Where Mark had been a lively baby and an adventurous child, Karen was quiet, indrawn, meditative. She was like her mother, measuring, cautious. She even cried quietly, but because she had not brought Mark's immediate, trusting allegiance to the world, she wasn't so shattered when the world did not act as she expected. There was, from birth, a guardedness about her.

Even the looks of the two children differed. Mark's hair was the color of dark honey and went darker as he grew. In summer he tanned a peach color so that he seemed to glow. Karen was like Helen, dark and elfin with fair skin whose delicate undersheen was like a pearl.

Anne was the third child, smaller at birth than the others. He was glad she was born last or he would have thought there was a lack in them as parents. There was something cranky and perverse about her almost from birth. Her cries were not howls as Mark's had been or mewings like Karen's, but peevish wails that sometimes went on for hours no matter what Helen did. She startled at being picked up and turned her head away from kissing. In his secret heart Eric had to admit that he didn't like her very much. Still, they were a family and he saw them all with a kind of wonder and he spoke of them with wonder, especially Mark.

"Is this the city slicker, the eastern sophisticate, the devil-may-care man about Aureole?" Roche had cried when Eric described some clever saying or new skill. "Tie him to a chair, Cady, and whip out your grandkids' pictures while I get mine."

They were only laughing at him, Eric thought, because he dealt in details and had not conveyed the essence of his experience, the depth and resonance of it, hidden as it was in the most mundane and even unpleasant details, spilled food and diapers and sticky doorknobs. "It's really a secret," he said to Roche and Cady.

"Wouldn't that be nice." Roche laughed.

But Helen knew, although she never spoke of it. Sometimes he would come on her rocking Anne with Karen in her lap and Mark lying against her knee, and he would see the soft, vulnerable, musing look on her face, and she would look up at him and smile, her eyes glowing, brimming, he thought, with love and pride.

She was still spare of speech and careful, but he knew she was happy. Now and then she sang in the house as she worked, in a pleasant, sweet voice. Her gestures, always graceful, were freer now, more creative, like the little extra steps, playing, that she tried when they went dancing. She loved the house and its small back garden and she lavished care on it, so that even with the work of the children, everything she touched had a serene order to it.

Sometimes she invited some of the women with whom she

sang in the choir for tea. He would see her as he left for work, beginning the elaborate preparations, setting the table in the small dining room with the luncheon set, little cups and matching sandwich plates, doilies, a centerpiece. It reminded him of a little girl playing house. He wondered where she had learned this elaborate style. When he asked her, she said, "That's how you have tea for ladies in the afternoon."

Helen's best friend was still Ernestine. They had worked at the commissioners' office together and later Ernestine had gone to work on her own as a temporary secretary, going all over Aureole. They still sang in the choir together and saw each other on Ernestine's free days.

Eric was surprised at Ernestine. She was a large woman, almost overpowering. Her clothes were bright and she wore two rings on each hand and huge loop earrings. She had a loud voice and a booming laugh. Her size made Helen look smaller and more fragile, or maybe it was Helen's smallness that made Ernestine look so large. In any case, Eric felt a little intimidated by Helen's friend, so he was pleasant to her but no more. Helen seemed to understand. The fact that Ernestine was divorced and had a small child made it hard for her socially, but Eric was relieved that Helen did not ask to include her in evenings with the Cadys and the Roches or some of their newer acquaintances. As it was, Eric had less and less time for social evenings or the building of new friendships. The year they moved, the Rivercrest development had come to Aureole.

In the 1880s, Aureole was a suddenly large, suddenly rich mining town with a population of thirty thousand people living in tents or shanties, running shafts and breakers up every mountain. Forests were cut for timber, river courses changed for sluicing; the mine shafts propped their beams on nothing, and the miners hammered tent-pegs on the wind, the ground itself being too valuable. A large area between the river's bend and Jackass Hill (now called Aureole Hill) had been undermined with shafts and test holes and the leaching of dumped tailings. The area above this land had already been built on, and it was the area of greatest cost and trouble for the city. Streets there occasionally caved in, houses sank, mains buckled, water made sudden violent whirlpools after heavy snows and disappeared only to reappear later, poisonously yellow, in people's cellars. Half the city engineers' time was spent in that area, shoring, pounding, and leveling. Eric had proposed a plan that all the land between hill and river be taken over by the city, leveled, and made into a park of some kind. It could be planted over with trees, which would cut the winds that tormented the town in winter and spring. There might even be a recreational area, and without the pressure of heavy buildings, parts of the land could, in fact, cave in, fill themselves, and someday reach an equilibrium that might support a small number of new homes. The council listened and told him they would give his idea careful thought. Done right, he had argued, the project might pay for itself in tourist dollars and be a source of recreation and enjoyment for the town.

He was working on his plan, and a series of statistics, when Lehti Associates (Denver, Colorado Springs, Tucson, Reno, and Las Vegas) came in with a proposal, in essence, that Jackass Hill be used to fill the undermined areas. New methods of packing, blasting, and compressing the earth would make it possible to use all the land between the hill and the river for high-density housing. Using retaining walls, the housing could come right up to the river itself, all along its course through town. Eric listened to the proposals in horror.

"Cady, they want to seal off the river, to move Jackass Hill. They call it 'landfill,' but with four-story apartments they plan to wall away the town's view of the river."

"Jackass Hill is tailings," Cady said, "and it wasn't there before the miners put it there. It cuts off the wind from that side, but it also limits the growth of the town. Done right, getting rid of it could be a good thing for Aureole."

Eric couldn't believe his ears. "Cady, the river—"

"Have you been down there lately? You know that when a thing belongs to everybody it belongs to nobody. That area down there is awful, scrub trees, garbage, rats. It looks quaint and old-fashioned from a distance, peaceful, but it's unowned."

"It should be set aside for a park—"

"And that means we'd have to hire supervisors, maintenance men, the whole thing, and for whom, tourists? Kids? People won't go any distance to a park when they can barbecue in their backyards."

"Boom and bust!" Eric cried.

"Progress," Cady whispered.

As the days went on, Eric heard from people all over town. The school principal liked the developers' idea: "That area has been dangerous for years." The Rotary, the Chamber of Commerce liked it, the Elks and the churches liked it. Some of the old residents were against it, but when he heard their reasons, they sounded petty and small-minded. Eric wanted to keep Aureole small—the same. Malcolm agreed.

Cady had hired Malcolm after begging the council for almost a year. The town's growth demanded they have a bigger department. Inspections had been doubled and trebled, repairs were not keeping up. "Don't you see," Eric had cried, "they want double the growth but they don't want to double this department. It's demand we can't keep up with."

"It's progress," Cady had said.

"It's blindness—the same blindness that wanted to bring the Olympics to the foothills! The growth will run away with us!"

Roche said he agreed with Eric, but he didn't back the park idea. The river had willow trees and wild shrubbery along its bank, which was nice to look at when it was summertime, but valuable land was being wasted and nobody really went there anymore—the land had been uncared for for years.

"But a park—"

"How many people go to the town park except in summer, and look at the mess Miner's Park is, out past the high school."

Roche had more or less taken over the job of running the culvert crews and doing maintenance. Eric had drifted naturally into planning.

"Fight, of course," Cady said, "but fight for compromise. Make the Rivercrest people do something extra—a walkway along the river, trees around the development—"

"At that density?"

"Fight them down on the density. They know they need to compromise. The commissioners will be conservative; it's their job."

"Half a plague?"

"No, it's only—"

"Don't say it, progress."

He told Helen most of it, although she often seemed too busy and distracted when he came home; Karen needed care and Mark was in kindergarten and she had to take him each day. There was laundry; she seemed always to be folding, unfolding, sorting, piling, gathering laundry. She would listen with a little line between her eyes, but she gave no opinion. It bothered him until he asked her and she said, "You get enough opinions. People are always telling you things. I like to hear what you think, and, telling me, you sound out your own thoughts. I think I help you most that way."

"This town is going progress-crazy. It smells money. I think Cady has made a mistake with Malcolm. I think Cady will have to retire soon; I know he's over the age. He does his work well, very well, but we should be bringing someone along to head the department after he goes—another *two* men, someone, not Malcolm, and someone to replace Cady in a few years."

"Have you suggested that to him?" she asked, brushing a strand of hair away from her eye. It had escaped from the head scarf she wore while she was cleaning. Her hair was still black, but on top in one strand there were now streaks of gray.

"I can't. It sounds disloyal. He *is* the department in so many ways. He would think I meant to move him on."

"Can Roche say anything?"

"He even less than I."

Eric thought he alone was aware of the problem, but a month later Cady left the office one afternoon and came back whistling.

"What's going on, did the mayor's house go down a pothole?"

"Better than that." Cady winked and disappeared into the files. Later he took Eric aside. "I went to see Billy Tyrrel this afternoon. My birthday's coming up; I'm a couple of years over retirement age. I wanted to know what they thought—if they would press the retirement. Billy said *he* didn't know when I was born—that until someone raised the issue I could stay on the job for as long as I wanted to."

"That seems a little wobbly to me. Isn't a decision possible?"

"No, in these cases the best thing is to play dumb."

Eric felt uncomfortable, lacking the courage to raise the issue of a new man to be trained against the day when Cady did retire. Besides, Cady was his friend. "I guess my birthday surprise is no go, then, the ad I had planned to take out in the papers—Happy sixty—what?"

"Ninth."

"—Ninth birthday, no billboards, no skywriting—"

"Skywriting's okay, but why not make the message read, 'Mark Gordon's godfather is a man of wit and sophistication.' "

"You pay for those by the letter, y'know."

"Oh, I had no idea!"

"I think we should get another man on now—not to replace you but because we need one."

"We just got Malcolm—he has to work in."

"We got Malcolm three months ago, and he isn't working

in. Besides, what we are doing now really needs a bigger office, more staff."

"You don't think Malcolm will improve?"

"No."

"It isn't just his looks or his manner—"

"No, or not only."

"I didn't realize you were having trouble with him. Roche is, too. We talked about it the other day—"

"I've been waiting, but I don't have much hope for him."

"I sort of like him in spite of the clothes, and he'd done all that stuff summers, dam construction, bridge building."

"He's too radical."

"A man's politics are his own business."

"If only they *were*. He gets into political arguments with the people he inspects. He called Old Man Garger a bloated bourgeois exploiter of the under class."

"I heard about that—I just don't know why he said those things."

"Well, Garger hires Melendez to do his repairs . . . apparently Malcolm was there when Melendez was working."

"Bloated, huh, Jace Garger bloated. Does he look bloated to you? I always thought that was bunchy underwear."

"Cady, this is serious."

"Not today it isn't. Nothing is serious today, but yes, I'll talk to him."

Eric hadn't liked Malcolm from the beginning. There was a kind of perpetually injured innocence about him that got on Eric's nerves even before the radical politics had made their appearance. He came to work in rope sandals and flowing hair, and the road crews complained that he was "preaching" to them about their colonialism and imperialism and annoying people with his dress and manner. Cady kept defending Malcolm. The office needed shaking up, he said. A person's choice in clothes was trivial. The language he used— well, Cady had asked him what *bourgeois* meant, and his answer seemed good enough; no one who was realistic would object to being called that. But the complaints grew, and as time went on, it became evident that Malcolm wasn't working very hard. "He's gifted," Cady said. "You've seen his response to designing problems. When he does work, he's excellent. Let me talk to him."

Cady must have said a good deal, because Malcolm, injured and grudging, spent the summer doing his minimum best. Lunches, which had once been quiet, easy breaks in the day, were now filled with Malcolm's talk about plots, the plots that had killed President Kennedy and Dr. King, and the plots that the FBI, the CIA, and big business were hatching against the people. They found themselves, unwillingly, defending points of view in which they were not interested. On the job, Malcolm was perpetually angry until at last both Roche and Eric begged Cady to fire him.

"I can't, without a cause, a case of clear incompetence, drunkenness, *something*—"

"He alienates everyone."

"It's not reason enough."

Cady was irritated, too, but kept arguing for more time. Roche laughed at Malcolm. Bierstadt, the crew foreman who supervised the trucks, was scornful of him, but called him a "pistol." Only Eric really hated Malcolm, and did so with a depth of feeling that he himself could not explain. He remembered someone once saying that people hate in others what they wish to hide in themselves. He knew what he had tried to put by in himself, what shamed him in his private moments, but he couldn't see where doctrine-spouting, grievance-pouting Malcolm with his long hair, dirty teeth, and pirate bandannas was in any way like him. Nevertheless, he was ashamed of the depth of his feeling and tried to keep it hidden. He stayed away from Malcolm when he could. His doing so changed the easy friendliness of the office, and that made him hate Malcolm all the more.

Autumn came. Eric was busy pulling concessions from the Rivercrest people. He was fighting almost alone and his opponents knew it, and he cursed the cheery optimism of the commissioners and the downright greed of the town council. Everyone had stars in his eyes. "They say it will give everyone work!" he cried to Helen. "And be good for business, but losing the river isn't all that will happen. In twenty years, at that density, we'll have an urban slum there! If the commissioners weren't terrified of scaring Rivercrest away, we'd have gotten so much more!" He bargained for lower density and for a public walkway by the river, wringing it from the developers, who had said they wanted access closed the length of the development. He knew even as he planned and mapped it that the developers had been prepared to concede more from the beginning if only the town had fought for it. But the town had played dead. Even O'Brien and Billy Tyrrel.

In the ordered, serene house, Helen tried to comfort him. He had never before gone against people he liked and respected to fight for beliefs he could not prove were sound. He wasn't used to the strain of being the dissenting voice, of "holding up progress" with continual objections. When he stood up in the commissioners' meetings, people sighed. It hurt and baffled him. Helen knew he needed the comfort of being physically close to her and the children, to have them around him when he studied plans in the evenings, so instead of encouraging him to go downstairs to the basement to work, she made a place for his desk in the dining room, and he read maps and wrote up studies to the sound of her dishwashing and the children's bed preparations. He worked, in some way calmed by their noise and the security of their presence and soothed by their rhythms.

The fight went on for almost four years, waking up and subsiding as though with a life of its own. In addition, there were the smaller daily strains of work. Eric was surprised to find himself a tough, tenacious opponent, but he took no pleasure in fights. Helen's sympathy and the family routine became a still point of calm toward which he came eagerly every night for refreshment. Although he often had to be late after meetings, he always tried to come home in time to carry Mark to bed; Helen took Karen. Anne demanded to go by herself. Eric would tuck Mark in and then go to Karen's room and kiss her good night. Their strange youngest would not be kissed and shrank from touching. He got in the habit of calling to her from the doorway. It made him sad but he had long ago learned how different children could be; a family gets used to the strangeness of its members.

Helen asked for a sewing machine one Christmas, and she began to sew for the house and the children. Eric was amazed. "Who taught you all that?"

"Mrs. Woodcock. I worked for her after Frances and Mary Anne did. Unfortunately, she wasn't a very good cook—"

"You've been improving."

"I have no flair for it. Ernestine says I'm too literal to cook well."

Eric was amazed. He had responded to Helen's carefulness by trying to be more tactful and more gentle. "Ernestine's a bigmouth."

"Ernestine will save you from eating rubber eggs."

In the middle of the winter, between snows, the office got a new project. "It's Miner's Park, and I'm giving it to Malcolm," Cady said. "Somebody's found money in the city budget for it, and the historical people want to fix up the eyesore it makes. They want to move the miner's museum there."

"Good that Malcolm has it," Eric agreed. He was busy enough; Roche was inundated, and it was probably fair to let Malcolm have something to design. By now his dislike of Malcolm had become routine; he thought he had gotten used to it. Later, Cady kidded him.

"You'd make a great international spy. Never crack under torture because they wouldn't need to touch you—just read it all on your face."

"Did I say anything? I understand your decision, and in spite of your snide remarks, I approve."

131

"Like the guy said before he drank the vinegar. Malcolm is happy about the assignment, and he's been better since I talked to him about it. He was afraid that because of his politics, he wouldn't get his share of the creative things. Oh, and he's coming to dinner next Friday—Roche and Phyllis and their kids—I'd like to invite you, too, you and Helen and the kids."

A sudden, premonitory anxiety went through Eric like a wind. "Why do we need to do that?"

"Good Lord, he's been working here for almost nine months and Esther's never seen him. She's been doing fine and really wants all of you."

Eric couldn't think why he was anxious. He hated to lose an evening at home, but there was no reason for anxiety, except for his dislike of Malcolm and the social discomfort of an evening with him. He opened his mouth to say something and then thought better of it. What Cady said was true, and if Eric and Helen stayed away the snub would be pointed.

Helen and Phyllis Roche each brought a cold and a hot dish. Helen set the table and handled the cleanup. Malcolm came and brought beer for everyone. He was dressed less aggressively than usual, and his manner was almost cheerful. He was obviously struck by Helen's beauty and stillness, and the children interested him, children being an article of faith with him: mankind as yet unpolluted by culture.

"I understand you live outside of town, out near Bluebank," Esther said during dinner.

To Eric's complete amazement, the simple statement had an almost magical effect. Malcolm's eyes lit up. "We have a place, a little place, our group. The idea is for us to work here in town for three years and put all the money we can into the land out there, and then pull out to it full-time and be self-sufficient. I'll be designing it so we can farm it and have sheep for wool, and I'm designing a wind-driven generator. The women will spin and weave and we can sell their work for things we don't make, the hardware and so forth, although one of the members of the community is learning to be a blacksmith."

"I was amazed," Eric said to Helen afterward. "He was an entirely different person. He was nothing like what whines and shambles in and out of the office."

"He must be difficult to work with," she said, "he prizes his truths a little too much."

"Oh?"

"He thinks honesty is a greater virtue than it really is."

"What do you mean?"

"When we were out in the kitchen, he told me that when I got tired of my middle-class rut I should bring the children out to the land and live with his community."

"What? What did you tell him?"

"I told him that rural poverty holds no charm for me. He shrugged, and I went on clearing the table."

By March there were problems at the water-treatment plant. Roche and Eric spent most of their time there. Malcolm was hard at work, he said, doing his inspections. Eric suspected that he wasn't doing them. The grade school near the river kept calling the office about sewage fumes, and Malcolm said he had gone out there three times and found nothing, but Eric was too busy to follow up on his suspicions. The growth of the city had doubled his work. There were continual problems with the old bridge, the sewage problem was getting ahead of them, and Eric was still fighting with Rivercrest. More roads, more drainage problems. More building, more erosion outside of town. More erosion, more flooding. Wider streets, more buckling. More streets, more freezing. More freezing, more salt and sand. More salt and sand, more sewage problems.

People's expectations rose. Although they made more garbage, they wanted fewer dumps. When they got more cars, they wanted less traffic.

"The old bridge needs repairs again," Cady said. "It was never built for the kind of use the town gives it."

"We need a new one, upstream from the old."

"I was hoping you'd say that. Scout out a place and make a plan," Cady said. Eric sighed.

Last year, two years ago, it would have been a pleasurable assignment. Now there was so much else to do that the search would have a hurried quality to it and would have to be pieced together between other trips. He remembered with a keen nostalgia the leisure of the easier days—when he had planned "his" municipal building and had taken the time he needed.

"It's all getting too rushed," he said to Cady and Roche.

"*We're* getting rushed," Cady said. "*We're* knuckling under to pressure. These are demands the council will have to face, but we may have to slow down or get men and split the office into routine maintenance and improvements."

"Although I'd like planning, it's on the routine things that you get a feeling for the larger problems—neighborhoods, traffic flow, water—they're all part of one another."

"I agree," Cady said, "but I'm afraid quality is suffering in the rush."

"Where has Malcolm been all this time?"

"Malcolm was a mistake," Cady admitted. "He hasn't been working at all. He's been going back to the commune two, three times a week. The men say he's been 'borrowing' equipment from the city shops. I've never fired anyone before—I'll have to study up on what to do."

"Forgive me, Cady, but why the hell did you hire him?"

Cady looked hurt. "I guess in some way he reminded me of you—someone trying for something better—"

Eric was shocked, then hurt. "I never dressed like that or spouted those politics or was lazy or whined or—"

"I know, I know, and now I know I was wrong. I'm sorry, I've made it tough on all of us."

A week later, Malcolm, without consulting them, submitted his plan for Miner's Park to the town council. Cady was fuming. "I had to find out what *my* office was doing by getting a call from Bud Lucas! I told Malcolm when he first came that work was done through the office, and the office stood behind it. What did he think I was saying!"

"What should we do?"

"You and Roche get back here for lunch. I'm going up to the town council to get those plans. I'll be back here at twelve-thirty."

Eric and Roche stood looking over Cady's shoulder as he sat at his desk with Malcolm's plan opened before him. They didn't dare look at each other for fear of touching off a murderous laughter. Malcolm's design was a kind of black-humor Disneyland—a guilt memorial to man's rapacity. The area was treeless, but had once had trees; stumps stood here and there in mounds of mine tailings. There were places to sit on rusted mine equipment and on what looked like metal-reinforced animal carcasses. There were no groupings of these "seats," they all faced outward and were out of the conversational range of one another. At the center of the park was a hill, and in it a mine entrance, a broken track running into it and an ore cart on the track. The mine interior was to be lit, it was noted, with a blue light. The technical drawing was excellent. Malcolm had thought to put fences—weathered slat fences—at the north and west sides of the park so that the wind wouldn't blow his tailings away; he had shown a good eye for detail, too.

"Had they looked at the plans yet?" Roche asked, at last.

"I don't know. Where is he, anyway?"

"I think he's supposed to be out at the elementary school again. They're talking about closing it as a health menace."

"Call them," Cady said.

Eric called the school. The principal said he hadn't seen Malcolm. Roche left to go to the school, still biting his lip and hiding his face from Eric.

"I know you both think this is funny," Cady said, "but it's compromised me two ways and I'm not laughing."

"The situation isn't funny, but the plan is."

"Tomorrow, maybe. Next year, but not now."

"Let's have fun planning who we'll get after you fire Mr. Malcolm."

"Someone staid. Someone very staid." And then they did laugh, looking at the plan. "The self-righteous idiot doesn't know, but this is exactly what the whole downriver side used to look like, out where it flows south. My dad used to take me there." And they laughed again.

Cady gave Malcolm his month's notice the next morning, and Malcolm disappeared from the office. He had done so little work that the place where he had been closed over without a ripple. Cady persuaded the town council to give them a new man, and a secretary who would take calls and coordinate the office.

Several weeks later, Eric saw Malcolm at the courthouse. He assumed Malcolm was looking for work. They greeted each other guardedly. Eric asked about the commune.

"We've got a completely self-sufficient system planned. We've already had people coming from as far away as Idaho to see it."

"I'd like to see it myself."

"It's not complete yet, but when it is, it will be a model for every biosynergic group wanting to live off the land."

A few weeks later, he saw Malcolm at the courthouse again. Now that the man was no longer working with him, he felt better about him. Their greeting was easier.

He didn't see Malcolm again. One Sunday in early summer, he and Helen and the children decided to take a trip out to Pickaxe with Cady and Esther and stop at the commune on the way. Their feeling against Malcolm had mellowed with time and none of them had ever seen a commune. Malcolm had described it well enough so that Eric thought he knew where it was. They took a picnic lunch and followed the Ute up by back roads, past Callan. There they found what they thought was the road, and followed it. Cady began to tell the history of the area. They saw no people, but the ground was full of blown trash of fairly recent making. Farther along, they came to one large and one small geodesic dome. The large building had been covered with plastic and was ingeniously planned, with vents top and bottom. No one was there. Papers and discarded clothing littered the cleared area. Chipmunks and mice had nested in the clothing and had shredded the plastic so that streamers of it, like women's hair, blew among the oil cans and plastic jugs.

"Part of a grand old tradition," Eric said, quoting Roche. "Get the gold and get out, bury your dead and cut your losses."

"Humph!" Cady said.

"Cady, didn't your folks come out here to get rich?"

"Nope. My granddad was what, with no particular affection, was called a 'lunger.' He had TB and came out here to get well or die. Grandma was a nurse in Denver. They were very sensitive about 'cut your losses.' "

"This place," Helen murmured. "I wonder where these people went."

"I wonder where the dream went," Esther said. "Do you think the people found some new place together?"

Helen looked around and shook her head. "I don't think so. If they had, they would have gone with some pride. They would have cleaned up a little."

Cady turned to her. "I never thought of that, that cut your losses means losses after all, and a sense of failure . . . and a sense of shame."

A week later, Cady got a call from the mayor. There had been letters—the same letter, actually—mailed to him and to the two local newspapers and to the state legislature and to the governor. It complained of favoritism in the engineer's office, keeping someone on who should have been retired because he was a crony of the men who ran things. "We've got to act on it. No one wants to, but the issue has been forced. It's a shame, really, a damn shame!"

There was anger first—the secretary in the mayor's office told Roche that the mayor had hit the ceiling. Everyone said the law should be changed, that it was arbitrary and wasted good talent, but everyone knew that feelings made no difference. Their anger relieved them, but did no good. For a month Eric and Roche thought things might blow over, but a directive came down from the town council that Eric was to be made temporary director pending a decision to raise him to the position of chief or get someone new in from outside.

For two months Cady haunted the place, making Eric uncomfortable and unable to take command. Eric tried to suggest that Cady go into private work as a consultant. Developers would be eager to use him, since he knew so much about the town and the river. The state and county would call him in by private contract.

"You've got the contacts and the knowledge—"

"I don't want to start all over again."

"That's the point—you won't have to. Everyone knows you—even the new developers soon learn who you are and how much you know."

They urged and begged, but what had happened seemed to have hurt Cady in a way that struck at the heart of his beliefs about himself and the town. He had never been able to find out why the letters had been sent. The signers were people Cady knew only slightly, one not at all. They were people who had had no dealings with him recently, who had no reason. "I can't understand it. It takes time and trouble to go into the records at the courthouse and verify everything·and then write all those letters . . ." Eric and Roche thought that Malcolm was behind it. Eric remembered seeing Malcolm at the courthouse, but beyond that there was only guesswork and wondering, pieces blowing like the shredded plastic at the deserted commune, a metaphor of loss.

So, like a victim of loss, Cady wandered the town, revisiting old jobs, or haunting the office, looking up obscure records on streets and bridges. He seemed to have lost color in his face, sureness in his gestures. Sometimes he stood in the office time-stunned, as though he had forgotten the day or the year. Sometimes he would begin to talk about the levees or shorings he had made at a certain spot years before, the history of a certain stretch of bank, as though to claim it as his before it eroded away. They saw his grief that he was not to be permitted any more wars except against his own boredom and Esther's pain. Someone at the mayor's office called Eric and asked about a party and presentation in Cady's honor. It was to be a surprise, but Eric asked Cady, who answered bitterly, so bitterly that Eric called the mayor and told him he didn't think Cady would come. Everyone was sorry it had all been brought up. A town like Aureole had once had the autonomy that allowed it to close ranks and protect its own, to make its decisions on a personal level. Now . . . Eric felt a twinge of anger. They're all very sympathetic, he thought, but only his family and friends have to see him wandering here and there, aimless and stunned.

"Cady, help me get some men—help me hire the two new people—"

"Me? After the wonderful job I did with Malcolm?"

"Do better this time. Help me fight with the developers. I know what you think about progress. Help me get concessions."

"The fight's gone out of me. I've gotten old and scared."

"Not you. Impossible."

"I am scared—I'm scared that Esther's sickness will get beyond me and beyond her—that I'll start hating her pain and want to be away from her and from it, and that she'll know. It happened twice this winter—and not for the odd minute of impatience at how slow she is, or that she can't think or talk about anything but pain or loss or her own impatience with it all, no, hours, days at a time, when I wanted to be free of her, this place, a life I once loved—"

"She gets better, whole months when—"

"Sure, and there's this new medicine and that new medicine. What's bad is the fear we both have now, she of the next attack, I of that anger at her, the guilt of it, that I wanted to be free of her and may want it again the next time . . ."

Eric wanted to say something, but there was nothing he could say.

"And now I've been retired and nowhere to go, no office to escape to in bad times, no other thing to worry about, no other challenges but ones I can't win."

"Surely—"

"No reason for her to get up, to try to conquer the pain. Neither of us wants to move south, but I guess we'll have to, eventually."

"Take the Rivercrest project over for me, be a citizen. Watch them. Make them give something to the town."

"I don't know . . . I don't know."

"I felt so sorry—and there was nothing I could say," he told Helen later. "Malcolm walked through here; he walked through and left an acre of blowing garbage near Callan and a man without a job—a good man, a man good and patient enough to have tried to help him."

"Cady was over the age. It would have come eventually," Helen said quietly. "You knew that and Cady did, too."

"He would have chosen it, then he could have faced it better. He haunts the office now, like a ghost."

"He won't anymore, now that he's talked to you."

It was true. Eric invited Cady to sit in on the interviews for the new man—the town council had okayed two and a secretary, but said that the second man couldn't be hired until the first had worked for a year. Cady declined.

Eric, Roche, and the town council interviewed four men and chose Gibner, who lasted eight months and got a better job. Luther Call drank and they had to fire him. Alonzo Smith lasted two years and the second year they hired a quiet Indian, a Navaho, Jimmie Yazzi.

140

Slowly, the style and character of the office changed. The men were more independent but also more isolated, each doing a single kind of job. It was no longer possible to share projects or even discuss them much because the work had increased. Eric did planning and coordinated the other services from Planning's little room. Roche stayed near the radio and had sole charge of the road- and building-repair crews, Yazzi managed the inspections, and Smith, and then the new man, worked with Roche or Yazzi where the need was greatest. They saw one another every day, but there wasn't time for anything but a quick summation at weekly meetings, and some of the time they found themselves arguing over a project, passing it from man to man. It made for a certain adversary feeling that had never been there in Cady's time, all part of the progress everyone said was so desirable. Eric and Roche talked about it in the beginning and tried to keep some of the old feeling alive by planning Sunday picnics or parties with each other, but the artificiality of planned relaxation changed things and the pressure of work during the day made Eric have to take extra things home sometimes. On weekends he had no desire to do more than be at home with his family.

10

When Mark was six, Eric took him skiing. Mark learned quickly, instinctively, as he seemed to do everything. He was daring, fearless, and a natural on skis. Helen made a red ski suit for him, and small and bright he dove down the hills, took terrible falls, laughed, and rose to fall again. Eric urged Helen to go with them, but her caution and slowness frustrated them and she soon stopped. In two seasons Mark was almost as good as his father. So the Saturday after Thanksgiving, the men of the family got their gear in order for the season, stalking importantly about the house in overbig boots, waxing and polishing and sighting down their poles, arguing the merits of various hills and runs.

All through the school year Helen sewed almost frantically. Often Eric would come home to the sound of the machine, and whenever she had a spare moment he would hear it whining away upstairs. Eric guessed that the passion with which she attacked each sewing project must have had to do with her own ragged childhood, although she never said so. Once Mark, in a school game, ripped and soiled his shirt. He went on playing, and came home late with it almost torn off. Helen was carrying food to the table on a tray as he slipped into his place with an apology. Eric watched her go pale, recover herself with effort, and go out to the kitchen, where she stayed for quite a while. He looked around the table.

Karen, who had just started school, was dressed to almost aggressive perfection. Anne also, distant and scowling, sat in perfectly matching clothes. Later he said to Helen, "No kid of ours will have your burdens. I can see our kids clearly. They're going to have lots of friends and be very popular. I can see Mark in school and then in high school and in college. He's going to have a growing up as close and warm and friendly as Cady had. You suffered as a child, being poor, but you won't have to suffer that as a mother. That's not going to happen to us."

She shivered. "Don't make those promises," she said. But he knew; he had seen the future in his mind.

Mark's teachers confirmed what Eric had suspected all along. "I've seen many bright children in my day," Mrs. Kramer said, "but Mark seems to have the added gift of finding ways to use his intelligence so he isn't bored. If I were you, I would think seriously of advancing him a grade or two in the next few years. His social adjustment is good; there's no telling when he'll become restless in classes that offer him so little challenge."

Helen was angry. "There's nothing 'different' about Mark. He's as bright as he needs to be. Why does she single him out?"

"It's not always *bad* to be singled out. She said he needs challenge."

"I don't like her putting a—a difference on our child." And Helen would hear no more about it.

So Eric tried in his own way to find where Mark's interests were. When a new engineering problem came up at work, he would bring it home and lay it before the boy. The two of them began to design things for the backyard: wind-powered barbecue turners, solar toys, gear-driven washlines, and a forest of pulleys and levers to raise this and lower that.

As the years went on, Mark grew increasingly to be a source of wonder to Eric that he dared not share with anyone but Cady. At work it sounded like bragging, Helen would hear none of it, and he did not wish to alienate the parents of

Mark's friends. The boy read a lot, but wasn't bookbound, asked questions, invented games that he brought to school and introduced to his friends; the yard was always full of boys. Eric loved the questing, the eagerness in Mark, a wide-open acceptance of challenge coupled with that remarkable power of concentration and application that he had seen since Mark's early childhood. Karen, too, surprised him. It was she, in her self-sufficient quietness, who began to interpret Anne for her parents. Anne separated herself from the family as soon as she could, but she seemed calmed by Karen, and the two of them would sit in complete stillness for hours on end, Karen watchful and very still.

Eric tried to have lunch with Cady once a week. During school vacations, Cady would pick up Mark and bring him along.

"He's such a bright boy; he's learned so much just since Christmas!"

"Don't let Helen hear you say that."

"Is she still upset about his being different?"

"Helen seems scared of difference, even when it's good. Last month Karen and Anne were playing outside and a reporter came by and took a picture of them. He wanted to put it in the newspaper, you know, 'Spring is here,' and she wouldn't allow it."

"Well, he is exceptional whether Helen thinks so or not."

"Then put your money where your mouth is. You know about town history, the names of trees and the local geology. Why don't you take the kid out and learn him good."

Cady paused a minute. "Are you doing this for me—give the old buzzard something to do?"

"I don't let my favorite son associate with buzzards."

"I've adjusted, really, I'm doing all right." Eric nodded. "But I'd like it," Cady said, "I'd really like it."

So Cady began coming over on Saturday mornings to take Mark to the places of his own boyhood. They went upriver and down; they visited the new developments and Cady explained their problems. They explored the old caves north of town. Now and then, a friend or two of Mark's would go along. Eric was happy for the easy sharing between Mark and Cady. His own family visited rarely; he and Helen had planned to take the children East once a year, but things came up and they hadn't taken more than three trips. Eric's parents were not comfortable with the children, and seemed almost frightened of Anne. At those times Eric watched his children more carefully and saw Karen trying to reach out to Anne; he admired her ability to understand the poor, sour little girl. At other times he was impatient with both of them. Anne was not ill; they had gone to three doctors, all of whom said she was physically healthy. She wasn't deaf or blind or palsied. There was no need for the elaborate stratagems Karen used to charm and interest her. If she wanted to stay behind and sulk, he would declare, she should be allowed to do it and not be coddled by Karen.

It was by living with his children that Eric saw clearly how people change in one another's presence, like chemicals or colors or the forces of physics. He had seen people in simpler terms before he married, but living closely with Helen and then watching the forming personalities of his children, he was conscious of natural changes as dramatic as anything the river did, or the town. When Mark was alone with his sisters, he showed a gentle tolerance, a little patronizing, but brotherly. As soon as any of his friends were in attendance, he began to posture and bluster with his sisters, giving orders and playing the master. Karen, gentle with Anne, was said to be bossy at school. Anne was Anne everywhere except with Karen.

Eric tried for a while to hide his favoritism for his son, but Helen's unspoken rebuke at the unfairness made him see that he was contributing to Mark's bad habits with his sisters. Eric decided to take time alone with each of his children. He began to go out with them in turn on Sunday morning for a long, private breakfast at the Waffle Kitchen. At first, these

145

Sundays were formal and uncomfortable—Helen insisted that the children dress for the event—but as time went by the very ceremoniousness of the day attracted them, and even Anne seemed content, as content as Anne ever was, to go.

Over the breakfast of their choice, he would ask them about school, their friends, their thoughts, and he would talk about his job or someone he had met or about his own childhood in distant, green Maryland, his parents, and his sister. It became a time to which Eric looked forward, also.

Helen kept no family traditions of her own, no national or religious holidays, no Christmas, Easter, Fourth of July. It was Eric who saw that the family celebrated those days. He had no idea how gracious his own youth had been and how deeply the American traditions were part of him until he encountered in Helen so complete a lack.

"You never had Christmas or celebrated any holiday?"

"There were holidays from school, but they only meant we had to be home and to work."

"But what about Charles's family?"

She looked up in surprise. They never spoke of that, or almost never. "Charles's family celebrated everything," she said, "big mass affairs. Charles didn't like them and neither did I. It was a duty."

"But a family needs tradition, too," he argued. "The thing doesn't need to be big or elaborate but I think it's important."

"If you want to do it, we'll do it," she said simply.

He wondered why Helen had no inner spiritual clock for these holidays. His mother and aunts always knew when to bake the cookies with faces on them, when to buy the pumpkins and dye the eggs. He remembered everyone's house filled with marvelous aromas, parties, visiting, games, ornaments. Helen had no such urge. Eric had to say, "The holidays are coming . . . time for turkey," or, "It's going to be July Fourth next week. There should be strawberry shortcake. We used to put whipped cream and the whole strawberries around . . ." He felt himself laboring to explain; she did as he wished. It made him feel the events were stagy and not natural, but it was better than nothing. If he persevered, the children might come to feel those rhythms as they grew.

Perhaps her journal marked her year—it would be typical, a thing so secret and personal. She was still writing in those lined composition books, with her old furtive habits. He might come upon her when she was finishing an entry or carrying a new notebook, but he never saw her sitting, musing, summing up the day, and he was never privy to what she wrote.

"You still never read over what you write?"

"What for? Once I've written it, it's free to go and I'm free, too. I don't have to worry over it—what I should or should not have done."

"Is your life happy now—do the days say that?"

She smiled at him. "Are you asking me if you have made me happy?"

"Well, yes."

"I'm content," she said. "You're a better husband and father than I thought you would be."

He laughed a little self-consciously. "That's the story of my life—better than I seemed at first."

"Don't be angry—it's why these questions are better not asked at all. The answers, no matter how good, always seem to make people unhappy."

But he knew she was content. She still saw her friend Ernestine every week or so. He would come in and hear Ernestine's laughter booming through the house and know they were in the kitchen together. She still had a fancy tea once a month for the church choir ladies with tiny cookies and tiny napkins and paper doilies under everything. They still went dancing sometimes, and although they didn't learn many new steps, they adapted the old moves to the new rhythms and the years made them smooth together, anticipating each other's pauses, breathing, shifts of weight. At these times, her wordless looks blew flowers at him, her gestures were relaxed and naturally graceful. She glowed. And there were other proofs.

She had divided the tangled, weed-grown backyard in two. In one half she made a flower and vegetable garden, neat and precise, but she left the other half wild for the children to play in. It was a concession that must have caused her constant, secret annoyance: old tires were mounded there, a packing-box fort, Mark's half-built shed, the forest of wires and gears of their inventions. Once, when he saw her looking over the child-torn wilderness, he came up behind her and put his arms around her. "This is going to earn you time in heaven."

"Do you think so?"

"Definitely. They'll grow up, and when they do, you'll have the whole garden."

She laughed. "The house is enough for now."

She had performed a kind of magic on the house. Despite his workspace and the children's toys, she had infused it with a feeling of peace. There was in its use of space and line a delicate aesthetic sense he knew she must have conjured up from nothing. She certainly had not experienced any of it in her growing up. The rooms breathed a serene airiness he had never seen in magazine pictures or anyone else's home.

And sometimes, when she thought she was alone in the house or that no one was listening, she sang, softly, to herself. She had a pleasant voice, unremarkable, but clear, and he would hear her in the other room or in the garden and think how happy her contentment made him feel.

The winter Mark was eleven, they took Karen skiing. Eric saw in his mind the years to come, all the children and maybe the grandchildren skiing these hills. Maybe they would go to Pickaxe together and stay over for a week each winter—a family tradition. It was a silly dream, he knew. Even now, Mark dared more than he, needed more challenge; Helen was still picking her way down the green-marked beginners' hills, skiing well, but with great deliberation and caution; he knew that if he demanded some kind of effort from her, the fun would become work, but his pleasant picture would not go away.

Karen learned to ski the way Helen had, slowly, tightly, even rigidly. She was afraid of falling, of losing control, of being wrong. He had to remind her again and again that this was a sport, for fun, for freedom, that it was a kind of wingless flight. "Yes, there are ways to turn your body and your skis, but first relax, enjoy it, feel the snow under your skis, listen to it, let yourself do it . . ."

She couldn't; she was too conscious of how she looked, of what was right.

"I thought kids—I thought she would take to it the way Mark did."

"The easily free think freedom is easy," Helen said, and then, "The way you ski reminds me of Hetty Richardson, when I was growing up. She lived on the south side of town—"

He was surprised and pleased; she so seldom spoke about her childhood. "Yes?" he said.

"It's no great story. I used to watch her walk. She had the nice clothes my sisters Frances and Mary Anne wanted so much, but I envied the walk she had. I knew that if *we* had those clothes, we would only look as though we had stolen them. They would make liars of us, for all the pleats and plaids, they would hang down on us the way our own clothes did. The secret was in the way she stood and the way she walked—*you* walk that way. You ski that way, you and Mark."

A clue. He thought about it a long time. First he thought about getting Helen a good fur stole, maybe, but there was no occasion for her to wear one. A special dress—no, an outfit—a whole ensemble, all harmonizing in some way, the way Helen liked to match all the clothes she wore. In the end, he couldn't trust himself to choose for her and he had to settle for a gift certificate. He got it from an expensive store in Denver. And he wrote her a letter with it, including a bus ticket, round trip, and a check for two nights at the Brown. She could leave

Friday afternoon, stay all Saturday, and come back on Sunday. He would stay with the kids. She was now, he wrote, a full citizen of the sunny side of the street on the good side of town. "You can walk the way you dance and give everyone a treat." She seemed moved by the gift and took a long time planning, waiting for winter things to go on sale. She even called the store three times before she was ready. She made her trip in the spring and came back with a nice but fairly conventional outfit. Years of sewing had made her sensitive to color and line. The outfit was a soft green that brought out the color of her eyes and the clarity of her skin. It was simple and would not be out of place in Aureole. She wore the outfit often to singing practice, shopping, or out with Ernestine. "My green," she called the ensemble, "I'll wear my green."

That spring, Mark surprised them all by asking if he could take piano lessons He was in his last year in grade school. Since Helen had continued to oppose his being put ahead, Eric waited for signs of boredom in him, and he and Cady tried to find things to stimulate him outside of school. When he asked for the lessons, Eric said yes without hesitation. "They have a piano at school," Mark told them. "I can practice on it, and the music teacher says I can stay late every day. She even knew some people who give lessons." And he produced a list.

Eric smiled. It was the Helen part of Mark to do such things. "Do you have an idea which teacher you will want to try?" he asked.

Mark beamed. He had questioned all his schoolmates who took lessons, found the three best-liked teachers, rejected the one who seemed "too easy," found out which teachers gave pieces individually, which taught theory as well as piano.

"Who is your choice?" Eric said, grinning.

"This one; Mrs. Browning."

"Well, shall we give Mrs. Browning a call?"

"Cool," Mark said.

The teacher lived in a suburb on the other side of town. It would mean that Eric would have to arrange a day in the office so that Helen could have the car. He had been wanting to do this for her anyway, to give her a little more freedom, a day to shop or go somewhere else.

The shape of their changed weeks became set by Mark's school and Mrs. Browning's schedule. Mark's lesson was Wednesday afternoon. Wednesdays, Eric walked to work and arranged to do office things, saving site work for the rest of the week. Helen changed her shopping day and her luncheon day and her volunteer morning at school. Mark stayed later at school and practiced for an hour each afternoon. Because he practiced at school, they didn't know what progress he was making until Mrs. Browning gave a small recital six months or so after he had started. Eric and Helen went to her home and heard her students play. Helen, in her "green," sat quietly, intently, listening. Eric watched her watching her son. He knew that she would not express delight, but he knew just as surely that she felt it. Mark was doing well and would do better. He had chosen his teacher wisely.

"Would you like to be a musician when you grow up?" Helen asked that evening when they were on the way home.

Mark answered slowly. "I don't think you could do it unless you're very good and work all the time at it. The boy who played the Brahms piece—Kenneth—he's like that. I think I could be good if I really put everything I had into it, but I don't think I'm that kind of person—I want to do lots of different things. I want to learn piano and keep it for fun, and maybe to put myself through school later as an accompanist or in a group—something like that. I think I would like to go into science."

That night in bed they talked about Mark, marveling that he seemed to be a blend of both of them, having her cool-eyed, realistic gifts of appraisal, his ease and love of variety. He laughed. "Your care, my flair." And she laughed, too, in the darkness.

"And Karen—what do you see in Karen?" she asked.

"I don't see much of myself in Karen, but in Anne I see my sister, Doris, when she was young."

"That's funny, I thought that was my sister Frances." And they laughed again.

He went away for a week to Salt Lake City to a conference of city planners. He listened to presentations about high-rises and presentations against them, about planned communities and the destruction of neighborhoods in "urban renewal," but mainly he heard about towns and cities overwhelmed by soaring populations and sagging municipal services, towns suddenly gone city, suburbs swallowed by cities that had once been miles away. Through it all, the voices of Cady and Roche, the boom-and-bust experiences of the Colorado towns, echoed in his mind. Had the world suddenly gone Colorado? He listened to it all and went out of his way to meet planners and engineers who worked in the small cities on rivers—towns that used their rivers well, some that didn't. He took notes, talked about Aureole, and tried to formulate his thoughts carefully to discuss later with Cady.

And in the conversations and the discussions he heard the changes in himself. The people from the coasts spoke quickly. They hopped from subject to subject, idea to idea. They were witty and did balancing acts with wit, and they savaged one another's reputations. His pace had slowed. He was now aware of how much slower he spoke, how little traveling he had done. He had seen neither London's cluster cities nor Tokyo's transit system. He found he wasn't interested in those places except as they bore on Aureole's problems. It saddened him, but it was true all the same.

Helen noted it in him when he came home. "You're very quiet . . ."

"I felt like a hick. My mind's gone slow; in ten minutes one man gave fourteen examples of what he was talking about from places he'd been."

"Did they shed any more light than six or three or one

would have, or was he trying to tell you he had been to fourteen places?"

"I don't know," he said helplessly.

"Poor man. If you'd grown up country, you would have been used to that by now; you'd know which it was. Brighter may not be smarter."

"I felt shoeless, tobacco juice down my bibs."

"Poor man," she said, and smiled at him.

Cady laughed. "They were playing *that* game when I got out of school. Men who worked on the Bonneville or the Grand Coulee would talk amount. 'Pour concrete—why you ain't poured concrete unless you've counted thousand-ton days.' The others would talk distance. 'Remote—why, you can't talk remote till you've been in the mountains of Bolivia—'"

"I felt so—so *provincial.*"

"You are. We all are, one way or another. The big-timers have gotten specialized. Your sophisticate does bridges, certain kinds of bridges, all over the world. Or platforms, or missile silos. He never has to live with his mistakes, and he never has to integrate a new idea with all the others he's had before. We live with every mistake we make. Keeps us honest. Keeps us careful and modest."

"You're trying to make me feel better—"

"I'm buttering you up because I need your help on something."

"Whoever said country was guileless? What's up?"

"There's a new ski area going in east of Pickaxe. They want to call it Gold Flume and they want me to help design it."

"Cady, that's great!"

"But I need a skier, a good skier, to help."

"I'd love it, but I'll need an assistant."

"Who?"

"Someone more thrill-seeking, more daring, with more flair than I've got. A certain Mark James Gordon."

Mark James Gordon yelled with delight. Mark James Gordon capered around the house. Mark James Gordon attacked the problem with an intelligence that astonished even Cady. He got the series of topographic and quadrangle maps that related to the area, and then began to make a large relief map. With Cady's help, he scaled it three inches to the mile. Then he took the three main hills and their valleys, where the runs would be, and made a map of them, six inches to the mile, working on a trestle table in the basement. The maps took months and Cady started coming over now and again in the afternoons and evenings to go downstairs to work with Mark on them. Then Cady took Mark out to the site one weekend and they compared the maps to the mountains with pictures and measurements. They charted small but important changes in plane and aspect that weren't shown on what they had.

More and more, the project became Mark's and Cady's. Eric had work of his own.

II

Eric and Yazzi had submitted plans for the new bridge. The plans Eric had made five years ago were no longer applicable. As he had expected, the town had built up so heavily in that area that a new, less desirable spot for the bridge had to be selected. He and Yazzi had scouted the land and made plans of how and where to change the present roads. Yazzi didn't argue well, but he was solid and knowledgeable and had begun to organize his inspections so that he was free for some of the more creative work of the office. They had projected future growth in Aureole to show that a new bridge was vital and that the sooner they started, the fewer changes would be necessary.

"It looks as though I'm going to have to lobby the council, send candy and flowers to each of them to plead the obvious," Eric complained to Yazzi.

"We can argue what's happened. Fifty percent increase in bridge use and the old structure isn't strong enough to take that kind of traffic for long."

"I think the council still wants it repaired."

"Money down the drain," Yazzi said.

The council voted to repair and strengthen the old bridge.

It was a bitter disappointment. Eric took the decision to Roche's office and dropped the papers on Roche's desk. "Maintenance," he said furiously. "Maintain it."

"With what? It's not going to stand the weight of everything that's been coming over on it."

"Repair and strengthen is what the proposal says."

Roche looked up at him. "You and Yazzi really busted your asses on this one. I'm sorry."

"Six months' work."

"Save the plans. Save everything. In a couple of years they'll have to look again."

"By that time the area will be built up and the town will have to buy it back."

"Maybe that's what they want." And Roche grinned.

Eric felt exhausted. He was having to become more and more of a lobbyist as the town's competing needs and interests multiplied. The time he spent convincing, lobbying, was time taken from planning. He began to think about the ski hill, to dream of it as a kind of spiritual resort. It was his play. He knew it was Cady and Mark's project really. Helen said that both of them were beginning to look like prisoners, pale from their afternoons and weekends in the basement. He had argued a little with her about it. "Let the boy dedicate himself to something, now that he has the chance. This kind of joy is rare enough. I had mine with the city and county building, and I had to wait until I was twenty-four."

"I hope his schoolwork isn't suffering," she said. "He mustn't fall behind in school."

"He won't, he won't. God, I'm so proud of him," Eric said.

"I know."

"And he's nothing like the kid I was, the bland, agreeable, easy-sliding kid I was. And he's not the scared, sad kid you were."

"I know."

"Doesn't it make you happy that he is none of those things?"

"I don't like—I—he still looks pale to me."

For his twelfth birthday Eric had gotten Mark thirty pounds of modeling clay, two sheets of plywood, Styrofoam forms for the insides of the three hills, a huge bag of plastic model-makers' trees and packets of balsa wood and wire. They began the actual models of the three hills, building them to the scale on the elevation map Mark had made.

"When this is done, the developers want to see it," Cady told Eric. "I've got some ideas for the lodge at the bottom and a warming house halfway up. Maybe there should be an observation deck at the very top—someplace out of the wind."

So Cady was dreaming, too. Before he slept at night, he, like Eric, must be sailing solitary, almost soundlessly, on long, slender skis, moving through sun-and-shadow groves and out onto open spaces, down easy slopes, through mogul fields, and down daring chutes. He thought he should tell Mark—there should be variety on each run, changes of scene, and small changes in the competence required for each, open places, narrower places, places of full sunlight and dappled sun and shadow; on the beginners' slopes some long, quiet trails through trees, gentle enough so that . . . And so he skied to sleep, over wide hills or snow-secret trails, leisurely as breathing, or in long, blue falls shot over the rims of the world into the sky.

It was a Wednesday. Helen had the car and Eric had planned the day in the office, but at eleven-thirty Bennett, the new mayor, came by and asked him to come out and look at something. A group of residents were complaining about traffic and drainage problems caused by the erosion caused in turn by the overbuilding of an area above them. He tried to tell Bennett that it was a maintenance problem, not planning. "The city never should have allowed building at the bottom of that area, but they did. I was against it and still am."

"The problem is not a maintenance one. I want you to come and see, because maybe some creative thing can be done, a way found . . ."

It was the southern tip of Rivercrest at the bottom of the hill, the worst part of the undermining about which Eric had preached and pleaded. In his basement on one wall was his map, his dream plan for the area, park, tennis courts, golf greens, none of the area stressed by the high density that now burdened it. He sighed as he thought of it. The mayor was relatively new to Aureole, and nothing bores a politician like something decided and done before his time.

"It's going to be complicated and expensive to fix this, and we're going to have to treat each of these streets like a river—a torrent, which is really what it is."

Eric made careful notes. There would have to be a system, something to slow the water and minimize . . . He hardly noticed Bennett leaving him, promising to pick him up at three. When the mayor came back, Eric was still working. Some things that could be done had occurred to him. He had talked to some of the homeowners along the three streets and had seen some of the damage himself.

"Let me take you home," Bennett said, "it's after four-thirty."

"I'd better call the office; the switchboard is probably closed, but it's worth a try." He called and was pleasantly surprised when there was a click on the other end. "Jean?"

"Is that you, Mr. Gordon?"

"Yes, I thought you might have gone—"

"We've been trying to get you. I thought you were at the mayor's office . . ."

"No, but I'm with him. What's the problem?"

"They want you to come back here as soon as you can."

"All right," Eric said, but she had hung up before he could ask who "they" were.

The municipal building was almost deserted when they got there. Most of the offices were closed and most of the workers had gone home. The building stayed open at the town-police entrance, and there was a state patrol car pulled up outside the main doors. Sometimes the police pulled in near there after hours to write reports, because it was out of the wind. His design, his and Cady's. Even today there were some high-school kids talking there on their way home. It made him smile. He thanked Bennett and got out of the car. As he walked toward the doors he was surprised when the state policeman got out of his car and came up the walk toward him. "Mr. Gordon—?"

"Yes?"

"My name is Officer Schilling. Would you come with me, please."

It was not a question. He found himself checking Schilling's name against the shiny metal plate on his pocket.

"What is it?" Eric said.

"There's been an accident, sir, would you come with me." It was also not a question.

"Who?" Eric said. "Who is it?"

Again, and he could not see past the guarded stare. "Would you come with me, please, sir."

It came to Eric that he could refuse, that he had a right to refuse. This was not like arrest. He was guilty of nothing now, and he could not be forced to acquiesce to anything.

"No, I don't think so," he said and turned away from the officer and began to walk and then to walk faster down the street. He was walking very fast toward the river, where he could think, because he was mindlessly, needlessly, terrified. The river would be calming now, it would quiet him, just to be there for a while. But he was getting winded, very tired. He slowed and turned and saw the police car following slowly, patiently. He thought he might outwit Schilling if he kept on, if he crossed over where there were no streets, farther down, but then he remembered that the development was there now, that the riverbank was changed, that there was a barricade, a wall there. How could he have forgotten all that, when he himself had been so involved—that open street had been closed years ago. He stopped, confused, thwarted. The car came on, following him very slowly. It stopped abreast of him and Schilling leaned across and opened the passenger door.

"Please, Mr. Gordon," he said. Eric got into the car. They drove to the hospital in silence.

Cady was there, in a waiting room. Walking toward him, he saw Cady get up, a Cady older, grimmer than he remembered him being. It was all very strange. He had seen Cady three days ago—why was he suddenly so old? And then his eye went past Cady to someone sitting on a straight chair that was obviously not part of the waiting-room furniture. It was Esther. Only then did Eric see to the enormity of what was waiting for him.

"Who?" he asked. "Who is it?"

"All of them," Cady said. "It was all of them."

12

He went home with Cady and Esther. They drove slowly, they walked slowly. All around them, Eric knew, was anarchy, roaring grief. The trick was to go through the narrow passages here, this street and then this and then get out of the car and go up the steps to Cady's porch without stirring it. Why couldn't he have kept walking away from the state trooper? If he hadn't been tired, winded, in some part of him curious to know what it was, he might be going still, not half-dead with this awful sickness, terrified of letting in all the rest. In the beginning he had bargained with Cady and the police. It wasn't possible that all his family should be dead. Children outlive their parents, for one thing. One can hear of a child dying, perhaps, but not of a whole family. Child by child he argued and bargained. How could they be sure? And if the accident had been so terrible, how could they identify the victims as his? And suddenly he had remembered that other family, the ruined car, the shoeless foot. He couldn't tell Cady how unfair it was. He had gone past the deaths of that other family so long ago, put distance between them and the man he had become, but as the law's punishment had been too little and too easy, this was too late, too awful, not just. He had once caused the death of a family. He had not had to see them in their deaths. He had had no part of the death of his family, and yet they had made him look at *them*.

Filthy, crumpled, wax-faced dolls had been dressed in the clothes of the people he loved. How could they dare to say that *Helen*, beautiful Helen, was this pallid, dull-haired, dry-toothed, gape-mouthed . . . He had raised his head angrily, and then another part of him, a drier, more objective-spectator part of him, had caused him to nod his head. It helped to do that because then they covered up the thing that was wearing Helen's clothes. He didn't really look at the children. Cady helped in that.

Somehow, he and Cady and Esther made arrangements. People were called, the papers informed, funeral plans made at Helen's church. Roche's wife, Phyllis, went to the house and got Helen's address book, and they spent the next day calling. They called Helen's sister Mary Anne and her mother and her brother on the farm. He called his parents and his sister and Uncle Tony in Denver, and two of Helen's friends in town, and Ernestine. They called the school Mark and Karen went to and Mark's music teacher. He could do this because he never mentioned the children's names. He said, "The Gordon children," or "the Gordon family"—his name. He knew that if he spoke their names he would say nothing else. His parents called him back and told him they would be coming for the funeral. His sister would come, too. "Stay at the house," he said. "I want to go back there but not alone."

Cady heard him and got Roche and Phyllis to help, and Esther and Cady came with him back to the house that once, a long time ago, way back yesterday, had been a family's home.

The order there seemed a revelation to him, now that he saw it with strangers' eyes. Nothing stood out to be done, no bundle of ironing, no pile of mending, nothing hurriedly put by, needing her hand. It was as though the house did not yearn. Upstairs, the rooms were as orderly, as ungrieving. He didn't go into the children's rooms or trust himself to see into the drawers and closets that were Helen's, but looking at his bedroom he knew he could sleep there because the room seemed so impersonal in its order.

His mother said something like that when she came, as though to praise Helen; what a wonderful housekeeper, how serene and restful she had made the home. Later, he heard her talking with Esther when they thought he was in the garden: "Was it always so perfect? Somehow it bothers me."

"I've only been here once or twice," Esther's older voice said. "It's so difficult—steps, my own and then these. I'm not surprised. She was a woman who gave very little ground." Eric was shocked at what Esther had said. He stood stunned and disbelieving.

"Such a horror, everyone gone," his mother's voice said.

Eric didn't want to hear more, so he went out the front door and back around to the garden. It was late in February, a Chinook day. It was as warm as spring. Tomorrow would be the funeral and after that the weekend, and Monday he would go back to work, and then this awful dislocation would end. He hated that he was here now, marooned in the winter garden in the middle of a day, and that there was nothing to do.

Not so. He had forgotten the basement, Cady's project, and Mark's. Maybe there was surcease there, an end to the awful restlessness. Because the restlessness was dangerous. If it made him wander off the narrow road on which he had to walk, the monsters would claim him, the uncontrollable, howling creatures of grief. If he could occupy himself putting trees into the clay of Mark's mountains, measuring elevations in the great bowls between them, plotting the location of the four lifts up the sides of those bowls . . .

He went in through the back door, into the spotless kitchen. The steps to the cellar were there—they were very steep because it was an old house, built before there were codes about such things. The thought suddenly annoyed him. Make all the codes you want to keep them alive, plan your plans, they will slip away all the same, all in an afternoon and not by such as these steps, a menace close and about which they had warned every guest and taught the children so carefully. He shook his head and went down.

163

Under the light was the miniature world, Mark's ski area: mountains, three of them made to scale; slope, aspect, and height carefully measured and marked with string. There were strips of crepe paper showing the three kinds of slopes—black for the expert, blue for intermediate, green for novice. There was a red line for the possible position of the lift, four on the bottom by the lodge, two in the middle of each mountain, fanning out to cover all three hills. That would have to be changed; it was too expensive. He would work on that problem over the weekend. Thank God he had it to do.

For an hour, two hours, three, he skied. He skied the beginners' slopes, soft, wide turns around the hill, yes, good; beginners like the feeling of competence, making those turns, wide hills and intimate trails through the trees where the land isn't steep. Here, here, here, it would have to be graded, though. Above all, oh, God, above all, for beginners, nothing sudden. "Yes," he muttered to himself, "they have to be able to see what's to come, to see and plan, to rest before, to decide, to . . ." Then he put the thought away and went to the advanced slopes. He heard a sound above him, Cady at the top of the stairs.

"Come on down," Eric cried, and Cady, hesitating, said, "You sure you want me down there?"

"Please come."

"They're making supper," Cady said, "Esther and Phyllis and your mom. She's a wonderful woman, your mom." Eric sighed. Cady went on, "Your dad's been keeping track of the calls and all that, flowers . . ."

Eric sighed again. Then he said, "Let's ski one more slope."

"Expert?"

"Intermediate."

"Those are the hardest to plan—it's hard to make them as varied as the beginners' trails, but not as steep as the expert. See what we've done on Cady's Cut?"

"Cady's Cut? You mean you've named them, then?"

"Oh, yes, from the beginning. Mark did. There's a list somewhere, and a map he did . . ."

"Just tell me, I don't want to look at his handwriting now."

So they traced Mark's Menace and Cady's Cut, Mom's Marvel, Karen's Joy, Little Annie, and runs called Don't Look Now and Omigosh, and a run, the hardest, the longest, the sheerest, called Father's Day, and Eric felt the awful roar on both sides of him for a moment until he turned his eyes away, back to the single narrow line, the winding road between the chasms.

"He has a terrific visual imagination," Eric said, hoping his voice was all right.

"Yes, he had," Cady said.

"Don't help me. Not yet."

"Sorry."

"Cady, how did they die?"

"What?"

"How did they die?"

"In a car, you know."

"Yes, but how? Was it because they swerved to avoid another car? Was it skidding, some ice, some water from the melt?"

"Well, you know, they were on Eighty-one, going toward Bluebank—"

"What were they doing *there*?"

"Didn't you know? Didn't Helen tell you?"

"No."

Cady looked uncomfortable. "I thought you knew all this."

"Maybe the police told me. I just wasn't listening."

"Well, the car was going north on Eighty-one, and, uh, it went off the edge of the canyon there on that shelf road about a mile south of Bluebank. It rolled, many times—do you really want to hear this?"

"Yes."

"Well, it rolled and landed on its side about eight hundred feet down."

"Did it skid?"

"The roads were clear."

"Was there another car?"

"I don't know."
"How can we find out?"
"State police, I guess."

So Friday he had something to do before the funeral. He was glad for it. He borrowed Cady's car and went to the police station and found the officers who had covered the accident. He read their reports and questioned them. They were subdued with him; even as familiar as they were with death and grave injury, they seemed anxious and offstride, afraid of his anguish.

The weather had been dry, the day clear. There had been no ice or rockfall on the road, no blowout, no skid marks, no sign of braking. No one saw the car go over, or if someone had, there was no evidence of it. Witnessing would have done no good as far as the victims' lives were concerned; they had all died instantly, or nearly so. There would have been no way to save them. If he wanted a summation of the injuries . . .

"No! How fast had they been going?"

The policeman was proud of his expertise in this matter. All along that road there were wrecks. Over the years, a mathematics had developed, a set of ratios, and at that spot, the distance of fall was directly related to the speed the car was traveling, because at certain speeds cars became airborne *here*, oversteering *here*, or not taking the curve *there*. At 40 mph they land on their sides at the edge of the highway; at 50 over once, still in sight, but up against the rock *here* (he was drawing as he spoke, the road, the falloff, the rock on the left side). At 60, cars fly and they roll when they land, missing the rock because, you see, they've gone over it, and down to land here; and at 70 or over, they shoot out into the open space, leaving the road six feet off the ground. The car in question had been going upwards of eighty miles an hour, oh, anywhere between 75 and 80 mph on a road posted *here* at 35, because it was curving and narrower than the rest because of the mountain on the east and the falloff.

"I see." But he didn't see. Helen had been traveling at a rate he had never known her to drive for a reason he didn't know to a place she hadn't told him of. He now realized that in some way he had been hoping all these hours that someone would call, some friend or neighbor, to solve the problem, explain how and why. He needed a reason for Helen to be on the road to Pickaxe or to one of the towns on the way with the children in the middle of the afternoon. Who was there in Bluebank or Granite for her to see—what field trip or party or meeting or sale?

There was no answer. They had her purse and some things saved from the wreck. They had him sign for them. If he wanted to inspect the car, it would be at Dover Wreckers out of Callan. Sign here, here, and here. They had wrapped the things in plastic and sealed them. Some of the things were bloody, many of the papers torn and indecipherable. They had done the best they could. Yes, thank you, yes. He got into the car with the packages and decided he didn't want to go home with them. With the mystery beside him, he went to Miner's Park, not yet a park, never yet a park since Malcolm's leaving, so it was a good place to be alone. He pulled up near it and sat in the car and unwrapped the packages.

Helen's purse: a comb, a lipstick, a mirror, a pack of Kleenex, a wallet and book of addresses, a shopping list, a sewing kit, a small combination key chain–flashlight, a tin of aspirin, a roll of mints, a change purse, a pocket calculator for the supermarket, a checkbook, a pen, an extra set of keys, a small notebook, a dainty, useless, and unused handkerchief. In the wallet: twenty-six dollars in cash, two credit cards, a driver's license and registration, a library card, a Social Security card, two raffle slips—no pictures, no special elemental part of her. In the notebook: pages of comparisons of prices, most recently of the freezer they had bought two months ago; note of a new dance place they had planned to try; a recipe she had copied, probably from a friend; and some household hints. At the end, there were more prices and a single, final statement: Tell E chains don't fit.

The rest: Mark's music things, Karen's stuffed bear, a blanket they always carried, a pair of sunglasses, and material and papers taken from the glove compartment, mostly pertaining to the car. A long, long time ago, two days ago, the papers had been important and valuable. He remembered scolding Karen for fussing with them when the glove compartment was open. Suddenly the bear was more important than the papers. He took the opened packages home, and put everything—dirty toys and bloody papers—on the clean, perfect surface of the coffee table, plastic and all. Then he went up and dressed for the funeral.

Knotting his tie over the clean white shirt, he saw a man who looked no different from how he had looked two days before. What was different was the weight of new decisions that were almost overwhelming him. He would need a new car. Could he stay in this big house alone without someone in to clean and cook? What would such a person be like? Why had Helen reduced him to this series of decisions and problems? Why had she taken his maturity away, reduced him to a tenth the size he had been two days ago, taken back fourteen years?

Ernestine was at the funeral, and some people from the choir. He saw some of Mark's friends; school people; Mrs. Browning, the music teacher; the Cadys; the Roches; Yazzi, and other people from the office. His parents, his sister, Doris, Uncle Tony, and Aunt Florence were there, and people he didn't know or couldn't place. The minister spoke, read, prayed, talked about Helen's work at the school and the church. She has eluded you, too, Eric thought. Her quietness and reticence, her orderliness, her "devotion," were all people saw. But he was seeing a piece of road with a falloff to the west, a shelf road, a good road, well engineered, but with a curve that no car going eighty miles an hour could take. He didn't see the car, only the road and the fall over the edge. The car had been airborne; there would be no tracks. But *before* it had lifted—all two tons of it, over his hypothetical head, watching—there should have been the desperate, instinctive jamming of the brake, the wheels clutching at the ground, a long, tearing brake mark, a shriek of rubber remembered on the road as the tires begged friction—keep me, hold me—before the inexorable centrifugal force tore the car away from the earth and out into blue air—flight—where no wheels print, where no weight is remembered.

She had left no such mark. Why not? Around him others mourned. He watched them. Had the house always been so orderly? Why had she left no mark, no Mark, ever again?

After the services he stood turned away from his mother and sister, who were speaking quietly to others. A woman came toward him and took his hand. "You probably don't recognize me, Mr. Gordon, but I'm Laura Flint; I was Mark's sixth-grade teacher."

"Oh, yes," he said, not, in fact, recognizing her.

"Mark was only twelve," she went on, and it was something he saw she had planned to say, "but in my class he gave so much . . ." She said more, but there had been a word that had stopped him from hearing the rest, a word she had put before him that grew as it lay in the air until it became a wall over which he could not see. Its sound grew also until it was a roar in his ears. Half-deaf, half-blind, he tried to reach out to her as she moved away, and he stood staring after her until his mother came and guided him out to the waiting car.

"What did she say?" he said over the roaring of the word. "What was she saying?"

"I don't know, dear, I didn't hear."

But Eric had heard. She had said "twelve." She had said that Mark was only twelve. That other one, the first one, had been twelve, too; "Lois Gerson, twelve." He remembered it from the policeman and from the lawyer, what was his name, yes, Rademaker, and from the court and Judge Hamblin, dead years ago of a massive stroke as he worked. Didn't that prove how long ago it had all been, that other family?

But the word "twelve" was how he came to stand wherever

he stood and not remember having been there. He had no memory of the car or who gathered at the graves or what was said or how they all got home. Inside his blindness he was seeing; inside his deafness, hearing the charges being made. That Helen hated gambling in any form, yet she had two raffle tickets in her purse. That the house, normally clean, was this time spotless, with a finality about the order—new soap in the soap dish, the sliver of old soap gone, the shoes in the closet all lined up, because no one would walk anywhere beyond this day. And silence. Do I have your attention, the closet said, now that I have you mute before me? And do I have your attention, the cabinets said, now that there is nothing to be said? The car had left no marks, no skids, no rubber from its tires offering a last bargain with the road. In a car. And what he had done to her, so she, on a Wednesday afternoon, even as she loved him and them, did to him. For the justice of it, because Helen believed in justice above all things. He had seen his children as special, particular, exceptional, and her act cried that Charles Gerson's children were special and were snapped off in the middle of their ordinary, daily breathing as easily as though they had wished it. The one who might have lived—she must have sat with him, begging and bargaining as Eric had done with the police. How hard she must have wished, but he had not obeyed and had flickered out. And there was Eric—Arnie then, young and careless—with a fractured arm that stopped giving him pain six months after the death of everything she had. Justice, clean as stone.

"Wasn't your love greater than that?" he murmured into the distant day.

"My father and my brothers said that love is irrelevant and that justice lasts," her spirit whispered back at him.

He knew that it wasn't Helen's spirit rising before him to say what she had said, but his own thought, an obscene thought, a nightmare that he was dreaming standing up. He found he couldn't rid himself of it, see around it to where reason was, weep and be cured, grieve and be healed. In time. He lay helpless in her justice as in a lake of ice.

On Saturday and Sunday he worked on the model. His parents and sister left Sunday afternoon. Cady and Esther left that evening, but Eric told Cady he would stop by after work on Monday. Esther said she would ask the people she knew if there was anyone who would come in to clean for him. So many details, things that related to the running of the house, the bills Helen had paid, the household accounts she had kept—his head buzzed with details.

And behind the details she stood without expression waiting for him to prove the truth.

13

Cady's house seemed to have changed since he had last been there. Like everything in Aureole, it was darker, more weathered, shabbier. Cady saw his look. He didn't have the energy to keep his face from any of its changes.

"Yes, the house needs a paint job," Cady said, and shrugged. "It needs a lot more than that, too. I thought I'd get to all those things when I retired. The truth is, it's dangerous to do repairs alone, and no fun either. I guess I should hire someone."

"Hire me," Eric said. "The evenings and weekends are going to stretch out forever."

"It'd be taking advantage," Cady said.

Eric waved him away. "I'll be here next Saturday with brushes. Be ready."

They went inside. Sadder still, an indefinable rancid smell hung in the air, and there was clutter he didn't remember. They had brought some of the things down from the attic, little tables, rickety chairs. There were newspapers and magazines in piles against one wall. "I keep meaning to get rid of this stuff, to read the magazines and get rid of them, it all seems like so much effort—"

"Don't you have those girls coming in?"

"Esther gets angry at them, and now that I have no full-time job, I feel like I ought to be doing the house at least."

"But the ski area—"

"That takes only a couple of hours a week. They hired an

172

architect for the lodges, we were only doing the slopes, Mark and I—"

"It's all right," Eric said. He thought Cady might weep, standing there. The possibility frightened him and he headed it off by walking past Cady into the kitchen.

They sat down in the once-welcoming room. Boxes and cartons stood in the corners—here, too, was clutter and disarray and that oily odor. It was the odor of unaired beds, unswept corners, of closed-off rooms, and closets never turned out, of yellowing cloth and paper going brittle. His house would go this way, if he let it—let it, then, let it!

"I haven't done very well," Cady said. "Somehow—somehow there was no reason to—"

"I haven't said hello to Esther. Where is she?"

"She's probably still asleep. She had an awful night last night and I thought I'd just leave her alone. She doesn't get out enough and I don't encourage her enough, don't force her. It all takes so long and hurts so much."

"Cady, I need your help and Esther's, too, and I need things done that I can't do because I can't get time during the week, and maybe because people won't talk so frankly to me—"

"What is it—what's happened?"

"Cady, why did they die?"

"Oh, wait a minute—"

"Why were there no marks, no brake marks, and what were they doing there anyway, thirty-four miles from town? Why was she doing eighty? What do the police *think*? They talked facts to me and the facts don't guess *why*. They're cautious, the police, but you have contacts—find out for me."

"Connell's retired. They have a new man now. My old boys aren't there anymore. What exactly are you thinking about?"

"I'm thinking about suicide . . . and murder."

Cady was very still. "Why?" he said then.

"Revenge—she wouldn't have seen it as revenge but as justice. Helen was fair. She went to church but she didn't believe in God or in religion very much, and I don't know if she even believed much in human love, but she did believe in fairness, in justice."

"You can't be serious. Revenge for what? Justice for what?"

"For something I did to her years ago."

"Helen loved you. She was a good wife and a wonderful mother and when she was here, a better help to Esther and me than we had any reason to expect. She couldn't have—not her own children—no mother could—"

"Prove it," Eric said. "Prove she couldn't have killed herself and them. Mothers do it all the time. She had another life in Omaha, a family life I don't know anything about. She had a past I never heard about and she was going someplace she didn't tell me for a reason I don't know, unless she was going *there* for the reason I just told you."

"You once mentioned she kept a diary," Cady said. "Has she been keeping it still?"

He had forgotten. His mouth dropped open and he stared at Cady in surprise. "Good God, could I have been so foggy that I'd forgotten?"

"You have been foggy and it's because of shock and grief. You can't make the grief go away by hating her."

"I want to find out if—if she did it."

"How could a man find out such a thing?"

"I don't know, and I need to know. I need to study what happened, what the police have studied: Why was she going so fast? Did she swerve? And where did she leave the road? Were there witnesses? Who found the car and how? Where had she been going and why? You and Esther have contacts, people who won't be as hesitant with you as they would be with me. I'll get the diary."

"None of your knowledge will bring them back—"

"Just don't change anything you find out to spare me."

"You want the truth, I'll try to get it for you."

"That's what I want, the truth."

He walked home. With no car, he had been walking as he did when he first came to Aureole. He was shocked and ashamed that he found himself so resentful of the new, galling daily problems to be dealt with. The insurance—it would pay for the funerals, which had been relatively modest; he would need a new car. He thought with a pang that Charles's insurance money was his at last, that he could even buy the little sports car he had seen in Halloran's showroom. No trouble now. He had paused at the car when they were buying the Rabbit last year. He hadn't really wanted the car, he had just stopped at it because it was so bright and would be so quick and sweet and responsive down the valley to Bluebank in the spring or down Gold Flume Canyon in the fall . . . Helen had come up to him as he stood looking and had said the obvious "But it only seats two," and they had gone back into the lot to the good used cars and had gotten the Rabbit. "I want to *know*," he said aloud. "I want to know."

He thought he would have to ransack the house to get to the latest journal wherever it was and devour it, but suddenly he saw the house itself as a clue, a series of clues, as an archaeologist must see a site on which only the surface has been disturbed. There might be, for example, something she had brought from the old place, some few letters or mementos that had been in the two small suitcases she had taken with her from her old room. She had an address book and there were signs to be read in the household accounts, clues of daily living. What if, for example, she had stopped renewing her library card or her magazines, had, in effect, stopped making plans for the future. Surely that would say something. And the children—if there were no new clothes in those closets—it might mean that Helen knew no one would wear those clothes, how many days, weeks, months ago? The house, a lonely cave only last night, was now a repository of wordless truth.

The days were difficult. Roche and Yazzi and Jean, the secretary, didn't know what to say to him. They walked around him as though he were so fragile and precious that the wrong word or sound might pierce his flesh and craze his bones; every word he uttered was like the shattering of glass in a cathedral. He needed their closeness—why were they so far away, why did they keep him so distant? Thank God for the work. Heavy trucking through town was playing havoc with the old bridge. He could route the complaints to Roche for that, but the same trucking was shaking the foundations of homes and businesses on the streets between the bridge and the highway junction. A new highway would have to be built looping the town and the town streets and roads would have to be adjusted to give access at at least three points north and three points south of the road. He fled into the work.

Eric had talked with the highway engineers before and he spent Monday afternoon with them, discussing these issues. They didn't know about his sudden, special changes; they spoke normally to him. He relaxed and forgot, for three short hours, emptiness and anguish, causes, tire tracks, closets, clothes, journals, and the horror of grief he was holding away from him, only barely. If anything was different it was his need at first to refer to the maps the men brought with them. He seemed to need this more than he ordinarily did, checking himself so that he would not drift away into a daydream and embarrass himself by losing the point or forgetting that a problem had already been covered. Too soon it was finished. At five, he asked the men out for a beer, but they said they had to get on to Callan, where there was work in the morning. They would be back on Wednesday and would stay over then. He was grateful to them. At five-thirty Roche took him home. It was two miles out of Roche's way but Roche said he would be glad to do it until Eric could find a decent car. He had looked forward to Roche's company, but Roche was so careful with him that the ride was stiff and formal.

He put a frozen dinner in the oven and started for the attic. Her other journals might be there, the old ones. He would see into her life with Charles Gerson at last. Beyond that, who knew what evidence of plan could be voiced in the finality with which a string was tied, a carton repacked? Had she been there recently? Was the dust disturbed on any of the boxes? The attic had been hers almost exclusively; he never went there, and it was almost bare. The baby crib, a couple of boxes of maternity and baby clothes, all carefully marked, suitcases wrapped in plastic, a carton of odd dishes and pots, another of jelly glasses. She made jelly in the summer. Had she known last summer that there would be no need thereafter for her canner, her jars, her lids, the other tools of summer housewifery? If so, why did she save them here, she who kept little beyond its need? Maybe last summer she had still not yet decided, not decided how or when to end it.

Another carton was on the brick-and-plank bookcase they had used at the Cadys'. The journals? Yes, there they were, more of them than he thought there would be—a whole carton of the lined composition books. He took the carton downstairs. He had decided to match her formality in this with his own. He would begin where she began and he would read a book a night. If there had been a plan he would see it begin, watch it grow, know it as she knew it. He would miss none of her thoughts, her justifications, her changes.

Because if she had planned this justice, this agony for him as punishment or in revenge, she would want him to know. There had been no note, no letter, no ugly sign on the mirror written in lipstick; there were only these books and the book in which she had written, perhaps the very morning of the afternoon she . . . He had not found it yet; he would look for it later. Her orderliness angered him. Let *her* wait now, he would be the deliberate one. He put the books by his bedside and then went down to the kitchen, ate the dinner without tasting it, spent an hour on a drawing he was making of the Ute River Road access, watched the ten o'clock news on TV, and went up to bed. Except for the silence at dinner and the soundlessness of the house, it could have been any evening, any ordinary evening of his life.

But going up to bed he found the stillness was oppressive. Even the house's own life-throbs: the breathing of the freezer, the heartsounds of the water heater, on and off, the buzzes and murmurs of electrical energy sounded different now that there was only one hearer. What differences had those others caused in the house that their absence so changed it? Physics—movement of molecules, rises in the heat level, the carbon dioxide breathed through lungs—would all those things together cause the air to flow, the house to echo so differently? Oh, the dreamers, who . . . "No!" he shouted in the hollow room, to keep away what was beyond bearing. Then he took up his reading.

Book One. Worn-looking and yellowing. He opened it to the first page, July 9, 1944. He had just been born; there was no war for him, no Nebraska, no world outside his crib. She would have been eight. He wished suddenly that there was a picture. Everyone has some pictures—perhaps the sister . . . The first entry was brief: "It's raining. I am punished. Mama says there is no use of me. A hole month and a half before school starts again." He turned the page. "Yesterday turned hail and the garden was runed so we picked what we could. Buck and Curtis fight a lot. They hit each other. Dad whipped Curtis becaus he was too sore from fighting for doing chores good. I can hear the sound of it the hole day after."

He sighed. The ugliness, the chill, even in that distant July, had permeated the pages. He read on, sampling the cold rage of this failed family. Helen was whipped herself a month later for "aruing," defenseless even before the whipping; there was only this journal to state the truths she saw and still saw even after the harness strap came down. He was moved by the beginnings of a sense of form in what she did. Here and there she crossed things out, refining her thought, a primitive aesthetic comfort. He read on. Hot spells, dry spells, the sisters fighting, her yearning for school. There was, there must be, even now, a secret race, a whole foreign race of children who yearn for school because it isn't home, whose vacations are dreaded and who watch the warming days of May creep over the desk tops with sinking hearts, made lonelier still, more bereft, because all the others count the days to summer and

178

swarm out of the schoolhouse with joy at the end of the last day, free.

He had little sense of "Dad" and "Mama" as he read, except as somewhat baleful presences to be avoided when possible. The sisters and brothers were more real and, for the most part, were tyrannical. Summer over, school, blessed school, began again, the neatness and order she craved, but here, too, social differences made life bitter. "Sellie and Martha laughed at my lunch." At November he read about a Thanksgiving party the teacher planned in her idealistic, grown-up's ignorance. Everyone was to bring something. Cake, three kinds, and one of the parents said he would give a turkey and cook it right there at the school, in a pit the way it was done in Indian days. There was to be corn and squash, pumpkin-bake and popcorn. For days the journal echoed her terror at telling her father about the party and asking for something. When she finally did, he must have raged at her and all of them, the school people and the town. Did they think he was a millionaire that he could waste his time on such foolishness? Helen didn't quote him, she hadn't learned to, only, "Papa got mad." Eric read the bitter rancher's anguish in the blank space that was the rest of that day. Her brother Buck gave her some horse blankets to take to school for the Pilgrims and Indians to sit on. They smelled of the stable as they would have then, in Pilgrim days, and the girls refused to sit on them, ranchers' daughters, farm girls and small-town girls, but with an acute, a very acute, sense of social distinction. He read and hated darkly and wondered if Helen had hated as darkly as he did, had learned to hate for years in silence in that classroom.

He read on. There were triumphs, too. Neatness and order could be cut from the chaos that surrounded it. Mama let her have a place in the attic, a corner behind the trunks and boxes, and her brothers, Buck and Curtis, in a sudden, un-characteristic display of kindness, made her a Christmas box—a wooden chest in which to keep her treasures, the very books he was reading now. A piece of lace was put in it, her Christmas cards, and favorite book. By New Year's, she was writing about a friend.

The entries were seldom longer than a paragraph. They didn't deal with hopes or things that should or might be. Many were as boring and banal as the life of an eight-, then a nine-year-old, but Helen was bright in ways that he was not—had never had to be. Even here there were flashes of her bedrock knowledge, the objectivity that so many people—sometimes even he—had seen as coldness: "Grandma Carberry came to see us. Mama cleaned the house and tried hard to show her we weren't poor, but it wasn't no use. They always argue later. Somebody's sure to get the strap after Grandma Carberry visits."

The spring came. Frances got work in town as hired girl for Mrs. Woodcock. Buck and the father left for the stock-show circuit. Curtis went into the marines. For a month there was joy in the house. Mama sewed and taught the girls to dance. They played radio music all day and did the things forbidden or denigrated when the men were home. They put up each other's hair. They siphoned three gallons of gas out of the tractor and two out of the car and sold them in town unrationed and went to the movies with the money and out for sodas after. Mama's face relaxed and in town that night Helen saw men looking at her and remembering that she was still a pretty woman.

All too soon it was over. July and the men were home. The army wanted Buck. Dad went down to the draft board and convinced them Buck was needed. Eric read on.

They sold skim milk (blue milk, she called it) to the government and butter illegally for high prices. They got a new horse. Frances left home to go to Cut Bank and work in a defense plant. A bitter winter. Dad grumbled, ready with slaps and the harness end for the least annoyance. Mama was vague and tired the way winter made her. The landscape snowblinded and deafened them, six feet deep to the ends of the world. A Tuesday afternoon. Helen, home from school and doing her homework in the icy front room, put the day's supply of wood in the wood stove, coming to the last piece in genuine surprise. Too late. It was already dark, the woodpile hidden under the snow. When Dad came in she was waiting for him, wordlessly, the harness end in her hand. None of the reasons were written. The whole thing was said on half the page, the letters no bigger, the writing no less ordered than the rest. Need for justice or just self-hate, or an inability to endure the tension of discovery, accusation, all the preliminaries that would end with the whipping anyway? None of the reasons were there, just the impenetrable order of the words. She didn't go to school the next day or the day after that. Bad weather, or what he had done? She was as mute as the snow. The book ended and Eric was free to sleep.

The state health department was concerned about septic waste leaching into the water supply. Eric spent all morning trying to develop the figures: how much water, how much waste, tests in the past, recent tests. There was a public meeting in the afternoon and so many interested parties that it all but ground to a halt. He read his figures and then was asked to interpret them. A long procedural discourse began among the departments of health and water and the commissioners. They were in the hearing room where he had recognized Helen all those years ago, handing papers to Tyrrel, now long retired. They used this room for large meetings out of the habit they called tradition. He sat in the paneled room's official drone and thought about her. Had she said, "I couldn't hate you after that. Yes, I forgive you. I already have." Or had she said, "*I* forgive you; *I* already have," meaning that for the part of the horror that had robbed *her* of husband and children, she had forgiveness to give. But for the horror he had done to *them*, there was no forgiveness. He tried to hear her again, back through the years. "I forgive you," but there was no way to call up the sound of her voice or the memory of her face, the exact memory. The head of the health department called on him again and he had to interpret the numbers and show where the statistics were incomplete. And at the edges of the room, in all the corners, Helen floated, now a wife, now a mother, now a nine-year-old absolutist with the harness strap in her hand. Why did she have those raffle tickets in her purse, she who hated "luck"? Then he thought idly: She always kept the house so warm—I'd come home and it would be seventy-five in there. I made her happy because I let her be warm. And he thought of the little girl again until he forced himself to put her away.

He had become immersed in the journals. He read one or two every night. They opened outward as she grew. Buck stupidly bragged in town about his deferment, and word got around and the draft board looked again, and then Buck was gone and there were only women in the house except for Dad. Then Mary Anne got the job in town with Mrs. Woodcock. Then, abruptly, written with what he saw were the wide-open eyes of fear and incredulity: "Dad said it wasn't any more use. We would never get good horses or be anything. I came downstairs this morning and he was still sitting there. He got up and did chores, but like someone who is sleeping."

But living beings need to continue living. Mary Anne began working at the five-and-dime and during the week stayed in town with a school friend's family, and Helen took her place at Mrs. Woodcock's, cleaning house and minding the children. It was at Mrs. Woodcock's—he found himself smiling—there were born the social manners he had seen her use all those years later: the tea in little cups, the paper doilies under everything, hat and shoes and purse to match, the social expressions, dead and dated in the forties that "nice people" in tiny towns in the Midwest were still using and that rang so artificially in Helen's speech years later. In that house she had been silent and had watched everything, heard everything, hoarded everything to build on the stubborn stone foundations of her life.

Cady came over on Friday evening to work on Mark's model. More studies and aerial photographs had shown that the mountain had avalanche potential in five declivities right above one of the bowls. Cady brought twenty pounds of potato flakes, and got Eric to rig a fan (prevailing winds) to try to make as many avalanches as possible and to match the model overhangs with the ones in the photographs. They dusted themselves and the basement and finally found what made the avalanches in different places—changing the "wind's" direction and then changing again.

"Leave the trees on this side—"

"We're above timberline from here up."

"Oh, sure, I forgot."

When Eric went to bed, Cady was still working. It felt good to have someone in the house.

The weekends were the hardest. This one was cold and bright blue. The house was a mess. Eric went down to the basement and got his skis, resolutely looking past Mark's and Karen's and Helen's—and a guilty feeling that he needed to act in some way, to get rid of the ski clothes and the skis and the woolen hats and all the toys. Other children—no, he couldn't think of that, not yet, not yet! His stomach turned with grief. He thought he would be sick. He opened his mouth and took a gulp of air and said to the empty house, "I don't have to," and he grabbed his skis and boots and poles and took them upstairs. It was only then that he realized that he had no car. He called Cady.

"Sure," Cady said. "I've got some questions about lifts, length, distance, anyway. I'll be glad to take you. I'll be there in half an hour."

The day was blue and silver, a surprise, because Friday had been ice-cold with more cold predicted. Eric got his lift ticket, put on his skis, and went up on the chair lift, trying to be mindless, without a memory. Had it been only three weeks since he had bęen skiing with Mark? Yes, only that, but so irretrievable now that it might as well have been three years or thirty. For a few panic-stricken moments riding up, cold and alone, he thought the skiing was a mistake. Everything would remind him—this tree where Mark had fallen, this hill where Helen had . . . He knew he had to be strong and resist the memories. If he let the memories come, none of the streets in Aureole would be open to him and he would never ski here again, and the world would close down on him still more. At the top of the hill he felt the need for caution, so he kept to the easier slopes, judging everything, measuring a new unwillingness of his body to bend and give, as though crevasses might open before him on those well-known contours, earthquakes begin, shattering the easy downhill drift of these slopes, trees spring up and bramble hedges, as they had for the prince in the story Karen liked, and, oh, God, Karen— why was he thinking of her now?

Yes, of course—this was Karen's run—had been Karen's run, and Helen's, this soft slope with wide vistas and few trees. Trees to the expert are lovely and magical—a challenge; to the beginner they are simply a hazard. The makers of the slopes know this and keep the trees wide of the beginners' trail. Karen's trail, Helen's trail. He would have to go into higher, colder reaches, where even Mark hadn't gone, places that bore none of their imprints, no matter how deeply buried by successive snows—emptier, colder, steeper.

He took the next lift to the top. It was early and the snow was unforgiving with cold, but he relished the high, wind-clean spaces and he stood for a while at the top planning his run. He didn't want to do any of the delicate, surgical kind of skiing, cutting his way around moguls or through the slalom course that had been set up on the far end of the hill. He wanted speed, soaring, a downward fall like a hawk who dropped over the rim of the world and then soared outward. There was a back trail—Tumbleweed—headlong to the bottom. He bent into his skis and pushed off for the back face of the hill.

He hadn't gone past the first steep drop before he realized his timing was off. Some mystical give-and-take between the slope and his instincts, body, and mind was missing. He was working against the hill, against his own body; turns came up that he took too wide and too fast, forcing him to slow lest he hit the trees. He took bumps that brought him down with teeth-jarring force. He fell twice and came near to falling many times because of soft sloughs he hadn't seen and had taken too fast, or patches of ice he did see and didn't go around. He was furious with himself. He stopped halfway down, hissing at himself. You came to be healed; then *be* healed! Give it your eyes, your mind. He said out loud: "Give it your attention!" Then he was careful and attentive and he did a little better, but the ease wasn't there, the very thing he had come for, to be lucky and free. He skied the intermediate slopes then, teaching himself his old moves, and for a while he was able to forget himself in technique, a more demanding and contriving thing than he had planned, and without any of the joy.

He met Cady for lunch in the lodge, thinking they might quit then, but Cady was so full of ideas and insights from talking to skiers and watching them that Eric didn't want to cut his day short. So after lunch they went out again and Eric went up to a run he had always enjoyed. In new snow, it was intermediate; in old snow, expert. He and Mark had done it earlier in the year.

Some of the old freedom came back. The ice at the heights had softened, the sun opened his spirit. He began to enjoy the day. He breathed the blue air with its odor of snow, crisp as new apples. "Now, let it go a little, just a little," he murmured to himself. He wasn't ready for wit, for clever cornering among the trees, fox-sharp, fox-quick, but the trail wound and fell off in long, tight chutes and because there had been a new fall of snow, the bumps and ridges were still small. Eric jumped, kicked, sheared in the narrow chute, enjoying for the first time that day the work of it. The trail opened and then went down through groves of pines and firs. The quietness was vast—he could hear only his own breathing and the sound of the motion of his arms and legs inside his clothes, the susurrant reassurance of his skis on the new powder. Those were the only sounds there were. The voices in his head quieted and went still. He pulled in the breath of that solitude. Then he whispered soundlessly, "be healed," and he went in that rhythm, unweighting right, left, "be healed, be healed," down and down, neater and sharper, wit-quick at last, blazing from the zenith like a comet, tearing the light.

Near the bottom he had to slow. The trails crossed and merged with intermediate and then beginners' hills that all ended together at the lift. When he was younger, much younger, he used to like to howl past the novices, announcing himself "On your left!" and "On your right!" closer than he needed, faster than he needed, for the fun of the flurry. Later, teaching Helen and the children, he saw how thoughtless, how childish it was as they wobbled and fell in the wake of one of those "experts," and when Mark began to do it, he spoke sharply to his son and was careful, more careful than need be, because of the example he set.

He saw her half the hill down, a small figure, stopped far over to the right where the hill seemed safest. Novices always cling to the edges. In spite of the bundling ski clothes, he knew somehow that she was a girl. He came closer, slowing. She was stuck there. She had the look of tightness about her posture that he recognized as the panic of a skier whose nerve has failed, who sees no way safe to go, no way but the awful fall. He skied closer and came up beside her gently. "Hello," he said.

She turned to him. It was Karen. It could even be his Karen. "Oh," she whimpered, "please . . . help . . ." Her face was tight and pale with the cold and the panic. "Can you help me?"

Gently, he taught her. "Don't look at the hill, honey, only to the next place you want to go. Can you turn? See that little bump there? Can you turn and ski to that? Good. I'll go there and be waiting." He did. She came toward him trembling but in control. Then they planned their next move and their next. Her confidence began to come back a little. She took the next turn, traversing wide, the way all novices do, so that she built up too much speed, and frightened herself again. He guided her. She began to move more easily until they were skiing slowly but companionably together down the gentle slope. Dread began to build in him. They would be at the bottom soon and he would no longer have her. "Sweetheart . . ."

She turned to him, a lovely child, but with a stranger's face out of the shadows of the little fur hood she wore. "Thank you," she said. "Thank you very much." And down and away she went, leaving two shining trails like tear tracks that gleamed behind her till other skiers crossed them with their own. Whatever Helen had done to him or not done, whatever long net she had set to catch him and bring him down, the children were not to blame. They had not known. They could not have known. The black wound tore open. He tried to hold it shut with his hands. He skied to a grove of trees while the agony leaked out between his fingers. "Not here!" he begged, and bit it back with his teeth, but it was too late. It tore from him in great sobs, which he tried to muffle with his gloves, leaning against a tree.

14

Cady had news: Helen's seat belt had been taken off in the moments before the car had gone over, and the hook had gotten stuck somehow in the door handle. Mark had not been wearing his seat belt and neither had Karen, who had quite literally flown out of the car on its second roll. There had been no gross mechanical problems with the car. The brakes were good; as far as they could tell from the wreck, the steering and other mechanisms were working when the car went over. Esther had talked to Ernestine at church. Ernestine said she had no idea where Helen was going that day. There were no special school programs or meetings in which she might have been interested, no sales to which she might have been rushing at eighty miles an hour. That the speed had been hers was now certain. Even after the accident, the accelerator had been free; one of the officers had tried it. The brakes were in good order. The speed had been by choice—Helen's foot on the gas.

After his breakdown on the slopes, Eric tried not to contain his anguish for the children so tightly, but to let it come slowly, bit by bit. He went to stand at the door of Mark's now airless room, at Karen's, at Anne's. Those ghost-haunted places were now the only neat rooms in the house. Something was making him want to destroy Helen's memory by attacking the things she held dear; "her" parlor was now his workroom, "her" kitchen now collected his greasy pots and unwashed dishes. Crumbs crunched underfoot and the room, uncared for, soured with his anger like the damp towels wadded behind the door.

In the journals the little girl was growing. Her work for Mrs. Woodcock was teaching her more than school had. The language she used became consciously "nicer," more "polite." How hard she was trying to be accepted at school with all those new words and nice manners, how self-effacing in her threadbare dresses. Eric found himself remembering the quiet, sad girls of high school years ago in Silver Spring, the girls from the farms beyond the town. He had walked past them for years and not really seen them. Now they were suddenly real for him because of Helen. How vulnerable they were, standing in the halls, clutching their books to their chests, their hands red and workworn, secret-keepers as she had been, quiet, "nice." They were never at the dances or the parties, and people breathed easier without them. Helen had been one of those girls—the mended, pilling sweater getting tighter over her new breasts—Helen had been one of those girls all her life until . . .

The Book of Omaha. Here the words became more objective still: the job at a store, then looking for work typing and filing, the cheapest room in the cheapest rooming house, and the night classes and the three meals a day out of paper bags and once a week a dinner out. Saving for the clothes, the shoes and purse that matched: respectability. Oh, that hunger—never spoken, never breathed—sang, cried out of her pages. She hadn't yet met Charles Gerson, but Eric began to wonder if that need by which she went hungry in order to come to the job in matching clothes, to walk to work on all but the worst days so that she could have a beauty-shop permanent, was the need that married her to Charles Gerson and, after him, to Eric. If so . . .

If so, no blame, no blame but a testimony to her single-mindedness. At other times, he thought of other things: how really hungry she must have been, how cold, in the Omaha winters. These years later, in the equivocating days of early March, he watched the secretaries at the county offices eating their sack lunches in the windless, sun-warmed areas he had designed for them. They looked so spruce, they dressed so pleasingly, they smiled and talked to one another so cheerfully, that he felt tears come to his eyes. Did anyone care what awful economies some of them practiced in secret to look so comfortable and happy on the lunchtime benches? He had read how Helen's stocking had once been torn beyond mending and what a calamity it had been. She could eat only one meal that day and went to bed trembling with the chill of her hunger. Yet with that resoluteness with which she denied herself the food she wanted in order to buy the new stockings, might she not also . . .

That weekend he helped Cady paint the house. They did the upstairs and they waxed the walls in the paneled upstairs front room. There were memories there that tore at him and Cady saw it and sent him downstairs to move furniture there. Esther kept him company. "I bless the day you came to Aureole to work with Cady," she said. "Here you are again and he never would have gotten the energy to fix up the place if not for you."

"You've had people up there since we left," he said. "You may just need someone else."

She smiled. "You were the best, you and Helen."

"Esther, tell me about Helen."

Esther looked up at Eric quickly and then away. "I wasn't comfortable with Helen."

"I know that, but why?"

"She seemed cold to me; it was difficult to talk to her. I thought she thought I was malingering in some way, as though my infirmity was a sin. When you both lived here it was difficult because she did so much to help. Her acts were kind, but . . ."

190

"But?"

"Why is this coming up now? She's dead. You should be grieving, not gnawing at this thing Cady's told me about. It's wrong."

"I want to know what you saw, what you felt."

"Helen had secrets. I got the feeling she was hiding something."

"She was."

Eric told Esther who Helen was. At first it was almost impossible to use the words. For so many years they had both guarded the day, the road, the every entrance to the telling. It had become so habitual a part of him to do this automatically that he censored himself in almost complete unawareness. Now that the words had to be said, he stuttered and backtracked, went red, felt his heart beating. When he finished, they both sat silent for a long time. Then Esther said, "It's a terrible tragedy. I've known about it for eight years or so, the way things come out in a place like this. And it doesn't change anything. Helen had secrets before that one, and I think she had secrets since, but I don't think she killed her children. I think you need to find her guilty because you prefer anger to sorrow. I didn't much like her, as I said before, but look how little she forced the children, for all the rigidity in her nature."

"She didn't need to force them if she didn't think they would outlive their childhoods. The pressure was off, then, she was as free to be as loving as she wanted."

"Impossible."

Eric looked at her. Pain had made her very old. She had suffered for years, fighting back ever less successfully. In her lap, her ruined hands lay knotted and twisted. Could such a person understand someone who could sail off the edge, leaving a spotless house behind her? "What do you know about the last few days of her—their lives?" he asked again.

Esther shrugged. "Things get around, talk. A tragedy like that in a town this size is gone over pretty carefully. Mark's music teacher, Mrs. Browning, teaches the granddaughter of one of my friends. Mark's piano lesson was that Wednesday; you've probably wondered why they were on Highway Eighty-one past Bluebank instead of at the lesson—"

"I forgot about Mark's lesson, that he was supposed to be there—"

"Apparently Helen called at the last minute and canceled, a thing she'd never done before. I think you should talk to Mrs. Browning about it. I think a person who is planning to end her life, especially Helen, who planned everything, would have planned better than that."

"Esther—"

"Yes?"

"How do you stand the pain, pain like yours?"

"Yours will fade. I keep hoping mine will, too. Sometimes it does. There are days of grace, whole days when I can't even remember what the pain is like."

"I see them—not Helen, but the kids. I saw Karen on the ski slopes and all three kids at the supermarket. I see them everywhere."

"And Helen?"

"No, not Helen."

"Dear man, I wish you could grieve for her!"

He went home pondering it. Helen had always been punctilious, even fussy, about the children's wearing seat belts. She had always worn one herself. Always. The fact stared at him with hollow eyes. If the belt had been found looped around the door, it meant she had taken it off during the trip—had had it on, by habit, and had taken it off consciously. And Mark's also. Had she ordered Karen to unbuckle hers? He almost gagged with hate.

He didn't want to read about the girl in Omaha that night, but habit was strong and the book was in his hand as he lay in bed. And he didn't hate *that* girl. She was resolute, tough-minded, courageous, qualities he once thought most admirable in her. He decided to think of *that* girl not as his wife, but as The Omaha Girl, another woman. She was a woman who made friends very slowly. They must have been put off by that resoluteness of hers, that propriety, and the stilted language she had learned from Mrs. Woodcock. She didn't fit in easily with the other secretaries in the office. She had few dates, and those she had were stiff and uncomfortable. Once she wrote simply, "I got quieter and quieter. I got smaller and smaller."

Then there was a job at the county assessor's office, a temporary job that she liked. She was taking courses at night in shorthand and business machines. One of the teachers was interested in her but he was married. She had fantasies about him that were impossible for her to write about, only, "I think about Mr. Lawson. I think about him a lot, but then I remember what wishing did to Mama. He is married. Let him make his wife miserable." The county job ended. She had made some friends there. She went to work at Prairie Home Insurance.

She was happy. Against his will, Eric found himself glad for it. She almost sang with relief, quietly, quietly. "I have been mistaken. I thought I should work in small offices, out of the way, but the smallness, the quietness, draws people's attention. In a big office I seem free. I go and come invisibly and I'm happy." Oh, look, she opens up a little: lunch with "the girls," shopping with Jill, Suzy, and Anne. It seemed sisterly, like the parties they had had back in Cory when the men were away. Had that occurred to her? Promoted to Mr. Carlsson's office. The typing-pool girls thought she would high-hat them after that, but she didn't and they were grateful and began to do Carlsson's casework first and to do Helen favors, which made Carlsson look good and he was advanced and so was she, and Eric grinned at The Omaha Girl, watching it all through her wide eyes.

"Oh, hello, Eric, I'm real glad you called." Ernestine's voice boomed over the phone. He heard the bracelets tinkle. "Listen, can you hold on for a sec, something's burning." She was back a moment later. "God, you wouldn't think anyone could burn *soup*, would you?" And she laughed that big, rumbling laugh of hers.

"I'd—I'd like to see you," he said, feeling helpless and inept. "I want to talk about Helen."

"I've got the weekend free," she said, "my place or yours?" She laughed again. "If you'd feel better, we can meet for lunch somewhere."

"I guess that would be more comfortable."

"Look at this mess!" she said, surveying the diet salad. "Ten-day shape-up, thirty-day beauty plan, fourteen-day diet. I've tried 'em all, and you know what? They don't change a thing. You got spared all that. Helen was beautiful and she didn't have to work at it. She didn't diet; she ate what she liked and her figure was better after six kids than mine was when I was nineteen."

"Did you envy that?"

"Let's say what the author of *A Better You* says: It was a 'challenge.' "

"You knew about the other family—that there had been three other children?"

"I knew about them and about Charlie—just a little. I knew it was a very formal marriage. Conventional. That he was very conventional. That's really all."

"Ernestine, I was her husband. I knew Helen as my wife. What was she like as a friend?"

"She was loyal, she was a very good friend, and she was what the kids in school used to call a crack-up."

"A crack-up?"

"A sketch, a card. She used to keep me in stitches."

"Helen?"

"The very same. God, I miss that broad!" She shook her head. "Y'know, she never said a word out of turn, no foul language, no 'jokes.' What she had wasn't wit—I've got that. It wasn't humor either. It was . . . she saw what was incongruous in things, where the paradoxes were and with a word or two—well, you just had to laugh, and she'd sit there with that straight-face look of hers like a kid with a polecat in a cakebox, and oh, Christ, I used to *look* at her and just crack up laughing. People didn't get her. The beauty fooled them." Ernestine shook her head. "What a disguise!"

"Did she laugh at us—at me?"

"Helen had a house. With rooms. Each room was kept separate. Each room had its own furniture, its own separate door. You were in one room, the kids were in one room, the past was in one room, I was in one room. She never commented on the *rooms*; she commented on the *house*—do you understand?"

"You say she was a crack-up—why didn't I see it? I'm not stupid or humorless—why did she never show it to me?"

"Oh, Eric, you were *a husband*. Husband was a role, not a person, and husband went into a very formal, careful room."

"Why? What for?"

"Think about Charmaine Wingate, beauty queen and ranch-wife, playing roles to her kids. Remember what Frances and Mary Anne did all through their girlhoods, faking, and the elegant Mrs. Woodcock, trying so hard out there in Cory. *You* weren't dumb; *she* was scared, scared and clever. I was a friend, my role was the one that allowed her her sense of fun. When Helen was with me, she was on vacation."

"Ernestine, did Helen kill herself and the kids?"

"No way."

"But you're not shocked at the question."

"Nope. I thought about it myself for about fifteen minutes when I heard. Same time of year as the—well, the other accident. Three kids, like the first time and both the oldest ones twelve. When I found out about the first accident, which I did *not* hear from her, I had to wonder what she was doing in Aureole in the first place, why she came and set up *here*."

"You knew about me, then—"

"I dated a state policeman then who remembered you."

"Did Helen make this thing happen?"

"She was a planner. If anyone was capable of that kind of long, slow windup, she was."

"Then why not?"

"Because the long, slow windup might have been her style, but I don't think revenge was."

"Not revenge, Ernestine, justice, fairness. The same justice and need for fairness that made her frightened of lucky breaks and something for nothing, that made her deny that Mark was special, brighter than other kids—"

"Oh, God, don't you know by now that Helen's wars were all defensive? You learn that early when your older sisters are homely as axe handles and you look like your mother did the day she was voted Miss Gorgeous!"

"I didn't know her sisters were homely, but what does that matter?"

"Oh, Jesus, I don't believe you said that!"

"Helen never told me her sisters were ugly. I never met them."

"*She* might not even have realized it consciously, but there were pictures . . . They must be somewhere. One of them is of the four of them that must have been taken for fun when the men were away."

"Ernestine, did Helen—was she able to love?"

"First tell me what that is."

"Well, you know, did she have the capacity to love anyone?"

"Oh, God . . . love, love, love. Do you love me, do I love you, what the world needs now—is it fellow feeling? I think she had a lot of that. Is it something you *feel* or something you *do* or is it a kind of emotional button you push or is it forgiving other people's faults or is it a soppy wash of emotion that makes the person feeling it think how wonderful *he* is? Helen gave you the best she had. If you wanted gaiety, well, she didn't have that to give. 'Rapture'? I think that died on the farm. The woman was faithful to you and those kids. She

196

kept a house that anyone would envy. She made a life with you. How can you forget that?"

"I'm not forgetting," he murmured. "I'm not forgetting."

He couldn't tell Ernestine or even Cady the most damning things: when she had seen him in the hospital almost unscathed, when she had looked at him in court, when she had met him on the ski slopes that day, she must have seen how little there was to him. Had she held a gun in her hand that day, skiing, she would have been given no justice. She had first to help build a boy into a man, to bring him to a man's depth and knowledge, before *he* could begin to be capable of such a loss. There would be no way to get that justice but by being part of it.

And she could be part of it in all ways but one. She could be faithful and giving in all ways but one and that one was by the complete release of her body in orgasm. That she could not give.

The seventh book—oh, here comes Charles. For a moment in the now messy bedroom, on a bed whose sheets were beginning to bother him with their odor, clothes left around with an almost adolescent aggressiveness, he felt a pang of shame. He had spied on her loneliness, visited the wastelands of her weekend life, over her shoulder he had counted the pennies of her meals. Now—what would come, pawings in the movies? Lunchtime in a motel? For a long moment he lay with the book open before him, not reading but staring at her pages of neat, school script. That, too, condemned her. Missed meals, torn stockings, finding a friend, rare praise from a boss, the solidarity of the secretarial pool, all of it written in the same, small, precise hand. Now, Charles, no doubt. Not even exclamation marks. So much control, so much patience, such power over the smallest muscles in her hand that they would not betray her. He read on.

Charles's interest was a surprise to her. He was only twenty-three but he acted much older, as though he was a set and settled bachelor. She worked in his company, though not in his department. She had seen him but he had not seemed to notice her. He had come into the office to settle a claim when his car had been run into. He was staid, attentive. They went out for dinner, a movie. He took her home and shook hands and left her at the rooming house with plans for another evening out. They went to a concert, they went to a club. Eric saw there for the first time, unwritten, that deadpan knowingness that Ernestine had described to him. It must have been there all along—how could he have missed it? Charles was checking her out: Did she spend money extravagantly? Did she drink too much? He was late once, and measured her reaction to it. He afforded her a chance to gossip about a small office matter, which she decorously refused to do. Each outing was carefully planned to show some facet, present some challenge. She didn't express anger that he was testing her, revealing only that unblinking gaze. My God, he thought, Ernestine was right. It was that open-eyed look she sometimes had, and he had missed it because it was soundless laughter, wordless wit, a measuring stare at the wild incongruities of the world. Years—and he had never known! And he had wondered why careful, controlled Helen could have been so incongruously befriended by big, loud Ernestine. Because she had seen . . . because she had seen . . .

Helen met Charles's large family at a picnic. They were sober, hardworking people, conventional, self-involved, and, Eric got the feeling, totally humorless. The measuring went on. They put her next to Grandma, who was cantankerous, and then stood back, not knowing that to a veteran of such wars as had been waged in Cory, and to a campaigner in the schools of Cory, this was a piece of cake. "The family test is over and Charles considers us engaged," she wrote at the end of four lines about the picnic. Eric shook his head in wonder. What came next he knew—the chastity test. And so it did. Charles made a pass, urged his need, urged his love. She saw it coming and deftly moved away. Eric sat up in bed and laughed and heard his laughter ring in the filthy room.

There was a letter pasted to the next page. "Dear Helen, It is my sad duty to take pen in hand and write to you"—oh, Mrs. Woodcock, Mary Anne worked for you, too!—"that our loving father passed away by being caught between a horse and a wall and all his ribs broke. At the funeral, Buck and Curtis got into it. So, Buck has the ranch and Curtis is gone off and Ma is staying with Buck and his new wife which is Clodie Simmons who you know. Frances is married. I married Floyd Euler and we live in Cut Bank. Your sister, Mary Anne Wingate Euler." Later there was an entry that Helen had written to Mary Anne and also to the ranch about her engagement and then about her marriage. If there was a response from them, it was not noted.

The Gersons ended up having to give the wedding, which they did with no particular grace. Helen came down the aisle by herself in something called a "faille suit," which she had bought over the family's objections. They moved into the family home.

Mrs. Browning opened the door and Eric introduced himself. He had called and told her he had music of Mark's that might be hers and for which, in any case, he had no need. She seemed glad of the opportunity to see him.

"I was at the funeral, but there were so many people there, and one gets shy. Because I had only met you the two times, it was difficult. Such a lovely, talented boy!" He gave her the music. She looked it over. "Getting most boys to play Bach is impossible," she said. "I let them learn on pop things, or jazz, and hope they will come later to other literature for the piano. Mark had an affinity for Bach. It was because of the engineering, you know, moving parts that fit together. His metaphors—our metaphors—described you and your work. He spoke of skiing, too. I'd never thought about the rhythm of skiing."

"Scarlatti is good skier's rhythm," he told her. "Scarlatti and Bach." She was suddenly embarrassed. He looked at her. She was a very short, heavy woman, with what could be described as a "good" face, plain and intelligent. "He liked you," he said. "He chose you himself and he liked you very much." She smiled. It was time to ask. He took a breath. "I've been tracing the events of that day. We don't know why—why my wife was where she was."

"I thought you knew," she said. "I didn't see them that day. Mark had only missed a lesson once or twice before, due to illness, and his mother had always called in plenty of time. That day, she called, but not until noon."

"What did she say?"

Mrs. Browning saw that she was in a situation where her answers would be sifted for meanings that she could not foresee. It made her cautious. "She simply called and said that Mark would not be coming to his lesson."

"Did you ask why?"

"I might have—I think I asked if he was ill—not to pry; out of concern."

"And what was her answer?"

"I think she said no, that something had come up and she was unable to bring him this time."

"Did she say 'this time'? As though she would bring him next week? Did she say, 'We'll see you next week'?"

"I don't remember—I was with another student and we didn't talk long. Mr. Gordon, what is this about?"

"It's about why Mark wasn't at his music lesson at three that day. He was lying in a gully at three, miles from Aureole, and nobody knows why."

She looked stricken. "Had he been to school?" she asked.

"I don't know. I haven't checked there yet."

She looked as though she were going to say something, then decided against it and stood facing him. "One reason I like teaching youngsters is that we are the same size," she said. "Short people spend their lives looking up into the nostrils of tall people, like perpetual children. Sometimes, when we are both standing, it's difficult to see the expressions on tall people's faces. I feel even shorter than usual right now."

"You've helped me—maybe the people at the school can help me, too."

"I'm sorry you needed my help. I'll miss that boy very much."

Book Eight. They settle down, Charles and Helen. She worked for a while. The days were recitals of details: she was learning Charles's life, his likes and dislikes, his parents, the home, their ways of cleaning and cooking. She sundered all the parts of her past that didn't fit and unmade any habit that would cause talk or friction with Charles's family. Colorado, he thought, boom and bust, clear away the past and don't count your losses. Three months, then pregnancy. Her first. She was terrified of her body changes but told no one for fear of being thought unnatural. The pregnancy was difficult—the details all too familiar. He skipped over the months as quickly as he could. Her labor was long and full of fear. Lois was born under some kind of spinal block, which gave Helen more terror than the pain would have. She didn't utter a sound. Charles said she was brave. She only knew she didn't want to be the mother Charmaine Wingate had been. She let the Gersons guide her movements as a new mother and she followed their guidance to the letter.

15

He had to conquer the children's rooms, to see the dust on their tables, to smell the airless, musty smell of unuse. He hadn't entered the rooms before, only stood at the doors. Now, because he needed the information, he had to search for their schoolbooks and the pieces of posterboard Karen had been given and a special pencil and eraser. Their rooms were as dead as the moon. In Mark's, two long lines of cobwebbing blew lightly in front of the window, as though the spider who had begun it had become forgetful, taken by the stillness of the place into the same daze of sorrow and loss Eric felt. Mark's room reflected him; it was, for all of Helen's influence, a little messy. There were piles of books and papers. The music Eric had returned to Mrs. Browning had been in the car with him. It had been a part of the material wrapped in plastic that the police had given Eric. There were only a few schoolbooks and a plastic-covered school folder to return. Eric sighed and began to look through the pile where he soon found them. How lifeless they seemed, how unfamiliar. All of it was lifeless now, useless, and beginning to smell sad and musty. He kept thinking he should get someone to help him box up the clothes and the books, the projects, bedding, and the old toys, and take it all to the Goodwill. Esther had mentioned getting him help; he just couldn't summon up the will to get started.

Karen's room was like Karen herself. At first, it seemed formal, almost impersonal, as Helen's rooms had been, but then Eric saw that it was simply private. As he looked, he saw her need for small, intimate things. Her tiny tea set was displayed on the dresser. The little glass animals stood on the sill, tiny dolls in a little box. There were many boxes, crannies, corners into which she had fitted her things. He soon found the pile of books and hurried out before the tea set made him weep. Anne's room: he went in knowing there were no school supplies to be found there, that what would be reflected would give him another feeling than the rooms of his happier, warmer children.

He realized then that he had almost never been in Anne's room. She didn't like people coming there. After tucking Karen in at night he had always stood at Anne's door and spoken across the space to her, in the near dark. The room was bare, almost cell-like. The walls had no pattern and there was none on the curtains; any toys there were, were out of sight. He walked over to the bed and the stark, bare little night table beside it and opened its drawer. He remembered then, the conversations half listened to between Helen and the girls about decorating their rooms, swatches, wallpapers—he had forgotten them, the buzz of words he didn't understand and in which he had had no interest. Helen had not done this to her youngest child, forced or even approved of this barrenness, this impersonal bare-walled room—Anne had insisted. There was nothing to see, almost nothing by which to remember his younger daughter. In the drawer were a small stuffed doll and a box of crayons and a bottle, a medicine bottle with a little plastic spoon held on it with a rubber band. He picked it up. It was half full. He read the prescription absentmindedly: Anne Gordon one teaspoonful three times daily. He couldn't remember any illness for which she was being treated—and it wasn't an old prescription. Had she had a cold? He couldn't remember. He looked at the name of the drug: phenobarbital.

Wasn't that some kind of narcotic? "What the hell?" he murmured quietly in the quiet place. He looked around again. The room's strangeness held him in something like fear. He took the bottle with the books and papers he was holding and left the room, closing the door. His heart had begun to beat harder.

This time he was tempted to skip ahead in the diary, to leave Charles and his not very interesting family, babies, breast problems, and meal planning. His daughter's medicine stood on his dresser, glowing red, like cough medicine. But it wasn't cough medicine. If he looked ahead, went past that other family, perhaps he could learn, know what was beginning to look back at him over the walls of his rage and grief. He glanced at the box of Helen's books; he was no more than halfway through them. In them were her reasons, her plans. He was learning her. He would keep on. He sighed and opened a new book. Charles's mother's birthday. "Whoopie," he said.

He had been six years old in 1950. Truman was president. She had written about the times—not much, but the entries, sentences here and there that dealt with the events around them, gave him a feeling for what the country had gone through while he was busy growing up in Silver Spring. Omaha had begun to grow. Japanese from the relocation camps in Colorado and Wyoming settled there. Negroes from the army who had passed through during the war came back later and settled; men from Nebraska farms back from the war married and moved to the city that blossomed into new tract suburbs, raw and bare and full of an excitement that seemed to be about freedom and independence from old family styles and an end to shortages and war. Booming. Eisenhower was president. Korea. Omaha read about McCarthy, and Eric remembered what his parents had called the Communist Witch Hunt. Far away from Washington, much farther than it seemed now, Eric thought, the noise came to the heart of the country muted, changed. If there were communists in the government, Charles said, it would be a good thing to find out. There was no anger in it, and no fear. None of the faces in the paper were faces of friends. Hollywood and Washington were worlds barely real.

Helen had another baby, Richard. She yearned to move to a place of their own but said nothing. After Richard was born she had not wanted to make love, but said nothing, and was glad later when distaste was replaced by indifference. She did volunteer work at the Gersons' church and the bookkeeping for Charles's family. Eric felt her drowning in the family duties and expectations.

She must have felt it, too, because she began to have nightmares and to feel far more tired than the days' activities warranted. This went on for almost a year, and then she did a typical thing. She stopped. With no explanation, even to the diary, she went into the attic and stayed there for one day and when she came down it was with a carefully reasoned declaration of her needs. The family was dumbstruck, awed. There was no emotion, no begging, no weeping. Not even confrontation. The church got one morning a week, she would continue keeping the family accounts, but she would like one day for herself, Tuesday, perhaps. She would do nothing that would cause talk, or bring attention to them in any way. All of her other household duties would remain the same.

Eric grinned. The surprise had defeated them as she must have known it would. Omaha's innocent tyrants were no match for a secret-keeper like Helen—they could eat their hearts out; they would never know what she thought or how she felt or even where she would go on those Tuesdays. Because they needed their peace, nothing would happen. That need was greater than their need to dominate her, and she had known that, too.

He looked around. Need had cornered him as well. He had run out of clean clothing; his socks stank under the bed, his sheets stank on it. He got up, angry at the imposition of it, stripped his bed furiously, hunted out the worst of the clothes under it, and put them all in the washer. By 2:00 A.M. he had clean sheets, streaked with the red and blue of his socks. The aggressive ugliness of his bedroom, the litter, filth, and jumbled clothes, had been a fist before her nose, because he saw how deep and secret her plans went, and how rational she was, even in Charles's deadening house, how silent even in the sexual distaste she had for him. Furiously, he read on.

The family adjusted to the open days. Charles's sister took the children on Tuesday and later began to leave hers with Helen one day so that she, too, could get out. Everyone congratulated himself; Eric could read between the lines the family's self-satisfaction, interpreting her cleverness as its "modernity." Why did he hate them so?

"Mr. Larson, I found this bottle when I was cleaning out the medicine cabinet and I wondered about it—phenobarbital—that's a narcotic, isn't it?"

"Oh, no, it's a barbiturate but in this mixture and dosage it's nothing to worry about. It's a recent prescription—let me just look at the records."

"What was it prescribed for?"

"Yes, here it is, it was one of Dr. Tremlett's prescriptions. You can ask him."

"No need to bother him—I thought it might be a one-time thing."

"Oh, no, it's been filled before. See this number? It shows this is the second time."

"Dr. Tremlett, I'm trying to get the hang of my wife's bookkeeping and I need to get some things straight."

"Of course. We were all sorry to hear—it was a terrible shock—"

"Yes, thank you. I was wondering if all your bills have been paid."

"I think so, let me get the record. Here it is, yes, your wife usually paid by the visit."

"And how many were there during the last year?"

"Well, two in January—Karen's strep throat, Mark's fall in May, Anne had chicken pox in June, and then the emergency call and the two visits for Anne, December sixth and sixteenth."

Eric combed his memory. Nothing. "A cold?"

"No, the seizures then, the first on the sixth, the emergency visit, and then the call on the eighth, and I prescribed, and then of course the one on the sixteenth."

"Oh, yes," Eric said, "yes, of course." Seizures? He was having trouble controlling his breathing.

"I suppose nothing had come back from the neurological exam at the hospital by that time, had it?"

"No, uh, you prescribed the phenobarbital for that, then."

"Yes, I put her on a fairly heavy dose to keep the seizure activity at a minimum while she was waiting to be seen—"

"And there were no other calls after that?"

"No, I'd been waiting for the hospital report, and then of course—"

"Yes."

"Well, is that all you needed to know?"

"Yes, thank you."

He talked to a friend of Cady's, who had been a nurse. "Sarah, what causes seizures in children?"

"Could be lots of things. That wasn't my specialty when I was in nursing, but it's not uncommon, a seizure at the onset of one of the childhood diseases or when there's a high fever beginning."

"Just one?"

"Yes, just one and then the fever."

"What if there is no fever and then there's another seizure, say a few days later, and then a third?"

"Well, you'd look for other causes then."

"What other causes?"

"You'd have to work up a profile to know—EEG, a skull series, blood studies, a neurological examination."

"And you'd have the child on, say, phenobarbital while that was going on?"

"What's this all about?"

"A friend of mine has a child—they're going through it and I didn't want to ask him any details, to pry—"

"Oh, I see. Well, the neurologist would be checking for brain tumors, brain damage, lesions, venous insufficiency, metabolic or hormonal disorders, but most commonly it's plain idiopathic epilepsy."

"Idiopathic?"

"Cause unknown."

"And how long does it take to find out which of those things it is?"

"Well, with the mess the hospital's in now, a month or so."

"I see. So they'd have to sit out that time before the child could be seen?"

"Well, seen and tested and the results gotten."

He sat in his office that afternoon incredulous and alternately furious and sad. He had never seen any kind of spell in Anne. Why had Helen borne that all alone, the worry, the planning? Why had she taken away his right to know and share his daughter's problem? Would she consider her justice imperfect if one of the children was flawed? No, that couldn't be true. Why, then, why? There was no pressing need now, no hurry. He would go to the only source he knew—the journals.

That fall, after her announcement, she took a class in flower arranging at the YWCA. The teacher's name was Naohito Sakai, a relocated Japanese, Nisei. She had it written carefully: Nisei—second generation. It was part of her Tuesday out, a study not aggressively practical, for the first time in her life. As the Tuesdays went by, the notebook began to speak of the class more and more. Words like zen, ikebana, haiku, cha-no-yu, began to appear, first almost obsessively defined and then used with greater ease. "Dr. Sakai said that

ikebana, the art of flower arranging, like cha-no-yu (tea ceremony) and noh drama, is the perfection of a balance between
law and example." "Dr. Sakai said we must stop pruning or
trimming each part of the arrangement at the moment when
each plant element is most like *itself* . . ."

The words and definitions grew. She began to make careful
discriminations, to grow in the study, to ask questions and
make connections between one phase of the study and the
others. Eric read on in wonder, knowing that she had never
once referred to the art, to any bit of this subject in all their
years together. Was she so frightened of difference, so terrified
of being singled out for anything, that she trimmed her needs
and thoughts the way she trimmed her flower stalks until only
an irreducible, essential self was left?

She began to read the haiku collections Sakai recom-
mended, first the poems of a man called Kikaku, who wrote a
lot about flower arranging, then the great masters. She had a
natural affinity for the Japanese style, emotions understated,
a dislike of excess, a hunger for the four principles she had
written: harmony, respect, purity, tranquillity. She fell in love
with Dr. Sakai.

A love like a tornado. Amazed, he read on. She began to
hate the dead, stifling center of her daily round: Charles,
Charles's family, her children, Mother Gerson's well-meant
meddling. Surrounding, isolating that center with as much
terror as passion was her feeling for Sakai, a feeling deeper
and more violent than she had ever experienced in her life. "If
only I had . . ." "His gentle face haunts . . ." "I see him
everywhere . . ." "I'm unable to sleep, to think of anything
else. I yearn for the nights; the mornings smell of disappointment like the smell of a burned city." "A pain I can barely
endure—a pain I could not bear to live without. It's more
than a hunger in the flesh; it's a yearning in my spirit, my
history, and my dreams." How she must have hated such
excess in herself! The class ended and a new one began. Bonsai—miniature trees. She stayed on and he began to acknowl-

edge her answers with respect. He invited her and two other students to the Japanese art exhibit touring the local museum. They walked together in complete silence for two hours, looking at the various bronzes, hangings, and calligraphy. "I have not interpreted for you," he said to them, "because I wanted you to see with your own eyes, not mine. If you wish, I will now speak of what we have seen." The other students were tired and left. When they did, he turned and said, "I am in a difficult position. I am very much a stranger here." She answered, "I am as much a stranger as you and my position is as difficult." He said, "Then a relationship is impossible." She said, "It is too late for that to be true." Nothing more was spoken—they spent the rest of the time walking the exhibit again, he explaining, interpreting, translating. The fourth of June entry was a haiku: "Issa, my favorite poet next to Basho, says: Simply trust/Do not the petals flutter down/Just like that?"

Eric cursed himself. Why was he so surprised at the cool and proper Helen, the cool and proper teacher? He had loved wildly as a boy and he remembered the ache of his having loved her. He felt for her suffering then.

They began to meet every week in the hour before the class and she stayed to help him collect the bonsai materials when the class was finished. They didn't touch during these times; they didn't dare, fearing someone would come in on them. She began to look drawn and she lost weight. For weeks the family didn't notice, but at a picnic on July 4, there were pictures taken and when they were developed it was seen by everyone. Helen wrote: "I felt caught, trapped as I had been at home. I said it was probably a touch of anemia. There are no classes until the fall." She did not tell this to the family.

"Mrs. Eric Gordon was my wife, Anne Gordon was my daughter. I want to find out when their appointments were and what the results of the tests turned up."

"You want records, then, but bring some identification

when you come in because we don't give out any information without it."

The woman at the records office was small and dark, and her back was to him, so for a moment he thought she was Helen and he opened his mouth to cry out and only then did he remember. Then she turned and he saw it wasn't Helen at all but someone entirely different, so different that he wondered how he could have seen Helen in her. "Can I help you?"

He explained. He gave the names and the doctor and the problem. She went back to the files. He waited the minutes away, nervous and impatient.

He had taken his lunch hour to come there, but in fact he had been giving very little attention to his work. In the beginning he had wanted work to save him; he had thrown himself into it like a suicide off a bridge: plans for a small airport, plans for the feeder-roads, the new jail, the new hospital. He had thought these things would keep him from the pain, but he seemed unable to concentrate. He stared at plans, grids, maps. He retrieved all kinds of information, made all kinds of studies, and when it came time to summarize them and make a plan, he was unable to do it. Yazzi had worked up the jail requirements and when he brought them in to discuss with Eric, Eric had confused them with a study someone else had done previously, and they had talked at cross purposes for half an hour before discovering the mistake. He had apologized, Yazzi had nodded in acceptance, but the mistakes were beginning to frighten him. How long could his mind be filmed over like the windows in an abandoned house? This morning he was looking yet again at Yazzi's impenetrable figures and he found himself wondering about what Sakai looked like.

Because leaving for work he had realized that the destroyed serenity and simplicity of his house, the clean-surfaced order, the careful placement of things so as to give—what had she written—harmony, respect, purity, tranquillity, these had been the aesthetics of her study. Sakai. Sakai in all of it, down the years, through all the changes, all the different rooms. In Omaha those years ago, Helen had journeyed spiritually to Kyoto and had come back changed. Even before his marriage, when he had gone to her room that first night, he had noticed how spare, how bare it was. He had thought it impersonal; he had looked in vain for the photograph, the memento. How could he have known that the whole room was a memory? Sakai, never mentioned, *lived*, every day for almost twenty years. And in their rooms at Cady's—why hadn't he seen, noticed, compared? Downstairs, Esther kept her past all around her—all the children's presents, all the photos, all the souvenirs of trips and friends; upstairs, zen spareness, Sakai. What love affair had he ever had, what passion in all his life had so permeated his consciousness, so ordered his acts, so transformed him as Sakai's presence had permeated and transformed her? He had asked Ernestine if Helen could love. That is love.

The clerk came back, popping her gum. "There's no record of an Anne Gordon from neurology. There's no record in the admissions or in general medical." She stood looking at him as though in accusation.

He stared back. "There must be," he said.

She chewed on. "How recent was this?"

"Well, I'm not sure—the prescription was issued almost two months ago."

"Lemme try something," she said and picked up the phone. "Get me Cathy on four," she said into it. There followed a conversation as much social as business. He saw that she was asking for a favor. "Cathy, there's a man here—yeah, I know it. He's lookin for a record he thinks is yours. Uh-huh. Uh-huh. Gordon, Anne. Yeah, a kid, uh—five. Yeah, thanks." They waited. No record. They tried pediatrics. No record.

He left the hospital more mystified than ever. No record at all. No record of the child, the tests, nothing. Could Helen have gone to the doctor about a child's convulsive seizures, gotten a prescription, had the child have seizures still, and done nothing more? Secret-keeper! Damn her!

That evening he came home, dipped into the mailbox automatically and as automatically separated his mail and the house bills from the fliers, catalogues, solicitations, and mail addressed to Helen, and threw what wasn't his on the couch where there was now a substantial pile. Her mail. "Oh, God!" he said to the house. "How could I have missed this?" Her mail would tell him what he wanted to know.

He spent the evening sorting it. There were numerous magazines and catalogues and form letters. These he put into a pile and took them out to the backyard incinerator. There was an invitation to a party and a letter from a Harriet on vacation, a letter of thanks from the school principal for some volunteer work, and a letter answering her letter of inquiry about a product. The bank mail: her last batch of returned checks. He flipped through them. Mountain Market Grocery, cleaners, Mrs. Browning, the doctor—here it was, yes, here— Ute Valley Hospital and it was for $600. It was dated January 16. Where had she gotten the money? Charles. She had cashed one of the certificates—she must have, all in secret, all in silence. Money, hospitals, seizures, doctors, fear, lessons canceled, trips made. Why was it taking him so long to unravel it all? Why had he not been able to think more clearly, to plan and proceed and trace in an organized way what she had done? There were links to be forged, ideas to be followed through, not only with Helen and what she had done, but at work. He seemed unable to think straight about any of his life. He was fragmented, haunted, his mind circling on itself in a dreamlike, useless way. Sakai—Helen and Sakai.

All that summer when she did not tell Charles and his family there were no classes they met on Tuesdays in a room he had rented on a quiet street. Sakai was a physics teacher who had the summer off from school but worked on the side as a free-lance editor of scientific textbooks. They didn't make love every time—some of the days were hot and sometimes there was work he had to do and then they would sit together talking quietly or she would work on a flower arrangement while he went over his copy. Once or twice they went on gathering trips into the country. He taught her cha-no-yu, the tea ceremony, and in September he made a ceremony for her in the backyard of his house, the first and last time she visited him there. His contract at the school would be up the following spring and he was planning not to renew. The fact of an end, a finite time to their relationship, made her joy half despair.

When school began again they could not meet during the day. He started a course in zen philosophy, and before the class they were together, sometimes skipping dinner to make love or eating together quietly and then going to class, separating before they got to the building. The months measured themselves out inexorably and then they were gone. He gave her a small jade vase. They demonstrated a tea ceremony to his class and she wore an antique kimono he had sent for from his family. Her brief entries were moans of grief. "Charles is a good man; his body is not gross or deformed in any way. Why can't I want him?" The school year flowed away week by week and then it was gone and Sakai was gone. For weeks she moved through his streets, passing the school on her afternoon out, his house, the place he had rented, like a dog scenting essences in the air.

Then one day Charles came home with an announcement. He had decided that they should move out of his parents' house. He had described Helen's looks and weight loss to a doctor friend of his and the doctor had said that the problem might be that they had been married so long and still lived with the husband's family. He found a house a mile away and they moved. She dove gratefully into the work of it, convincing Charles that his decision had been correct.

"Cady, I can't go to Pickaxe during hospital business hours this week, but I have Helen's check and the bill from Ute

Valley. She went there instead of Memorial. I'll write a note giving them permission to talk to you. Jean can notarize it. I only want you to find out what you can."

"I'll be right over," Cady said. "I have some news for you, too."

Cady came in through Eric's front door and Eric saw his eyes widen. "Don't tell me you got a raccoon as a pet or something?"

"Is it that bad?"

"No, it'll be okay if you have maps printed."

"I'll—I'm going to start swamping out this weekend. For a while, I couldn't stand the order, the neatness—"

"No danger of that now. What's that smell?"

"I don't know. I guess I'll find out when I come across whatever it is that's making it. Cady . . ."

And Eric told Cady about Anne. The telling ordered things for him. He didn't tell the story as it had unraveled itself to him but as it must have happened: a seizure, probably febrile, the doctor said, no cause to worry. Then another seizure and another and the first prescription, then perhaps another and a recommendation for a neurological examination. Why had she not gone to Memorial, the closest hospital? Telling it to Cady, he saw it for himself. The woman who didn't want her son singled out for special notice would certainly want to save her daughter from the comments of a gossiping town. They were likely to see people they knew, run into school acquaintances or someone from the choir. In the middle of what must have been panic, Helen was thinking clearly, even coldly. Why couldn't he be the same as he followed her in sorrow and anger? She had not only kept secrets from the town but from him. Why? Why?

Helen had written in her diary, "The art of the Japanese, the art of tea and of life, is the acceptance of the Buddha-nature of each thing, the thing itself . . ." Why was he thinking of that now? He felt tired of the puzzle and at last disgusted with his sloth and the ugliness of his surroundings. "You said you had some news?"

"Yes. The ski-area people like our plan. They want the model in their new offices."

"It's not finished yet."

"It's almost finished. One or two more sessions and it will be. It's the best way of visualizing the area. Mark did a wonderful job and I got them to promise they would keep his names for the runs with minor changes."

"I hate to see it go."

"I know. How are we going to get it up? I've got some men and a truck when you're ready, but I don't want to take it sideways up the stairs."

"Mark and I figured that out. There's the coal bin that opens out into the backyard. Give me a week, will you, to play with it?"

"Okay. We'll come for it next Saturday morning so you can be home."

"When do you think you can go to Pickaxe?"

"Monday. I'll stop by at the office for your note."

16

Helen's despair did not lift; it diluted like tears in water. It was almost a year before she was able to look at the night coming on and not ache for Sakai. She was grateful to be in her own house, to cry the four walls, as she said. Lois was growing, and Helen found delight in the quick, appreciative girl. She became pregnant again. Eric read quickly because she wrote sketchily now, feeling her real life was over; this would be her last pregnancy, she would get older, old, and die. She was living by imitating herself and part of that imitation was the continuation of her day out once a week. Now she took only practical courses, sewing, household management, upholstery, gardening. Richard went through a series of childhood illnesses. Eric's heart caught. Nothing like Anne. Another pregnancy. Patricia was born. He read on. The minutiae of her days weighed on him. He wondered if they weighed on her. Kennedy was assassinated and Helen wrote about the incident that he remembered her telling all those years later, all those years ago.

Wheels of days. Charles's mother had a gallbladder attack and then surgery. Her sister-in-law miscarried. At each of her birthdays she summarized the year. She couldn't have known, because she never looked back over the books, how much her style had changed. There was growing in her not the Buddhistic quietism she yearned for, but the open-eyed mother wit that Ernestine had described. Love and loss had given her that wit, acceptance without question. Almost, but not quite. Her realities were not gentle, but they had too much of her love of Sakai to be cruel. Years turned. Children in school, summer vacations. He sighed.

Did they see those measuring looks, Charles and the children and the in-laws? Did she let them see the wide eyes, the almost imperceptible turn of the head, underlining one of her literal, serious-sounding comparisons? Did *they* think she was a "crack-up"? He had missed it, or she had chosen not to show it to him, or maybe she had tried a few times and when he hadn't noticed, she closed up and saved the art for others who could appreciate it. Nineteen sixty-six came and went. He knew that in 1967 her life would be riven apart. It was coming. He knew what she couldn't have known. Charles's office had a party. By now Eric knew her feelings about holidays: the Gersons celebrated everything with huge family gatherings. For Helen, whose deep pleasures were all personal and even secret, the loud, brash Christmases, the noisy, crowded Thanksgivings, the ear-ringing July Fourths were— Oh, God, here it was. Not so soon—it couldn't be so soon. The trip, the trip west over the mountains, their first trip away from Omaha since their marriage. He gritted his teeth and read on.

It was a company prize that Charles had won. They started out, driving west. The Plains made Helen think of her childhood, and although the land changed not at all as they entered eastern Colorado, she was glad to be out of Nebraska. The first night they spent near Denver and Charles pored over his map. It was Helen who, in a rare demonstration of her wishes, chose the route. The second night they stayed in a a small town in the mountains . . . They must have been on the road early, a little before six the next morning . . .

Nothing. Three blank pages. She must have set those aside to write in at the end of each day. Oh yes, her collarbone had been broken—she must have had the arm in a sling for a while, and then . . . She had said she never went back. He wondered if they had given *her* a plastic-wrapped package of bloody, dirty papers. He thought about the last child dying. Her next entry was icy with shock. She wrote about calling the minister of their church, seeing to all the details to which Eric had so recently attended: Where would the funeral be? Was there a will? Who needed to be told? In her numbness, strange details stood out: the people on the bus she took back to Denver, a conversation overheard in the bus station, what she ate. The family had wanted her to travel with the bodies back to Omaha. She acquiesced in everything and did what she wished. She saw the bodies onto the train and took a bus to Omaha.

The ride was healing. She got on the bus in Denver, sat down, and let herself feel the pain. The bus wasn't crowded. She sat alone and wept silently out of sight of the mountains, late morning to early evening, getting to Omaha as she wanted, quietly, even secretly. She took a cab to her house, locked the door, took the phone off the hook, and stayed by herself for two days, "crying the four walls," as she had said before. Then she called Charles's family. The bodies had come back, the funeral was set; she appeared at the church as if by magic, composed and self-possessed. The family members were as furious as they were astonished.

They told her what she must do. No need for the big house now—she must come to live with them. There was sure to be a job for her in Charles's company. That would be after a suitable mourning period. "I asked them if they knew who the last person was who had seen Charles and the children alive," she wrote, and Eric cringed. "It was a drunken boy looking through the windshield of the cars. I want to see the person who could do such things." The Gersons were scandalized. Their shock was so great they couldn't reply.

She asked them to dispose of the house and all its furnishings. She took the money in their joint bank account and told Charles's lawyer where she would be—seeing the person who had changed her life. The lawyer said he understood; but he pleaded with her to stay away from the scene and the people involved. There would be a trial or a hearing—the law would do its work. "The legal part of this must not concern you," he told her. Society proceeds according to law, not vengeance, maybe not even justice. And to "personalize" it is to take it back a thousand years to the vendetta, and the blood feud. She wrote down his reasons and, seeing them written, must have decided that she had given them a suitable hearing. She said good-bye to him, went back to the bus station, and bought her tickets.

It was late, but Eric couldn't stop reading. He knew that the next day he had to be at work, where he was finding it increasingly difficult to concentrate. Yazzi was patient. They were all patient, but a month had gone by and another, and people were beginning to wonder when he would take hold again. His mind flowed in and out of focus no matter how hard he tried to command it, and he came home drained every night from the effort.

But Helen was back in Denver and he couldn't stop. When was that—March, April, May? What had he been doing in those months—1967—oh, yes, trying to look responsible, keeping his head down because of the hearing, listening to Aguilar, seeing his lawyer, Rademaker. He groaned.

There hadn't been much money in the joint account. She got a job as a temporary office worker in Denver, staying at the Y. As soon as she could, she came to Aureole, looked up the local news coverage of the accident, went to the courthouse, and found out the date of the hearing. A week before the hearing, she quit her job and came back to Aureole. There were four hotels near the courthouse. She soon found where he was registered and simply waited. His registration was for Thursday night, he and his lawyer and the secretary. He was Arnie, then.

220

She saw him first, eating in the hotel, with Rademaker and the secretary. Now as Eric read, as he watched her watching him, he felt caught out, pinned by her cold stare; it was a sick, guilty feeling. She did not say what she thought of him then. Even at the hearing, she did not describe him or Rademaker or the judge. The evidence was put down in short phrases. "EAG was half-drunk—a party in Pickaxe. He left at three. He picked up Bressard, a hitchhiker. Bressard had a cylinder of nitrous oxide. EAG said he did not know the contents of cylinder. The judge is considering. Decision is held until Monday."

Good God, she was following him, tracking him. She sat four rows behind him at the movie he went to that Friday night; and after, she walked the dark streets behind him. There was no comment on his actions, nothing more than where he went. "Saturday. EAG had breakfast in hotel. He left at eleven. He walked to river and back. He walked to the park and met girls. They talked and laughed," she wrote, and then a few blistering words: "Let him play. Justice comes Monday."

Still following. She saw them skating, bowling, playing tennis. The girl on Saturday, the girl on Sunday. She saw the laughing and the beers and the hamburgers he fed a girl bite by bite, all the phony, too easy intimacy he used to practice so well. It made him cringe. There were details he had forgotten or changed in his mind. And ending the exhausting day, of course, was bed. "They went to her motel room. Sunday. A late start. The girl left. He found another one. Swimming. Tennis again and then another swim. The girl drank and danced." Helen, exhausted, left them there at ten.

The courtroom. "He has come in sick-looking under his tan. The judge looks at him with sympathy. Even his lawyer is surprised. But it's a hangover and too much sun and too much sex. His guilty plea is accepted. His sentence is deferred." She was writing in the present tense. She must have taken the book to the hearing with her. The page said nothing more; there was no cry for justice. Why hadn't she stood up and told the judge what she had seen? Why didn't she remind them all that she sat there widowed, childless, utterly alone? He felt himself shrivel with shame.

So she had known all along what he was. When she spoke to him on the ski slopes, it was with the full knowledge of how he had spent the weekend of his hearing. And she must have known in that cool, rational way of hers that she would never get justice except by her own means, in as long and slow a distillation as she had the power and the patience to make. She had to marry him, to build him, in order to give him a life worth destroying: a home, three children. The law could not give such justice—only Helen knew what justice was required. She had to give her justice a meaning. She had let him fall in love because justice equaled the deaths of four people—a spouse and three children, the eldest of whom was twelve years of age. It was two-thirty in the morning. He put the book aside and thought of her patience and her strength and the length of her love for Sakai, that could also be the length of her revenge.

Yazzi was waiting for him when he came in. "May I speak to you for a minute?"

"Sure, what is it?"

"It's about the old bridge, repairs on the old bridge."

"They were done last month—I saw the report—"

"Two months ago. There are problems. It's been two months and cracks are starting to show in the surfacing."

"What do you mean? Crazing?"

"No, sir, cracks, cracks two to three centimeters wide and four centimeters deep."

"That's impossible—we haven't had any extreme weather. Didn't they let the surface cure before they ran cars on it?"

"I don't think that's the problem, Mr. Gordon."

Yazzi was young but his style was as formal as a man generations older. He was able, but not easy to know. He had been working in the office for three months before Eric felt comfortable enough to invite him over for dinner. He had come a few times since and seemed to get along well with Helen. Eric had planned to have him more often, but by then Yazzi was courting a girl in Pickaxe and then there was . . . Eric could no longer think the word *accident* when he thought about "it." Now he didn't ask Yazzi because he felt the assistant would come out of pity, and the house looked so bad he couldn't have anyone but Cady anyway, so they had not gotten together after working hours. Yazzi stood in front of him, a stolid-looking, chunky man, blocking his escape. "What *is* the problem?"

"Mr. Gordon, the surface was to have been laid on a repaired base. It wasn't. The base was never put on and the surface is one-fourth the thickness of the specs."

"That's impossible," Eric said. Yazzi stared at him impassively for a moment and then looked away. "Did you see Roche about it—repair and maintenance is Roche's department."

"Yes, sir, I did. He said I was mistaken. The inspection is not due for a year. Mr. Tugwell was very careful to tell me that."

"Well—"

"Well, I went out there again and took measurements and samples. There isn't an inch of surfacing on that bridge."

"Surfaces compress under weight—maybe you got a bad spot." Yazzi waited silently. A voice said in Eric's mind, "Go on, skier, slide away down, turn past the trouble." He said, "What led you to look into this?"

"I brought my fiancée down for the weekend so she could see the town, get to know it. We walked across the bridge. Actually it was she who first pointed out the cracks."

"And you did tell Roche, you said?"

There was a long pause. Yazzi knew Eric and Roche were friends, that the families had grown up together, that Roche had been working with Eric back when the old guy was there, when it was a three-man office.

"Yes, sir, I did," he said quietly. "He said I was mistaken. Then I went back and took the samples. I took three of them. It's substandard, sir, not the difference between three-ply and four-ply, not the difference between one-inch base and three. There is no new base and the layer of asphalt is just a film on the old stuff."

"What do we have on this morning?"

"Town council meeting, about Miner's Park, and the two new grade schools." Yazzi's answer had no inflection in its tone. No wonder he and Helen had gotten on well. They had the same clinical objectivity, the same realism. What Helen had done she had done even while she loved him and without real anger, equaling up the score until it balanced and then canceling the equation.

"What after that?"

"Our study for the airport. There are three sites . . ."

He knew that. It annoyed him that Yazzi had added that, just because he had forgotten a meeting about the sites last week. "The mayor, the council, and the commissioners this time—"

"Yes, sir."

"We'll have to cancel that for today. Tell Jean to reschedule."

"Yes, sir."

The morning meeting had been long and wearing; now they were on their way to the bridge. Eric had not told Roche. Maybe there was some mistake, some other reason that would show why there had been an error, why Roche had been slipshod. Living where he did, Eric didn't use the bridge, and after he had lost his battle to build the necessary second one upstream, he had routed all complaints to maintenance and had stopped thinking about it. Now . . .

As they drove to the bridge, Eric told Yazzi a little of its history: what Cady had told him about it back in the mining days, Eric's first plan, his second.

"I'm glad you're telling me these things," Yazzi said. "My professor used to say that engineering is more of a social science than people think."

"Oh? How is this an example?"

"Well, the bridge is local and the airport is, uh, regional. The bridge is more mundane, more practical than the airport. Many more local people will be using it, but the commissioners turned down a new bridge and went for the airport instead. That was a cultural, not an engineering, choice."

"And you think Roche figured that—that he was free to go short on it because it was just the Divide Street Bridge?"

"I don't know if it was Mr. Roche's idea. Danforth and Aitken did the construction. Maybe the mayor knew, maybe a commissioner or two—"

"And Roche?"

"Yes, sir."

"And there was money all down the line for people who knew?"

"I figure they divided about seventy-five thousand dollars among them."

"Why did you decide to ring the bell on this?"

"Because I thought you weren't in on it."

There was no mistake, no quick, careless job, no bad-weather error. The bridge had been resurfaced on its old subcode, worn bed, with a thin glaze of asphalt to make it look as though something had been done. It didn't even take study. In the two months since it had been "fixed," lacerations had opened all the length of it. The bedding layers were so scanty that the bones of its cross-bracing showed here and there. No attempt had been made to bind or curb the edges or to treat them to prevent runoff from seeping between the skimpy layers. In a year, the surface would be buckling. In another year, some heavy truck might go through the eroded places. Until then, the surface would throw up great boils caused by the pressure of wet fill expanding. Moisture would seep down to the bracing and work away at it, and the bridge would begin to leak.

"I've seen enough," Eric said, "we can go back now."

Yazzi went silently after him.

That evening he dove into Helen's book to escape thoughts about the bridge.

"I loved the children; I was fond of Charles and grateful to him," Helen wrote, "but they are gone. I don't want to stay in Omaha. I don't want to stay in Denver. I have written to Naohito to ask him if I might come there and be with him on whatever terms he will have me. I can wait in Aureole for an answer. In Aureole I am that much closer."

Ten days. She walked by the river, drove up into the mountains. For the first time in her life there was no whip behind the door, no grinding need, no responsibility. It was her first vacation. She came to it fully prepared. Sakai had given her eyes to see the beauty around her. She quoted the haiku poet Buson:

> The spring morning
> The butterfly asleep
> On the temple bell.

She enjoyed everything profoundly, gratefully. The anguish eased in her a little.

A letter came from California. She did not quote it. There was only the brief "He writes as beautifully as he does ikebana. I now have a sample of that handwriting. The limitations of love are something of which I myself should be conscious." No more.

But the Ute had caught her, the huge sky and the low stars, the bare, spare mountains—stands of trees, a feeling of time and silence, and the healing of leisure and thought. The town had caught her, too, the other side of boom and bust, which was freedom, an informal joyousness in new starts, an acceptance of difference, an admiration of personal initiative, and little history given. There were also jobs to be had, a feeling of the town breathing in, expanding. She applied at the county and city and took the tests involved. Eric smiled. People had called him crazy, too, but Helen, at last, was doing what she liked.

He was glad to read about Helen to take his mind off Roche. He didn't want to deal with what Roche had done. He kept hoping there would be an explanation, a purpose that would explain it all. Perhaps Roche was researching some new wonder substance, some technological break-through, that would make—he cursed himself. Ski past it, slide past it, let the new fall of snow cover it so deep that not a sound is heard and all its contours are smoothed. It was fraud. He went in the next day and looked at Roche's records, which were in the general file where Yazzi had put them. It was all there, signed by Roche. Materials that had never been used, layers that had never been applied, promises that had never been kept, money that had come in and not gone out. Back in his office he saw his own disorder with new eyes. It was a horror. It looked like his house. How could he have let things get so bad? No wonder Roche could have done what he did; plans and reports lay everywhere, unorganized, without priority or place. As head of the department, he had administrative responsibilities also, and the papers generated by other papers were piled here and there. It had been two months since he had truly concentrated on any of it. He was too busy tracking the preceptress of justice and injustice, reading her hidden messages—or was she that? She had seen him and followed him, had been disgusted and fascinated by him, but she couldn't have known that he, too, would be coming back to Aureole, and her decision to stay had more to do with Sakai and mountains and a need for peace than . . .

And here he was, lost again in Helen's books and Helen's mind and Helen's motives while his job blew away around him in a scatter of papers and maps and missed opportunities. Roche had just come in. Skier had come to the bottom. It was time. Past time.

Roche stood in Eric's paper-piled wilderness and listened without a word. He had gone a bit pale in the beginning but when the telling was over—Yazzi, and Eric's disbelief, and his going to the bridge and what he had found—Roche was expressionless and silent. "Well—"

"Well, you saw."

"Good God, man, *why?*"

"The money. You argued for years about the need for a new bridge. No matter what we did to repair it, this one just doesn't have the strength to stand what the town wants to put on it. I saw that when I started the renovation. In two years we'll have to get a new bridge anyway. I thought, Why not just surface this one and be done?"

"You weren't the only one; who else took money?"

"Honor forbids me to—"

"*Honor.* How much did you get?"

"Ten thousand."

"Oh, Hank, Jesus! All the years, Cady and you and I, and all for *ten thousand*, on what must have been a hundred-thousand-dollar piece of garbage? Why, for God's sake?"

Roche shrugged. "I guess I'm not an honest man."

"What do you mean not honest? Cady and you and I worked for years together. You were honest then!"

"You mean I never stole anything—then. Remember how close we were. Every project was shared, in a way. You and Cady and I all knew what the projects were—there was no chance to take anything without the two of you knowing."

"So—"

"So Cady was honest, really honest, and you were trying to be what Cady was, and I—I guess I was honest because you were looking."

"And one day you looked around and nobody was there?"

"Not exactly. If people think you're above that kind of thing, they won't come to you, they won't tell you what's going on. I knew about the water commissioner and stuff some of the contractors did, but when they worked with me they didn't try things because it was this office."

"Well, then, what started it?"

"I didn't know about myself then, either. But it got to be 'Give the dirty work to Roche, let Roche do the crummy pothole work, the boring, endless stuff.'"

"But you didn't want planning or inspection, you said so."

"Not what, *how*. You took me for granted. I was in the background, I played support and even before Helen and the kids—I'm sorry to mention it—but even before the accident you were so busy with your ideas and your plans you didn't care how I was doing or how my side of the department was doing so long as the calls came in and the work got done."

"Why didn't you tell me?"

"You don't say that kind of thing: care, give a damn. I'm not blaming you, either. This just happened. I had a chance and I took it, I needed the money. Jimmy is planning to go to college—no one was going to be hurt—you were looking the other way and in a year, two years at the most, the damn bridge wouldn't have mattered anyway; you were right all along—"

"Don't you know I've got to fire you?" Eric said wearily. "Don't you know I'll have to make a report about what happened and send it to the authorities? There'll be an investigation—a prosecution."

"Nope," Roche said. "As soon as this gets out, the council will vote for a new bridge. In a month, before any evidence is gathered, a new bridge will be voted and then it will be in nobody's interest to yell about the old one. Let me go. I've been working with Russell's part time. I'll get on one of their projects somewhere else and if you keep quiet you'll get your new bridge, and you'll have the clout to get its quality as good as you want it. Think it over."

Eric was amazed. "Everyone around me," he murmured, "has secrets they're busy with. Tell me, can I fire you at least, or is this part of some vast plan including the FBI and the CIA?"

"Fire me."

"I can't believe we're saying these things. Don't you remember how we all stayed up nights to dispatch the snow crews—how we laughed at Malcolm's plan? And you like the work, I know you do."

"I've stayed here long enough, stuck in Cady's idea and yours. My heritage is boom and bust—like we said about these towns."

"You're not like that, you couldn't be."

"Then, let's talk about Malcolm, about how it was back then with Malcolm and his commune."

"All right."

"You told me how you and Cady had visited there, seen it all blowing away after Malcolm's bunch had left it. You hated all that, you and Cady. I didn't say anything, but I thought, Why not? When the dream dies, why stay and wallow in it? My folks did, in a dying town, calling it virtue when it was only laziness. Fire me, Eric; it's time for me to go."

"You're fired, Roche; you've got thirty days."

"This was once a good office with you as brother and Cady as father. I'll get someone good to take my place—someone honest. It'll take more than a month, though. I'll need time to get my next job—give me sixty days, will you?"

"Okay, sixty days," Eric said, and he turned away into the report-strewn room. He wished he could cry but he was only tired and confused. He felt like a child, a small child in a room where grown-ups argue in grown-up language. There were reasons he could not fathom, ideas that baffled and blurred, and a terrible sadness separate from his grief.

"They wouldn't tell me much," Cady said, "because there wasn't much to tell. You'll have to go to Pickaxe and find out more. Helen was there only twice."

They were in the kitchen, Esther sitting with them, propped up in a chair with cushions. It was one of her difficult times, May, when spring still alternated with wet, heavy snow. They were trying a new treatment that didn't seem to be working. Eric had come to hear about Cady's hospital visit and to tell Cady about Roche, but looking at Esther he didn't have the heart. He sat still and said nothing.

"The hospital in Pickaxe has the records. The man there is Boningsberg, in neurology. Helen went there soon after Anne had the second seizure. She paid by check—no insurance—and the next time she came back it was for the workup. The findings . . . well, you'll have to get those, but I got the impression that there was something—something serious and long-developing."

"Cady, why didn't she tell me? Why did she go to Pickaxe when we have a hospital here?"

"Surely you know!" Esther said. "It's the essential Helen—she couldn't have done it any other way."

"What do you mean?"

"Secrets," Esther said, "the secrets she kept, the awful pride she had in keeping them. It was what I respected most and liked least about her, that pride. Didn't you ever wonder why she wouldn't let anyone praise Mark?"

"I always thought she was afraid of the limelight for herself or the kids. When she was growing up, being special in any way meant trouble."

"But the secret joy does as much damage as the secret grief. She wanted to be the only one who saw those gifts in Mark. When joy goes underground, it swells to arrogance. Helen's joy was secret, so was her pain. Under the seeming reserve and modesty was a terrible pride." They said nothing. Eric went home and read.

She saw him in Aureole walking with Cady, talking, and couldn't believe her eyes. Carefully she asked questions and found out that he was Eric now, not Arnie, but the same man, that he had moved to Aureole and was living in an awful hole of a place and had gotten a job at the engineer's office. Why? "What could such a job in a town like this mean to him? Easy conquests and easy living are his style. Towns ask questions. Towns notice. He won't stay."

But he did. She began to hear about him. "Nice man, hard-working, serious," people said, "goes out very little." There was even a rumor that he was homosexual ("that bike an' all"). In the room that no longer had a vestige of Sakai, Eric laughed his first full laugh in two months. He read on. Kitty Springer, who worked in the secretarial pool, liked him and followed his movements. Which one was she, he wondered; he had been so busy he hadn't noticed. It was his not noticing that alerted Helen to a change in him. "Why doesn't he flirt with her? She's pretty enough—she's obvious enough—always delivering papers down there. I saw him at the courthouse today. He didn't recognize me—my hair was up and I must have looked very different in the context of the office—a worker, not a widow. He looked at me with interest, but nothing of the sly male coyness he used in May, with the girls he picked up—no little grin. He lives at the Cadys' now. He helps Esther Cady, who is an invalid. I don't understand. No liquor, no dope, he really isn't driving, and he is serious about that job. I don't understand."

He came to the moment of recognition at the commissioners' meeting. "He knows who I am. He looked at me and went white. I thought he would faint." "Saw EAG again at the office; he turned pale and stammered." "Kitty misinterprets what is happening and is jealous." "EAG at the bank. We will be seeing each other in town like this again and again. He runs from me, hides. When he sees me with the commissioners he goes pale and can't speak. It's embarrassing. People in the office notice it. They think it's love. The mayor's secretary laughed about it at lunch. Commissioner Tyrrel mentioned it this morning, asking what I was doing to Cady's new engineer. I can be happy here. He will not drive me away."

A week, two. Her days were filled with work but she didn't make friends easily and except for Ernestine at the office, there was no one to whom she felt close. The evenings and nights were endless.

And then came the meeting at the ski area. She saw him sitting alone and a chance to stop the embarrassment. "He has changed in some way I can't express. Before, he would have been busy looking for girls. He sat alone, quietly. When I came up to him he erupted with clumsiness, but under it all wasn't fear anymore, but pain, grief—it's an awestruck look, not the look of someone in a bad social situation—not what I had expected. I said my piece and left him. Later, I saw him on the slopes. I was helpless and miserable, stuck there, cold and frightened where I had fallen and couldn't get up. Skiing is awful. You slide away like dying and can't stop. He helped me. Then, for a reason I still don't understand, I let him take me up again and teach me. Maybe I was curious about the sport, or about him, maybe I was tired to death of being alone, tired of the awful ache of it—I did something I have only done once before—I let something happen because I wanted it to happen. I was thinking of Naohito and snow, and Issa saying, 'Simply trust.' The hill was beautiful, the day was beautiful; maybe I wanted to see it that way, just that. Later I saw Eric ski alone, and I thought of Naohito again. Eric's skiing is like Naohito's ikebana. It is sufficient, developed to simplicity; there is no shamming, or showing off, no self-glorification. He wastes no motion. He is complete. I want to learn which man he really is, the serious, quiet man who skis without tricks, or the man who smiles too easily and can't be alone."

So she let him try to teach her, and as he did, she saw his anguish as he strained toward what he wanted to become. It surprised and moved her. She was awed; she wrote that she had never seen anyone try such a work on himself. It wasn't what she had tried to do at Mrs. Woodcock's, a change of style, of manner, of speech—it was nothing less than a renovation of himself from the inside. As the weeks went on, she watched him struggle with the parts of his personality, pruning, correcting, in a blind hope that the final self would be worthy. He had no one forcing him in this, not even poverty.

It was a spiritual venture solely; she had never seen anything like it.

She began to like him, to open and warm to his company. She began to see that for him, too, the law had afforded no justice, that in his need for justice he was lonely in a way she deeply understood. They became lovers. When he urged that they marry, she wrote in her cool, detached way, "Of course I love him, but love is irrelevant, the personal feelings are irrelevant."

He read the sentence she had written so long ago. There was the proof for which he had been looking, that for her, love was irrelevant to justice. She might love—she did love—and still do—what she had done.

He was tempted to skip ahead, past the years they lived together, to get to her last months, Anne, the seizures. He was dumbstruck by the degree to which she had hidden Anne's problems from him. Was it pride, as Esther said, or the need to protect? He knew by now that there would be no why; the why was the whole story, in small phrases and sentences. He read on.

"I'm so damn sorry!" Cady said. "We should have watched Roche!" They were sitting in Cady's kitchen. Eric had come to help do repairs. It was better than staring at his own deteriorating house. He kept intending to get someone in to clean but never had.

"But you always said—we both thought he was honest—"

"He was. I forgot he had never been tested—not really. Roche came up in a small, close town where there were lots of eyes. Many people in small towns are decent and honest; some of them are that way because the neighbors keep them so."

"And that's all? That's what prevented him from taking bribes then?"

"Things were smaller when you first came, closer, more personal. A bad project would have gotten back to us sooner, and Roche knew it."

"I know. He said so. And it was my lack that let him go crooked; he said that, too. I was so busy fighting for this and against that . . . How did *you* do it, Cady, how did you keep us together, eager and honest and happy?"

"Things were smaller all around. There was less to do."

"Maybe I could have seen this before it happened. I've been busy grieving, busy being angry, busy doing God knows what. He must have felt me slipping away. I stopped caring and he knew it."

"Take your part of it, but don't take all of it; he could have quit *without* the graft "

"I don't think so. I think he needed a real break—something awful that would do it for him. Cady, why didn't *you* ever steal anything?"

"How do you know I didn't?"

"I would have found out by now."

"I suspect it was lack of ambition. I had Esther and all the money we needed. I'd traveled my fill during the war. I liked the job and the town and I liked being respected. I had no reason to be dishonest."

"And Roche did?"

"Yes, I guess he did. In any case, it's a hell of a blow."

"Should I let him get me a new man?"

"Sure, he owes you that. Small-town people are very keen on justice or at least fairness."

"So it seems."

The doctor knew Eric had taken time off from work to see him. He had the file on his desk. "What you said over the phone astounds me—that you never knew about any of this. You weren't separated, were you?"

"No, but apparently my wife felt the need to . . . well, I didn't know until after the accident. What was wrong with Anne?"

"What can that matter now?"

"I don't need to be protected. Please tell me what I want to know."

"We ran the tests and they were indicative but not definitive. Our next step would have been to send her to Denver for a CAT scan, because we strongly suspected a tumor. Most tumors in children—the overwhelming number—are malignant and very rapid. Because of the history we thought this was different, something slower-growing. You see this X ray—look at this part here—nothing easily spotted, but something's pushing *this* off center—see where it doesn't quite match the other side? Her neurologicals were ambiguous, too, not much off. There were things she'd learned to compensate for—balance, for one. Kids don't complain because they don't yet know what normal is. And of course, then, the seizures."

"Yes, the seizures. Were they coming to see you that day?"

"We weren't expecting them, not until the, uh, the twentieth. They were down for more tests then. Of course, they didn't—"

"No, they didn't."

Driving back from Pickaxe he came through the valley of the Ute in its short-lived spring green. The water was high and fast, fed by the runoff of the mountains whose heights still wore cockades of dazzling spring snow. Torrents had been born in the crevices of rocks, and from impossible rootholds in the faces of cliffs aspen trees found their precious inch of earth and sprang outward with small sprays of fragile-looking leaves. The road led upward from the valley on to the shelf, winding the mountainside in a spiral up and up. He came to the spot where the car had gone off, approaching it from the opposite direction. Who would attempt this road at eighty miles an hour? Take off a seat belt? Deny the brake? The road showed nothing. Already he had lost the exact spot on the curve where the car had left the highway. Already new growth, spring beauty, and a haze of weeds had covered the gouts the car had taken out of the earth. The earth healed; when would he? "When I see the truth and know it. When I know the person my wife was," he muttered, and went home to read.

236

17

Her reluctant courtship spread out before him: the meeting in the courthouse attic, the groundbreaking party for the municipal building, dinners, outings, the meeting with his parents, their making love, their waiting, their marriage. Little was there but the facts, yet day by day, he saw her picture of their life together. He saw how much closer was her woman's absorption in the details of living—things he had forgotten or taken for granted, seen now as she had seen them. There was the second terrible pregnancy and the loss of that child, then Karen. He was reading quickly, skimming the years, and suddenly, halfway lulled by the dailiness of her routine, he came on it and was skimming it, too, when its meaning stopped him in midsentence and he had to go back and read it again, slowly. September 24, 1973—Mark would have been four or so, Karen a baby. "Making love last night," she wrote, "something collapsed inside me, then filled and ran over, and I was in an urgency, like riding a river, then I was the river. Then I went over the edge. It must have been orgasm, all that shuddering fall, and it lasted a long time! I had thought it would be a kind of spasm; no one ever said it went so long. After all these years I had not expected it." He stared down at the writing.

And this, too, she had not told him! Damn the secret-keepers and their pride! Can a person be faithful and a betrayer at the same time? He had no doubt that, vengeful or not, she had been physically faithful to him. Indeed a vengeance like that would have demanded such fidelity, but here was a kind of evidence, a proof of authenticity, that he would not have questioned and which, in her silence, she had denied him knowledge of. He flipped ahead, reading quickly. Perhaps she would mention it again—but there was no more about it. Then he thought it would be logical not to mention it if it had begun to happen regularly. She would note it only if it stopped.

He read on. Mark's growing prowess and cleverness—not praised, even in that most private of places, but all of it noted, day after day, year after year. Every "A" paper was mentioned, every compliment from someone, every sign of beauty, talent, charm, or wit—entered, counted, saved. Karen. Anne. He had not seen this counting with the old family. Lois, Richard, Patricia—perhaps she thought she had taken them for granted. Their lives had been directly experienced, not used for anything but what they were. Her justice came with such measuring—the new family was being judged because it was a replacement for the old, directly, three for three, as though with equal signs, mate for mate, child for child He read on. A time he remembered. It was Malcolm's year. Yes, she was mentioning the trip they made out to Malcolm's ruined commune. She described the blowing trash briefly, the sadness. He was reading on quickly again when a word, another word stopped him. "Warm today. A woman at the shopping center said we were a lovely family. At supper Eric told me that Cady was sixty-eight. The law says sixty-five is retirement age. Something should be done. He should not demand that the office break the law for his sake."

Eric stared at the page. They had never spoken about Cady's forced retirement with anything but sympathy. No—*he* had never done so. He was learning in these books that what he had thought was their opinion had often enough been his alone; her silence had not been assent at all.

Could Helen have inspired those letters about Cady? Who

had signed them? It had happened so long ago, he had forgotten. He knew she would not have written them, or had them written, through malice or anger or to advance Eric into Cady's place, but as a matter of justice, the justice that was for him and his friends easy accommodation and was for her the harness end, a shattered family, the denial of suffering. For an instant he felt with her a flash of righteous anger. For the favored man the law lay curled like a sleeping cat. For the unlucky, it bared awful teeth.

He lay in bed and thought about Helen and justice. She had known a passionate love, but not with Charles. She had always been able to separate love from necessity, but she had never, from his reading of the diary, acted to make justice happen. She had borne her father's violence, her brothers' bullying, Cory's scorn, Charles's family's benevolent tyranny, without trying to get her own back again. Did something at last cry out for action? When was justice no longer to be simply seen, but finally to be done? Had she suddenly looked at Cady, happy in his work, and said to herself, I'll start now; I'll start with him? Then, had she watched her husband, happy in his job, successful in town, enjoying his family, all sins forgiven, all deaths forgotten, and thought, Now?

Eric sat up in bed and turned on the light, trying to silence his mind. It moved like a mole, digging in a blind search, cutting roots, turning into old caverns and burrowing new ones in a circle back to the beginning. Night work.

And he was back to Cady and the letters. They were from people to whom Helen had no access. He knew she would never have written the letters and signed them with the names of those men—the forgery would have come out. How could she have gotten to them? When the letters had come out, everyone had thought it was Malcolm.

And then, simply, he thought of Ernestine. Helen could easily have told Ernestine, sitting over those dainty sandwiches, that Cady was already sixty-eight and, Helen might have asked, How far would it have to go before they got someone in to fill his place? It could have been done in a moment over tea and cookies. Ernestine worked all over town, everyone knew her, everyone called on her for filing, for tax season, or inventory. A word or two was all that would have been necessary. He sighed. So instead of an easy, graceful transition, a department that brought in a new man slowly, letting Cady teach the ways they worked, building trust and continuity, there was a disaster and three men in three years before Yazzi, and the way lost. He thought again. Maybe she had not told Ernestine. Maybe it was only for the journal, that small disagreement, and put aside, a secret, like all her others, for the book only, like the orgasm after all those years.

Helen kept everything locked in the rooms she had built to house them. A smile might escape, a fragment of song, a single spray of a blossom in a small vase on her night table. Perhaps people of such pride and silence think they are the only ones who feel deeply, who need love at all, who treasure its evidences . . .

The next day, he called Jean into the office. "A new day has dawned," he said. They cleaned the room, divided and sorted the different kinds of paperwork, separated the problems, mounted the new maps, and took down the old ones. The order pleased him. He thought he might like to return to such order. When Yazzi came in from the field he stopped at the door and his round face broke into a grin. "What's this?"

Eric smiled back at him. "I thought Indians were inscrutable."

"White people seldom give us anything to scrute about. To what do we owe this change?"

He didn't answer, because he didn't know himself. Perhaps by digging, his mole had entered a familiar chamber and sensed that although the digging was blind, the direction was known—not a circle, this time, but a way to the center.

18

The next day instead of eating lunch, he went to the library and sat down with a Merck manual. He read the section on neurology, subsection convulsive disorders. He was appalled. The word *seizure* had meant something—tremors, unconsciousness. The reading brought the reality to him and its sudden onset, the uncontrollable shout or cry, that children pitch to the ground, flailing in spasms. He had never seen Anne do anything like that; there had been nothing but her dark-minded reserve. He hadn't loved his daughter, but the doctor had thought she might always have been fighting some subtle, awful pressure that was pushing against part of her brain. If there was a place in the brain that measured joy, called love by name, answered "Yes!" and "Here I am!" that part must have been closed off by the pressure when she was a tiny baby. The darkness had not been of her making, or of theirs.

But the seizures—Helen must have seen them. There were different kinds the book described. Which kind had Anne had? Now he would never know.

"Yazzi, have you ever seen someone have a seizure? Have you ever seen a child have a seizure?"

"Yes, two different kids."

"What were they like?"

"They don't only happen to Indians, you know. White people have them—kids who have had the best of everything . . ."

"I know that. I'm not asking idly. I need to know."

Yazzi described the cry, the pitching forward, the falling. "Those things are not the scary part," he said.

"What is?" Eric asked, wondering if there could be something worse.

"Well, they stop breathing. They turn blue and they're not breathing and you can't get them to breathe and it seems like forever before they start again—three, four minutes."

"They go without breathing for that long?"

"Yes, or so it seems. Sometimes a seizure will happen and then another and another after that."

"Yes, uh—status epilepticus—I read about that."

"What's this all about?" Yazzi asked.

Eric took a breath. "You knew my younger daughter, Anne, didn't you?"

"Well, I saw her the times I was at your house and then when your wife came by."

"Oh, when was that?"

"The day she—the day they—uh—died."

"What?"

"The other two were in the car. She had the little girl with her, sleeping in her arms. She came up to tell you she was going to Pickaxe and not to expect her, that she would explain it all later."

"My God, I never knew that!"

"The little girl—was it the little girl?"

"Yes."

"They came by, assuming you would be here because it was Wednesday, but you had gone out with the commissioner—with all that happened later, I didn't tell you—it didn't seem—well, and the message was irrelevant—that they were going to Pickaxe."

"Of course. I—Yazzi, I've got to go somewhere. I'll be gone for the rest of the afternoon. I have to check something out.

That day, when she came by, what time was that?"

"Oh, about one in the afternoon—twelve-thirty or one."

Eric drove toward Pickaxe again, living Helen's last day. It had been a Wednesday, her day for the car. Earlier in the morning she must have put the house in order, and because it was always in order, it must have been easy to check each room and give the final touches—shoes lined up, the new soap in the soap dish, the breakfast dishes washed and put away. She and Anne would be dressed for their outing, Anne to perfection, protected by those clothes from the cruel laughter of another place and time. They had their plans for the day, Mark's lesson, their shopping. Getting ready she must have heard that fall, that cry from Anne's room. There must have been a terrible wave of panic in her that despite the preventive medication there was *this* seizure. It must have happened around noon because he had read about what was called postictal state, the grogginess, sleepiness after seizure, and Helen had appeared with Anne, a five-year-old child, sleeping heavily in her arms, at the office at twelve-thirty or one, with the other children already in the car. She must have picked them up early at school while Anne slept her brain-drugged sleep. She had also called Mrs. Browning quickly to cancel Mark's lesson. Dear God, the logistics of it all!

He drove past Callan and Bluebank. He was halfway to Pickaxe when he realized that if Helen had wanted to stand before him like an avenging ghost, she was facing the wrong way! The accident with Bressard was *south* of Aureole in the canyon the Ute cuts as it flows east-southeast away from the divide. He was going north and west to the shelf road that was a cliff, not a canyon—the symbols were wrong.

Why had it taken him so long to see that? Had she meant to show him what *he* had done, she could easily have gone to the spot where the first wreck had taken place, turned, and taken the curve the way Charles had tried to do, and because there was no other car, kept on going into the mountain wall.

Perhaps she had thought of that, and the horror of a head-on crash was too much for her, memory of the smashed bodies of—he was twitching at the wheel. He pulled over close to the mountain wall and stopped. Once again he saw them, saw clearly what he had always tried so hard to put away . . . He and Bressard exploding into another car, rags of clothing, upholstery fluttering, bodies, his touching flesh and bone that gave under his hand as he struggled upward blindly to free himself from where he was. Then, standing, shivering, at the side of the road and seeing, sticking out of the window of a car on its side, a single bare foot, a child's foot. Later, bodies at the side of the road. Helen's children. He began to cry, long, tearing sobs, not for Mark or Karen or Anne or Helen, but for that old horror from which all his undeserved good fortune had sprung, those children, and a man he had never really seen, and a woman who was then a stranger. Crying, he began to cry for Mark and Karen and little Anne and her mystery, and for the first time, for Helen, his love, his wife, keeper of secrets, fearer of difference, prisoner of her lifelong defenses against the casual brutality of the world.

After a time he was able to pull himself together. His eyes were so puffed and swollen it was hard to see and he had difficulty swallowing. But the road was narrow and there was no place to turn around. He realized then that he was already on the shelf part of it and that he would have to pass the spot where the car had gone over before he could turn around. He went on, slowly. He saw clearly how it must have been: Mark, perhaps angry at missing his lesson; Karen, silent. Had *she* ever seen Anne's convulsions? Anne in the back seat, groggy. What if there had been another seizure, the sudden cry and spasm and the child flailing away in the back, hitting her head, terrifying the others, no one able to hold her or end the seizures that could—the book said so—end in death. What if that was happening while Helen drove on, desperately trying to reach the hospital before it was too late? The fear would have gone to terror—Anne's face blue, the children trembling,

Karen crying, Helen going faster, much faster, then taking off her seat belt to turn for a moment without realizing how fast she was going, to Karen, helpless in the back, and not nearly strong enough—"Hold her head up!" or "Don't let her hurt herself—Mark, quickly—can you get back there and . . ."—her foot involuntarily pressing the accelerator as she turned and then they would be in the air, unbelted, leaving not a hint of tread on the road they had left behind them.

It would be so easy here—only two lanes and Helen's attention not on the road at all, but on Pickaxe, where there was the hospital and the doctor who had tested Anne, a hospital Helen had chosen with the same need for secrecy with which she had lived her life. Or what if during the moments of Anne's seizure, when Helen's foot was heavy on the accelerator and Karen screaming in back, what if, in the awful feeling of dislocation and unreality such moments have, there was a sudden closing of the circle, year for year, month for month, child for child? Perhaps that dislocation made her relive the nightmare she, too, had denied and forgotten. Had she looked across again at Mark, her gifted son, whose gifts had caused her so much anxiety, and seen there another child, and heard again the sounds of that other day, other children's voices in that other car, and cried "No more!" and shot out beyond both nightmares into the blue air? Either way, what happened had been, moment by moment, not a betrayal years in the ripening. Perhaps it was not a betrayal *by* Helen but *of* her by a past she had not wished to examine. He had destroyed her twice. Years after the need to hide all feelings, all fear, to appear perfect, to be inconspicuous, to turn away envy or ridicule, she had done or not done something in a moment and left her memory to his awful slander.

He was past the shelf road. The way led down into the Ute's wide and gracious valley, splendid with pouring water. He pulled over to the side of the road and cried again, unrestrainedly, this time for the tiny dark-haired little girl who had brought to school the horse blankets on which no one would sit, and who later arranged all her rooms with the serene, spare beauty of her ikebana.

Helen's rooms . . . When Anne had her seizures, it must have seemed the most natural thing in the world to Helen simply to open one more of them and put there one more secret, to find help as far away as the car could go in a day and still be back for dinner, thinking there would be a way, a time, a method of telling him when the room was perfectly ready, serene, orderly. Then he cried for his wife.

When he turned the car around and began to head home, it was getting dark. He passed the place of the accident. They are sometimes arrogant, the people who have suffered terribly in their youth. They think their capacity for suffering is greater than anyone else's. He had suffered nothing in his early years. He lacked the words for it, the defenses against it, but he also lacked the pride she had developed in her capacity to endure it. Soon, he would be passing the exit to Bluebank and he would see its lights coming on for the evening. He thought about Bressard and wondered about that family he had never seen. He came to the cutoff where Malcolm had had his commune. By now Malcolm, miles away, would barely remember the details of the land, the people; it would be easy to forget the time he had spent in Aureole, the dreams and the death of the dreams. Eric would probably remember Malcolm's commune longer than Malcolm would. The road and the land would be there to remind him. Bluebank was where he had stopped with Bressard. Pave it over as they may, put up hamburger places and subdivisions, condominiums, and all the signs of prosperity there; he would still remember. The Ute narrowed a little and picked up speed. He realized he was thinking about Bressard, Malcolm, the commune, the road on which he traveled with a clarity and in a stillness he had not had since Helen's death. There would be more anguish, more sorrow, but the contending voices, the blur of feelings, the fury and despair were gone. The night was very still around him. He pulled over again and sat for a

246

few moments, relishing the silence. The first stars; no wind. He could hear the river, "his" river flowing toward "his" town. He started the car again and drove on. Aureole. People were talking about a highway bypass to ease the traffic. He smiled. The street on which he drove was full of familiar stops and associations. A friend of Mark's lived there. He passed the house and felt no envy. The new school, the corner that always flooded, something Cady had told him. Aureole's history was now his—snowbanks, traffic patterns, old problems solved, old problems with them still. His.

In green Maryland where he had come from, history was much longer. Wandering the backroads in the hickory, red-oak, sweet-gum summers, it was possible to come on abandoned farmsteads whose eroding lintels bore dates in the 1720s, before the war that came before the war between the states. People lay their dead four, five generations deep in those drowsy towns and wars blooded the ground, giving the people more reason to stay. In the towns along the Ute the dead were strangers to the living; those who had buried them had long since moved on. Eric had familiar dead in Aureole now. He felt them lying on the evening like a color or a sound, wishing him peace.

It no longer mattered whether Helen had yearned in some part of her soul for a simple, savage act of justice, or whether her foot had pushed the accelerator while she tried to save her threatened child. She had had thirteen years with Charles and thirteen with him and perhaps she had, or perhaps she had never, not even in the deepest part of herself, made the psychic connection. The evening deepened. He passed their neighborhood stores, the school, learning the new sorrow which was not anger.

The house was cold and forbidding. Though he had stopped littering it to spite her, there was a bleak, untenanted look to the outside; the inside spoke his rage and despair: ugly, uncared for, sour-smelling. What had Helen said all those years ago about Malcolm's group—something about loss and shame. He must not allow himself to be ashamed any-more, to run from his loss. Now that he no longer hated the loss, he could begin to think about the house as he should. He hadn't been able to get anyone in to clean, because he knew now he wanted to make the place his own, doing for himself. He saw it as it had been, spotless, uncluttered, consciously serene. He smiled in the dimness. Perhaps a little too formal for his taste, a little too ordered. He would now make peace with the house: wash the dishes, pick up the clothes, dust it, maybe sell it and move away, but not in hate anymore and not in guilt.

The journals were almost finished. He would read her ver-sion of the final days, Anne's illness, the doctors, the plans made. Helen had sought to protect her children as Char-maine Wingate had never protected hers, until the very end, but the last thing would not be in her power to write about. Eric would have to have the last word—not certain what that truly was—and put the books away, take back his house, at-tend to his roads, and walk his town, a dweller, a native, blooded.

He felt as old as Cady, but there would be a summer and the two of them might walk a little in the mountains and camp out as they had always said they would, and work on each other's houses through the golden fall. When the winter came again and the new ski area was built, the two of them would go, run by run, long and slow, down Mom's Marvel and Karen's Joy. Eric would ski Mark's Menace and Father's Day, a challenge to the skill of the father for whom it had been named. People would be skiing those runs for years and never know who that Mark was, or that Father. The native gets supplanted by the newcomer, but it is his privilege to name the places from which he disappears. Eric had a sudden picture of the sight down the basement stairs to the back of Mark's head as he sat drafting, planning with Cady. He caught his breath. When would that pain be bearable? Next week he would sell their skis, give away their woolen hats and winter scarves, clean the house, and feel the grief. He remembered Cady's saying that small-town engineers have to live with their mistakes. They also live with years of compromise. Newcomers, tourists, are heedless, accepting without understanding, riding the dawn down-canyon, conscious of the beauty of the river without knowing it in drought, in freeze, in flood, all undermining its shorings year after year. His relationship with Roche had been a kind of heedless acceptance, sprung from the same source. He sighed and put another frozen dinner in the oven. When it was done, he ate it, again without tasting, and then he felt ashamed. He wasn't a newcomer anymore; dwellers cooked. They lived in their houses and cooked and ate full meals. He began to be eager for the discipline of the dweller's self-love—cooking, cleaning, caring for himself.

He threw the cabinets open—country he had never visited—her pots and utensils, baking equipment, kitchen towels, plastic boxes—he had no idea there was so much. Surely with all this equipment he could learn to make something he could taste. The books were in the cupboard over his head. He took one down and opened it: "Sear the cubed chuck in a Dutch oven." What did that mean? He sighed. He would have to learn. A bereft feeling, a terrible helplessness, overwhelmed him. His life suddenly seemed too large to fit him even though there were so many fewer people filling it. In the empty, ghost-ridden house, the phone rang.

"Mr. Gordon, this is Sarie Crocker—at choir– uh—your wife, Helen, was a friend of mine. I know it's an imposition, but among her possessions did you—were there any raffle tickets?"

"What?"

"My tickets—you see, Helen found them and she wanted to throw them away, but they were for a quilt I really wanted, so I said I would take them. I had the kids with me and my hands full and she was leaving, so I said, 'Just put them in your purse, I'll get them tomorrow.' So I think she did and, well, there was the accident. But you see, she won—that is, I won. They said they would hold the quilt until I could get you and ask you—"

"Yes," Eric said, "I know where to look, I think. Helen was a very orderly person. I'll bring the tickets to work tomorrow. Can you come to the municipal building, room o-fourteen at about noon?"

He hung up the phone. Outside, a spring snow had begun to fall. Half rain, it would weigh down the newly opened leaves of the town's trees and break their branches. It would crush the flowers coming up in all the gardens. The people moving into these mountains always ached for the greener, more generous climates they had left. They brought their maple trees and elms, their snowball bushes and lilacs, their grape-ivy and hybrid roses, and planted them in the spare, cold, star-chilled nights of these high mountain towns, talismans against loss and homesickness. A tree might grow four years, or five; a plant might root and struggle for a handful of seasons; but a May freeze or a June snowstorm would be waiting—impersonal as justice—to ride out on the sudden wind, beating the freezing rain or layering the snow deep before it with what always seemed like malicious rage.

But even dwellers, natives, don't stop hoping. Helen had quoted in her journal that haiku:

> Simply trust
> Do not the petals flutter down
> Just like that?

So the dwellers plant again, the seeds of the greenest, the cuttings of the tenderest flowering vines, and the loveliest of trees that might, perhaps, survive.

1

Greenberg, Joanne

The far side of victory